The Shadow of Justice

ALSO BY MILTON HIRSCH

Hirsch's Florida Criminal Trial Procedure 5th ed.
(James Publishing 2002)

The Shadow of Justice

Milton Hirsch

ABA

Defending Liberty
Pursuing Justice

Criminal Justice Section

Cover design by Kelly Book

Printed in the United States of America.

08 07 06 05 04   5 4 3 2

Cataloging-in-Publication Data is on file with the Library of Congress

Hirsch, Milton, 1952-
The Shadow of Justice
ISBN 1-59031-15090-328-3 (pbk.)

Discounts are available for books ordered in bulk. Special consideration is given to state bars, CLE programs, and other bar-related organizations. Inquire at Book Publishing, ABA Publishing, American Bar Association, 321 North Clark, Chicago, Ilinois 60610.

www.ababooks.org

DEDICATION

To my wife Ilene and daughter Shana, whom I
love up to the sky and around the world.

ACKNOWLEDGEMENTS

Many, many thanks to Terry Escobar, without whom this book would never have been completed; and to Paul Rashkind, without whom it would never have been published.

*"I count myself in nothing else so happy
As in a soul remembering my good friends."*

—Shakespeare
The Tragedy of King Richard II,
Act II, Scene 3

Prologue

He cursed the moon. It was the sort of moon that brought tourists to Miami, the moon they put on picture-postcards of Miami, full and fair and bright. But he wasn't a tourist, and the moon's brightness was all too bright for his purposes. He couldn't allow himself the luxury of cursing aloud, but he ran his fingers through his long dirty hair and cursed the moon harshly in his heart.

He had planned to sit in the parked car for a few minutes before going about his errand. He wanted the few minutes to satisfy himself that the street was dark and still. But it occurred to him that the longer he sat in his car, the greater the risk that a neighbor, glancing out a window, might notice him and wonder what he was doing. It would be wrong to get out of his car too quickly, but it would be wrong to wait too long either.

Quietly, he exited the car. He was dressed stylishly, and all in dark. He dressed in dark clothing because he hoped not to be seen. He dressed in fashionable clothing because if he were seen or stopped by a cop he could explain that he had gotten lost on the way through Coconut Grove, and then he would ask the cop for directions. That, he thought, was very clever. The trendy parts of Coconut Grove — the bright lights, the sidewalk cafes, the party crowds — were only a few blocks away, and people were always getting lost going to or from there. He would say he was going to meet some friends, or a girl, and had gotten lost.

He carried a lightweight sportcoat slung over his shoulder. That, he thought, was clever too. Carrying any kind of package in his hands would be asking for trouble. Cops were always drawn to things in your hands, and anyway, why would a young guy hitting the bars in the Grove be carrying a couple of packages? But a jacket thrown over your shoulder on a warm Miami night could easily conceal a package or two, and no cop would have any reason to give it a second look. Very fucking clever, he thought.

He had parked, not in front of the house, but about half a block away. He followed the sidewalk as far as the driveway. It wasn't really a driveway, just a gap in the fence where a pair of tire furrows ran from the street onto the property. Not all houses in Miami have garages, particularly in a poor section of town like this one, but this house lacked even a carport or canvas awning to shield the car from the sun. The car itself was as it had been described to him, a Ford Taurus, dirty, and the license-plate number was the one he had memorized.

The driveway was no more than a dozen feet long, maybe less. Beyond the front of the car was the house itself, and it too was as it had been described to him: small, run-down, large Bahama shutters in front. No lights were on in the house, but he glimpsed the soft, flickering colors and heard the buzz of a television. Good.

He stood by the gas cap—it was on the driver's side—and allowed himself a furtive look around before he knelt to his work. He removed the cap and set it down beside him. Then he reached into one of his jacket's outside pockets, took out a small baggie, and pulled it open. He poured its contents into the gas tank, crumpled the baggie, and put it back in the pocket from which he had taken it. He wiped the area around the gas cap with the sleeve of his jacket, in case he had left a fingerprint.

The house and the street were quiet, but he looked quickly at the one and then the other. The street lights, as was often the case in poor neighborhoods, were either burned out or nonexistent. That was good and it was bad. It was good because he was less likely to be seen in the darkened driveway. It was bad because he was about to open the car door, and the interior compartment light would come on, all the more visible in the darkness. He looked up hurriedly at the moon, still full and bright, but he couldn't spare the time to curse.

Crouching low behind the car door, he used the jacket sleeve to work the door handle. The door opened. No light came on, and he breathed heavily with relief. What he could see of the interior of the car was a mess: fast-food wrappers, beach towels, loose papers or perhaps magazines, he couldn't be sure. He held the jacket over the back-seat floorboard and tore the vest pocket open. A package fell heavily on the floor, fell without his having to touch it. Good; no fingerprints. The package was rectangular in shape, larger than a brick, wrapped in plastic and duct tape. He stared at it, just lying there, for a quick second. Then he closed the door with his forearm, looked left and right to make sure he was still unseen, and stood up. He made an effort to walk slowly, casually, back to his own car.

He started the engine, rolled the windows down, shifted into drive. It was a stupid waste, he thought, but a deal was a deal. He drove away from the curb slowly, but not too slowly — cops pull you over if you're speeding, or if you're being too careful not to speed. He drove past the house — there was nothing, he thought, absolutely nothing to show that he had ever been there — and headed west toward U.S. 1. As the warm, damp air filled his car, he wiped his brow with his forearm and realized he had been sweating, sweating pretty heavily. He stuck his head out the car window and looked up at the moon, still full and bright. Fuck the moon, he whispered; but he smiled when he said it.

* * *

I tell you now that these things happened, but of course I was unaware of them at the time. It was only later that I learned of them. Only after it was too late.

Chapter One
Friday

They woke me out of a deep sleep to tell me Ed Barber was dead.

Standing in the open doorway, not having caught what they said, I started to mumble about not being the warrant-duty judge that week. Yes, said the senior of the two, they knew I wasn't the duty judge that week, but the lieutenant had remembered that Detective Barber and I were personal friends, and thought that ...

I nodded, motioned them in out of the dank pre-dawn air. They had said something about Ed Barber? The senior man, the one in front, glanced at his partner, and then he told me. No preface, no warm-up, no wasted attempt to make it easy to hear. He had been a cop a long time, and he knew that nothing makes it easy to hear, and nothing makes it easy to tell. So he told me. He told me how, and when, and where. He told me everything but why. That much I remember.

"Honey." It was Miriam's voice, softly. I looked up. She was standing in the kitchen doorway, adjusting her housecoat. I looked down. I was sitting at the kitchen table, staring at so much of the frayed white terrycloth bathrobe as covered my legs. I suppose I had been sitting for five minutes.

"Honey?" It was Miriam's voice, again softly. Behind her, in the middle distance, the two officers stood uncomfortably in the hallway. "Are you all right?"

Was I all right? "Clark, the officers are waiting. You've been ... you've been just sitting there for fifteen minutes." I stood, straightened the bathrobe, tightened the belt, motioned for the two men to join me at the kitchen table. Miriam started to put up coffee.

They were standard-issue Metro-Dade homicide bureau. The one who had spoken to me was black, heavy-set, dressed in shades of dull. His partner was white, slightly smaller, badly in need of a shave, dressed in shades of dull. They handed me paperwork. They handed it to me carefully, as if it might hurt me.

The warrant affidavit was written in cop-speak, the same phrases and expressions that repeated themselves in countless arrest forms, offense incident reports, and warrant applications. It stated that the affiant, Det. Harold Ray Washington, had been a Metro-Dade police officer for eleven years, the last five of those assigned to the homicide bureau; that he had, during that time, investigated approximately so-and-so-many homicides; that at approximately oh-three-something that morning a 911 call had been received from a citizen residing at such-and-such an address; that the citizen identified himself as a long-time next-door neighbor and friend of Metro-Dade Homicide Detective Edward James Barber; that the citizen reported receiving a telephone call from Detective Edward James Barber in which Detective Edward James Barber seemed to be crying, confused, and threatening; that the citizen started to go next door to the home of Detective Edward James Barber, but while he was in the driveway the citizen heard what he took to be the sound of gunshots coming from the house of Detective Edward James Barber; that marked patrol units were then dispatched; that three dead bodies, later identified as those of Detective Edward James Barber, Mrs. Dianne Barber, and Edward Barber, Jr. ...

Miriam interrupted to ask how the officers took their coffee. Both asked for heavy cream, heavy sugar. I declined coffee, began to read again.

But Washington had something more he wanted to tell me. He spoke gently, as if his words might break my bones. "Judge, the warrant-duty assistant state attorney said we probably didn't need a warrant in a case like this, everyone dead and who would we read the warrant to? But the lieutenant said that you would understand us not wanting to take chances, not maybe mess something up, because Barber was one of ours."

One of ours. I studied Detective Harold Ray Washington. He had worn the same badge as Ed Barber, probably knew him, might even have worked with him. Now Ed Barber was dead and Harold Ray Washington had been chosen to bear the news to me, and he wanted me to understand that he was as sorry to tell me as I was to be told. I was only a circuit judge, but Detective Edward James Barber had been one of theirs.

I suppose I skimmed the rest of the affidavit and signed the warrant. I remember the officers leaving; if I learned the white one's name I don't recall it. I'm a little sketchy about having shaved, showered, dressed. The next thing I remember clearly is the sound of my own footsteps clack-clacking along the linoleum on the fourth floor of the Richard E. Gerstein Metro-Justice Building, until I got to the door marked Chambers of the Hon. Clark N. Addison.

Carmen was already at her desk in the reception area. She said good morning and then, motioning with her head toward my office added, "Sheridan is inside."

John Wentworth "Blackjack" Sheridan IV was folded into the one good chair opposite my desk, his long, bony left leg hooked over the chair's arm. He still had his sunglasses on, covering eyes even redder than usual, so I didn't have to ask, but I did.

"You heard?"

"Yeah. I've still got friends in Homicide." *Aah've* still got friends, he said, because he was from generations of Southerners. "In another couple of hours, it'll be all over this courthouse." All *ovah*.

Blackjack Sheridan was a shade over six feet in height and so thin that his bones must have felt cramped for space. His sandy blond hair was straight and had not yet started to thin or recede. The skin of his face was perpetually red from sunburn and drink. He was a handsome man careless of his looks, a talented lawyer careless of his talents. He owned a small sailboat named The Blackjack, an on-again-off-again southern accent, and a liver that a cat wouldn't eat.

A thousand years or so ago, Jack and I had been trial partners in the major crimes division of the Miami-Dade County

State Attorney's Office. I was young, ambitious, good with law books. He was young, lazy, magic with juries. He mocked, in his good-natured way, my ambition and my bookishness. I envied, in my secret way, his effortless success with jurors, women, life. We became the most successful trial team in the office. Our last three or four convictions were splashy, high-profile murder cases that carried Jack into private practice and made me the youngest circuit judge in Miami-Dade County. Ed Barber had been the lead detective on those cases. The friendships we had formed were the closest I had ever known. Now Ed was gone.

I pushed away from my desk, turned my back on Jack and stared out my office's one window. The handful of scraggly tabebuia trees in the parking lot were dropping their last pink blooms.

"Why?"

Jack made no reply.

"Had you spoken to him lately? Did he complain of anything? Was he in any kind of trouble?"

Jack sighed. "He had some problems with his boy."

Not good enough. "He had the same problems every father has with a teenage son. They weren't as close as they could have been. They didn't understand each other as well as they should have." I shrugged, swung my chair around to face Jack again. "Ed Barber had an ordinary job, an ordinary wife, an ordinary house, an ordinary son, an ordinary life. If he had a complaint I never heard it and neither did you, and we would have. But half-a-dozen hours ago, Ed Barber put three bullets in his gun ..." I didn't complete the thought. "Why? Tell me why."

By way of answer, Jack reached inside his coat pocket and took out a small silver flask. Now nobody, but nobody in this day and age carries whiskey in a small silver flask in his coat pocket, but Blackjack Sheridan does. The flask is elaborately monogrammed "JWS" and was, according to Jack, originally the property of John Wentworth Sheridan the First. The sharp dent in one side of the flask was put there—again, according to Jack—during a crucial battle of the Civil War when a Yankee rifleman let fly at Blackjack the First; proof once again of the life-saving power of Old K-Mart, or whatever liquid Jack was now pouring down his throat.

I rotated my chair to face the window again. A cloud passed briefly across the sun, and I glimpsed my own reflection in the window. I am not an old man. If middle age still begins at forty, I am almost but not quite middle-aged. Miriam, who has known me since we were children, says I was never a child. I was born an old man, she says, born to have dark serious eyes and a pale serious face. I had never really thought about what she meant. But the dark eyes and pale face that I saw reflected in the window seemed to me now to be the eyes and the face of an old man. The cloud passed, and my image with it, and I had no occasion to regret the passing of either.

Carmen poked her head into my office. "Judge, it's time." I make it an invariable practice to be on the bench a minute or two before 9:00. Jack actually helped me on with my robe.

"You have anything on my calendar this morning?"

He responded with a sudden energy. "That kid Linden is on for a motion for reconsideration of bail. It's just bullshit that they've still got him locked up when ... ."

I cut him off. "We'll take it up in court in the prosecutor's presence. Your Rodriguez case is first up for trial on Monday, isn't it?"

"Right."

"Ready for trial?"

"Ready for trial." We started to head for court. I put a hand on his shoulder.

"Jack, can you come to the house for dinner tonight?"

He took his sunglasses off, folded them and put them away. Then he smiled that old Jack smile, ruddy skin stretched tight across cheekbones, eyes bloodshot but bright, teeth untarnished by oceans of booze. "Probably not." Still smiling, he turned and walked away. That was Blackjack Sheridan.

My courtroom is on the fourth floor of the Metro-Justice Building. Like all courtrooms in the building, and the building itself, it is a relic of an earlier day. It is decorated in a style known to lawyers and judges as "court noir." The walls are panelled in a cheap, dark wood. Lights peek out of a high ceiling here and there like distant stars on a cloudy night. In the visitors' gallery at the back are fixed rows of ancient fold-down chairs with arthritis in their joints. A brown carpet, dirty and worn, covers the floor of the courtroom. To one side is a brown table for the prosecution, and to the other a brown table for the defense. Behind each table are several chairs, but no two chairs match. Directly before me, as I sit at the bench, is a desk for the clerk of the court. To the right of the bench is the witness stand, and against the right-hand wall is the jury box.

Behind me are the flags, American and Florida, and on the wall high above me a placard with the motto, "We who labor here seek only Truth." In truth, we who labor here seek many things. Truth is a luxury. Defendants seek a break, prosecutors seek a conviction, defense attorneys seek an acquittal and, if they are very lucky, a legal fee. Jurors seek relief from boredom, visitors seek entertainment, victims and family members seek closure. I have no leisure to consider what it is that I seek. Miami has America's busiest criminal courts. The caseload of a judge in Miami is, on average, three times that of a judge in Manhattan. I seek not to drown.

Every morning the office of the court clerk provides each circuit judge with the day's calendar. A Monday morning calendar will run thirty or forty pages, each page listing half-a-dozen or more cases. The first section of the calendar lists cases set for arraignment, the formal entry of a plea in response to criminal charges. No jury is needed for morning calendar, and none is present. Instead, the jury box is used to seat the morning's defendants, natty in their manacles and Dade County Jail jumpsuits. Arraignments have a formulaic sameness about them, and if the lawyers before me are experienced I can arraign at the rate of about one defendant per minute: As the prosecutor announces the filing of charges and hands a copy of the indictment to the clerk, I ask the defendant how he pleads; as I ask how he pleads, the defense attorney answers with the speed and in the monotone of an old-time auctioneer that his client waives formal reading—enters his plea of not guilty—notices his intent to participate in discovery—demands trial by jury—

and requests fifteen days to file motions. The court reporter, who knows the drill by heart, gets it all down correctly whether the attorneys do or not. Next case.

The last section of the calendar lists the cases set for trial. In a given week, a couple of dozen cases, maybe more, will be called for trial. I cannot preside over more than one trial at a time, and over the course of the year I will not average more than one trial per week. The remainder of the trial cases— hundreds and hundreds of them—will have to be disposed of in one fashion or another. And they must be disposed of rapidly, because hundreds of new cases are coming to take their places.

Between the arraignments section of the calendar and the trial section of the calendar lies the motions section of the calendar—a kind of personals column for litigants. Single, incarcerated defendant seeks order suppressing evidence obtained in violation of his constitutional rights. Clean-cut, well-dressed young prosecutor seeks order compelling defendant's handwriting exemplars. Disgruntled bailbondsman seeks surrender of defendant and discharge of bond. Some of these motions are readily granted; others just as readily denied. Still others will require me to hear testimony. Until I resolve these motions— and everything else on the calendar—I cannot turn my attention to whatever case I am trying that day.

Friday calendars are always light. That Friday was no exception. There were few arraignments. A trial had just ended, the next one would not start until the following Monday. And the only motion that would require a hearing was the one Jack had mentioned to me in chambers.

"Page 19 of the calendar, State vs. Linden, defendant's motion for reconsideration of bail. Counsel please state your appearances." Jack stood and came forward, as did the assistant state attorney assigned to the Linden case.

"Eleanor T. Hibbard for the State, Your Honor."

"John Wentworth Sheridan for Mr. Linden, Judge."

I glanced at the case file. "We're here on your motion, Mr. Sheridan." Jack opened his mouth to speak, but was cut off by the prosecutor.

"Your Honor, I object to this proceeding. Bail was previously set by the Court in this matter after a plenary hearing. There are no newly discovered facts or changed circumstances to justify a second hearing. He's had his one bite at the apple, Judge."

Eleanor Hibbard was the prosecution's division chief in my courtroom. She was a "lifer," having spent her entire legal career in the state attorney's office. She brought to her work a great deal of determination, a beautiful speaking voice, and a feeling of absolute certainty that everyone charged with a crime was guilty not only of that crime, but also of several undiscovered crimes. She was a heavy-set woman. She wore loose clothing to mask some of her bulk, but otherwise gave little attention to her appearance. She did not woo jurors to convict. She hurled argument and evidence at them relentlessly, bristled with righteousness, then dared them not to convict. Few had the courage to take the dare.

Jack spoke. "Your Honor, we have witnesses and evidence that were not available to us at the time of the initial bond hearing."

"This is a charge of simple possession of cocaine, one count?" The lawyers agreed that it was. "I previously set bond in what amount?" The question was addressed to the court clerk, who replied that I had set the standard bond in such cases, five thousand dollars.

"This defendant has priors, Judge," said the prosecutor. "There's no reason to go below standard bond."

There probably wasn't, but Blackjack Sheridan and his client were entitled to their day in court. I translated the thought into judge-speak. "There may not be, Ms. Hibbard, but the defendant is entitled to be heard. All right, Mr. Sheridan, you may go forward on your motion."

A corrections officer escorted the defendant from the jury box to counsel table, where he sat next to his attorney. Linden was an ugly, scrawny kid, medium height. His hair was almost shoulder-length, straight, brown, dirty and greasy. He had a complexion like the surface of the moon. Jack leaned over him to confer briefly in whispers, then turned to address me. "Your

Honor, the prosecutor has referred to Mr. Linden's prior record. I now ask the prosecutor to stipulate that Mr. Linden has four prior arrests, one of them involving a felony; that in every case Mr. Linden was released on some form of bail; and that in every case Mr. Linden faithfully appeared for trial."

I looked to Eleanor Hibbard for her response. "For purposes of this hearing only, so stipulated."

Jack began again. "I call Mrs. Rhonda M. Halstead." A woman sitting in the second row of the gallery came forward. Rhonda Halstead was probably in her early fifties. She wore elaborate make-up, but her hair was carelessly combed. She was overweight, and her clothes were too tight. As she raised her right hand to take the oath, I saw that most of the polish covering her talon-length nails had been chipped away or chewed away. What remained was candy-apple, fire-engine red.

"Where do you live, Mrs. Halstead?"

"Naranja." Cow country in far south Dade County. Out of the courtroom, John Wentworth Sheridan IV would probably have described Rhonda M. Halstead as trailer trash. Inside the courtroom, he would treat her with all the old-South courtliness he could muster. His witness might not come across like a lady, but he would treat her like a lady, and in so doing perhaps he could invest her with the credibility, the believability due to a lady.

"And ma'am, what is your relationship to the defendant, Randy Linden?"

"I'm his mother."

"In the month that he has been locked up in the Dade County Jail, have you visited him, Mrs. Halstead?"

"Yes, sir. As often as they'll let me."

"And have you attempted to find the money to post his bail?"

"Yes, sir."

Jack gestured toward me. "Tell His Honor what efforts you have made to raise bail for your boy."

Mrs. Halstead turned to face me. "Judge, Your Honor, I've asked everyone in the family for money. I've asked all my friends and neighbors." Jack paused, as if unsure whether to ask his next question. He may have been expecting a more detailed answer, but that was the answer he got. If he wanted more from his witness, he would have to go get it.

"And were you able to raise five thousand dollars?"

"No sir, I sure wasn't."

"Were you able to raise anything close to five thousand dollars?"

"No, sir."

"Is there any chance of you, or your family, or your friends and neighbors, being able to raise five thousand dollars for Randy's bail?"

"No, sir." She faced me again. "There's no chance of that, Judge."

"Thank you kindly, Mrs. Halstead." Jack turned to Eleanor. "Your witness."

Eleanor brought a yellow legal pad with her to the podium. She studied it briefly, then turned her attention to the witness. "Your son wasn't living with you prior to his arrest, was he, Mrs. Halstead?"

"No, ma'am."

"Where was he living?"

"Um ... I think in Hialeah."

"But you're not sure, are you?"

"I'm pretty sure."

"You don't know his address in Hialeah, do you?"

"No."

"You've never visited him in Hialeah, or wherever he lives, have you?"

"No."

"You don't know who he lives with, do you?"

"No."

Jack's direct examination of this witness had been conducted to the slow, deliberate cadence of a funeral procession, intended to create the image of a distraught mother bereft of her child. Eleanor had begun her cross at forced-march pace. With half-a-dozen quick questions, she had raised the inference that Mrs. Halstead neither knew nor cared how her adult son led his life.

"And because you've never set foot in your son's residence, you can't tell us whether that residence is full of cocaine, can you?" Jack objected and I sustained. It was a throw-away question. Eleanor moved on to another area of inquiry.

"Before you came to court this morning, ma'am, you met with Mr. Sheridan, your son's attorney, on several occasions, didn't you?"

"I spoke to him. I don't know how many times. Not very many."

"And Mr. Sheridan explained to you that His Honor Judge Addison would only consider lowering your son's bail if you could show that your son wouldn't flee, that he would show up in court whenever he was needed; isn't that right?"

"Um ... yes."

"The truth is, Mrs. Halstead, that if your son is released on bail, you don't know where he'll go, do you?"

"Well ... he can come stay with me if he wants to."

In the war of cross-examination, Eleanor Hibbard's weapon was her voice. It was the accentless, perfectly modulated voice of a radio announcer. The witness had given an answer that displeased Eleanor, so the volume and focus of the Voice would have to be adjusted. And not slightly adjusted; the witness must be punished, must be bludgeoned with the Voice.

"Mrs. Halstead, your son hasn't lived with you this year, has he?" Perfectly modulated tones came hurling toward the witness at high speed and decibel levels.

"No." The answer seemed small, nasal, hushed.

"He didn't live with you last year, did he?"

"Not ... not that I recall."

Eleanor pointed at me, extending her arm to its full length. "Can you swear to Judge Addison that the defendant, Randy Linden, has lived with you at *any* time during the past five years?"

"I couldn't absolutely swear to it."

"And if the defendant were released on bail, you would have no way to force him to live with you, would you?"

"I ... no, I couldn't force him to."

"And you would have no way to force him to come to court, would you?"

Mrs. Halstead got the point. "I guess not."

Eleanor had been standing behind the podium, slightly to the left of it. She paused, then moved two steps to the right. It was lawyer body-language. The message was: I've made my point, I'll move on to my next one. The witness shifted her weight in the witness seat.

"You testified, Mrs. Halstead, that you've visited the defendant in the Dade County Jail on many occasions since his arrest, is that correct?"

"Yes."

"And on any of those occasions, did the defendant discuss this case with you?"

Jack was on his feet. "Objection, discovery. This is a bail hearing, Your Honor."

I turned to Eleanor. "Sustained, unless you can show relevance to the issue of bail." She put up token resistance, then conceded the point and terminated her cross-examination. I asked Jack if he had any re-direct. He had none. Rhonda M. Halstead, visibly relieved that the criminal justice system had no further need of her, returned to her seat in the gallery.

"Mr. Sheridan, do you have any other witnesses?"

"The Court's indulgence for just one second, Your Honor." Jack was conferring with his client. Watching them, I had a sense of what it was like to view an old-time silent movie. I couldn't hear what they were whispering, but their animated, almost comically exaggerated gestures and facial expressions spoke volumes. Like many a foolish defendant, Linden wanted to testify. Like any smart lawyer, Blackjack Sheridan wouldn't let him. Any courtroom veteran could have supplied the dialogue: What is it you think you want to say? That you promise not to flee, and to come to court for trial? Look, I'll tell the judge all that in my argument, your saying it isn't going to make any difference. That you're innocent? Then the prosecutor will get to cross-examine you. You'll end up compromising our defense at trial. Besides, do you think the judge is going to believe you're innocent just because you say so? Listen to me, I know Dade County Jail is a shithole, I know you want out, but think about what's really important: This bail hearing, which will decide where you live for the next few weeks, or the trial, which will decide where you live for the next three to five years?

"Mr. Sheridan, let's move along. Do you plan to call another witness?" The silent movie came to its dramatic conclusion. Linden slumped down in his seat, pouting. Jack stood and addressed me.

"We have no other witnesses, Your Honor, but we do wish to make argument." I gestured for Jack to proceed. "Your Honor, at the previous hearing on this matter we established that the defendant, Randy Linden, is a life-long resident of Miami-Dade County with ties to no other community. He does have priors, Your Honor, but as the prosecution has stipulated, he has always appeared for court when required to do so. He has established, in his prior cases, a track record as a dependable defendant, a reliable bail risk." It is one of the ironies of our criminal justice system: The defendant with prior arrests who has never jumped bail in the past may be set free on bail the next time he is arrested more readily than the first-time defendant. In the same way, I suppose, the consumer with a heavy load of credit-card debt who has always made his payments may be issued another credit card more readily than the consumer who has no debt, and therefore no credit history, because he has always paid cash.

Jack moved on to his next thought. "Your Honor, the standard bond amount in this jurisdiction for simple possession of cocaine is $5,000. As we have made clear, that amount is far, far beyond the means of this defendant or his family. The court might as well have set bond in the amount of $50,000 or $500,000. The effect is the outright denial of bail. I need hardly remind this Honorable Court of the Supreme Court authority for the proposition that bail should be set in an amount sufficient to insure that the defendant will return for trial—not in an amount calculated to insure that the defendant will never be released."

He was heading for the home stretch now, the part of his

argument lawyers call the peroration. The Old South came well-ing up in Jack's voice. "Your Honor, setting bail in an amount that Randy Linden cannot hope to meet and should not be re-quired to meet is simply a device"—a *devahs*—"for punishing Randy by locking him up in a cage called Dade County Jail. But the court has no right to punish Randy Linden. As he sits be-fore Your Honor, Randy Linden is presumed innocent. That presumption of innocence sits as a mantle of protection upon his shoulders. It is placed there by our Constitution. Thank you." Jack sat down.

Lawyer-talk. Mumbo-jumbo designed to impress the client, to show him how hard you're pitching his case. So I said, "Thank you, counsel. A very well-presented argument. Does the prosecution wish to be heard?" Eleanor gave me about ten minutes of the hard sell.

"Mr. Sheridan," I asked, "what bail are you seeking?"

"Release into the personal custody of the mother, Mrs. Hal-stead." Eleanor started to rise but I gestured for her to remain seated.

"That's not a realistic suggestion, Mr. Sheridan. The defen-dant is charged with a serious crime, and has a history of drug-related arrests. I will reduce his bond to $2,500, coupled with Nebbia conditions." Nebbia conditions meant that before the defendant could be released on bail, he would have to prove that any money he put up for bail was clean, that it wasn't drug money. I turned my attention to the defendant's mother, seated in the visitor's gallery. "Mrs. Halstead, $2,500 is a very reason-able bond in a case like this one. Your family can meet it by posting that amount, or by letting a bailbondsman hold prop-erty in that amount, and paying him a bond premium of ten percent. Mr. Sheridan can explain all that to you."

I had noticed, while I was addressing Rhonda Halstead, that the silent movie was being replayed at the defense table. Whatever Randy Linden was telling Blackjack Sheridan, he was telling him lots of it. Linden's face was flushed and he was ges-turing with as much animation as his handcuffs permitted. He retained enough self-control to keep his voice down, so I could-n't hear what he said, but he was the one doing the talking.

Jack was trying to placate him. He wasn't getting far. I intruded on their private moment. "Mr. Sheridan, is there anything else on this matter?"

And then I saw something that I had never seen in any courtroom in my life: I saw John Wentworth Sheridan IV completely lose his self-control. I have, over the course of the years, seen Jack *pretend* to lose his self-control in court. I have seen him feign outrage, indignation, shock, hurt feelings, and even loss of hearing. He once faked a heart attack in a trial that wasn't going too well. But as he stood before me, Blackjack Sheridan was not feigning, not faking. He was pale, shaking, sputtering. My ruling was an outrage, he said, and he repeated it again and again because he was in no condition to think of anything else to say. I had seen first-year public defenders come unhinged like that, but not Blackjack Sheridan. Never Jack Sheridan.

I have no gavel—in Miami they steal those—so I raised my arm and brought my open hand down hard. The sound of flesh hitting wood was as close as I could get to giving Jack a slap in the face, and it had the same effect. In the ensuing silence I spoke. I did not shout; the judge who shouts has already lost control. My voice was low, still, hard.

"Counsel, approach the bench." Jack came forward. I spoke again, my voice so low that the court reporter strained to hear me. "Mr. Sheridan, this court understands that certain events of last night have placed a great strain upon you. But you will control yourself in this courtroom at all times and in all circumstances. Do I make myself clear?"

Jack's composure had returned as suddenly as it had left him, and now he was blotchy-faced with embarrassment. "Yes, Your Honor. I'm so ... I apologize, Your Honor."

I think back on that moment now as one of the few times, perhaps the first time, that I did not like being in the judge business. In the week to follow I would have occasion to think much worse thoughts about the judge business, but of course I could not know that then. All I knew then was that I felt sad, I felt tired, my shirt was sticky with sweat. I rose, announced the noon recess, and was glad to leave the bench. The last thing I saw as I left the courtroom was the corrections officers leading Randy Linden back to his holding cell. His head was turned and he was looking over his shoulder at Blackjack Sheridan. His face told of an anger for which he could never have found words.

Back in chambers, I dropped my robe over a chair, grabbed my suitcoat and threw it over my shoulder. Carmen looked up from her word-processing. "Where you going, Judge?"

I was already halfway out the door. "Got to see a man about a hat," I told her. Five minutes later I was heading east on the causeway, toward Miami Beach. When I reached Collins Avenue I turned north.

* * *

The best location on Collins Avenue is occupied by the Hotel Antibes. This is as it should be. The Antibes is the most glorious remnant of the glory that was Miami Beach. It is the biggest, the most expensive, the gaudiest. All around it Miami Beach is in a state of constant change, for better and for worse. The Hotel Antibes wishes only to remain exactly as it was.

In the lower lobby of the Hotel Antibes is a gallery of shops, open to all comers but catering principally to the South American tourists who visit in the summertime. About half-way down on the right a marquee reads, "Antibes Mens Wear" and underneath that, "First with the finer things of fashion." In the window are mannequins modeling fruit-colored blazer sportcoats—banana yellow, lime green, tangerine—sportshirts with elaborate floral patterns, and panama hats. The front door is glass, and a bell jingles when you open it.

"Hello, Uncle Billy."

The old man, dressed like one of his mannequins, was leaning against a counter leafing through the scratch sheet. He isn't really my uncle. None of my real relatives are as glad to see me as he is.

"Young Adelstein!" And then, with elaborate mock ceremony, "I mean, 'Your Honor!'" I pointed to the scratch sheet. "How are your investments?"

"Come to Hialeah with me tomorrow?" I shook my head. "The most gorgeous goddamn racetrack on earth and nobody wants to go!"

"How's business?"

His face puckered as if he had french-kissed a lemon. "The *shmatte* business isn't what it used to be." It was the gospel according to Billy Eisenberg. The *shmatte* business isn't what it used to be, never will be what it used to be, and never used to be what it used to be. I ask only because he would be disappointed if I didn't. "And how's the life of a big-shot judge?"

A small counter runs along part of the wall inside the door of the Antibes Mens Wear. On top of the counter is the cash register, charge slips, paperwork. On the customer side of the counter are two bar stools. I sat. "Billy, I think I want my old job back."

"Fine. I've got some dress shirts in the stock room that need to be run into inventory. You can come every afternoon straight from high school." I was looking down, not at him. Worse yet, I wasn't holding up my end of the kibitzing. He came over and sat on the second bar stool. "What's the matter, kiddo?"

I looked over at him. "You remember Ed Barber?"

"Your cop friend?" I nodded. "Sure, I remember. Big guy, maybe 46 long. Why, something happen to him?"

I took a breath and let it out slowly. "Last night—actually, early this morning—he shot his wife and son to death. Then he called a neighbor, talking gibberish, you know, crying and carrying on. The neighbor came running over, but by the time he arrived, Ed had killed himself."

To his credit, Billy said nothing. He put his hand in his right pants pocket and jingled the loose change, which was his nervous habit. He had been, in his day, a tough guy when he had to be. He had served in the South Pacific during the Second World War. His wife, whom he adored, had spent years dying of cancer. He knew enough of life and death to refrain from saying something stupid, like what a shame it was or how sorry he was for me or how maybe it was part of a greater plan.

"Billy ... Ed Barber lived in the same house for as long as I knew him, and I never heard him say he was unhappy with that house. He worked at the same job for as long as I knew him, and I never heard him say he was unhappy with that job. He was married to the same wife for as long as I knew him, and I never heard him say he was unhappy with that wife. What the hell possesses a man to ... Why? Why would he do a thing like that?"

Billy shrugged; a small shrug, more eyebrows than shoulders. He spoke softly: "That's your department. Why do guys kill, steal, rape? Judges have been judging killers and thieves and rapists since King Solomon. You do it every day. How do you decide why they do it?"

How do I decide why they do it? Is that what people think lawyers and judges do? I got straight-As in law school, but I never once had to answer an exam question about why men commit crimes. I prosecuted criminals for almost a decade and I convicted them by proving that they did it, but I never once had to prove why they did it. Then I became a judge, and now every day I sit on the bench and sentence those who plead guilty or are found guilty, and not once, not once have I ever been called upon to consider why they are guilty. The court of appeals will never reverse one of my rulings for failure to ask "why?," like the kids' game in which you lose if you forget to ask "Mother may I?"

Billy was speaking again. "Did anyone actually ... you know, see it?"

"Two uniform patrolmen arrived when the neighbor called 911. They were the first ones on the scene."

"Yeah, but I mean, by the time they got there, everyone was already dead, right? I mean, they found the son dead, and the wife dead, and your friend dead with his own gun in his hand, right?"

I tried to remember what I had read in the warrant affidavit. It occurred to me I really knew very little of the details. "I guess so."

"It couldn't have happened any other way, could it?"

"I guess not."

Billy reached over and put his hands on my shoulders.

"Clark, listen to me. These things happen. We don't make them happen; we can't keep them from happening. What Ed did he did to himself and to his family."

I nodded. "That's right," I said. "He did it to himself, and he did it to his family." I hopped off the bar stool. I had come to talk about it, and now I didn't want to talk about it.

Billy got off his bar stool, ran his fingers along the lapel of my suitcoat, mumbled something about "X-make." I knew what was coming. "A gentleman in your position should wear a hat. It isn't right, not to wear a hat with a suit."

"Billy, nobody but nobody wears a hat anymore."

He snorted. "All my customers wear hats. I have some beautiful panamas I can show you..."

"No thanks."

"A fedora? They're back in fashion. Young people wear them."

Young people? "Really, Billy, thanks, but ..."

"Something conservative, in a houndstooth pattern, with a small brim. Very distinguished, perfect for a member of the judiciary."

"Billy, are you coming for *Shabbat* dinner tonight?" The torrent of salesmanship stopped. He smiled, rolled his eyes.

"What a question!"

As I was leaving, a customer was entering. He was an older man, Billy's age at least. I can't recall the shirt he had on, but he was wearing polyester pants in avocado and peach. His shoes were white bucks, and he was sporting the kind of tan only tourists have time for. I glanced over my shoulder to see Billy putting on his Friendly Salesman face. Here, clearly, was a young person in need of a hat.

* * *

There was nothing doing back at the courthouse, no afternoon calendar, no trial. Friday afternoon was often like that, and I usually use the time to catch up on paperwork, but that Friday my heart wasn't in it. I told Carmen to have a nice weekend and I snuck out early.

I was ahead of the traffic and I had a little time to spare, so I took a detour. Ed Barber lives — lived — in an unincorporated section of Miami-Dade County a few miles west of U.S. 1, not quite as far south as The Falls shopping mall. It was one of many residential tracts that had been developed in one of many South Florida boom cycles coming between two of many South Florida bust cycles. A concrete slab is poured, a CBS house goes up, a coat of paint in a pastel shade is affixed to the walls, and security bars are affixed to the jalousie windows. Garages are a rarity, attics and basements unheard-of. When the bottom drops out of the economy, the last finance company to buy the mortgage from the bank will get the property back, unless a hurricane has come along in the interim and knocked every-thing ass over teakettle. Once upon a time all this land was a part of the vast, foul-smelling, snake-infested swamp called the Everglades. Then the ugliness was natural. Now it is man-made.

I pulled into the Barbers' driveway and just sat there for a minute. Yellow crime-scene tape still barred the doors, but in all other respects the house looked just as it had the thousand times I had been there. I thought about getting out of the car ... and doing what? Knocking on the door? Looking in a win-dow? Ringing the bell?

I rolled down my car windows, turned off the engine, felt the hot, damp, late-afternoon air fill the car. I was about to go when a car pulled into the driveway alongside me, an off-white Mercury Marquis. The tall man who got out started to ask if he could help me and then, recognizing me, asked, "Judge Addi-son?"

"Yes. It's Lieutenant ...

"Cabrera."

"Yes, of course. Lieutenant Cabrera." We got out and shook hands. It was an awkward moment, neither of us too sure what to say. I thought about saying goodbye, just getting in the car and leaving. But Cabrera's arrival afforded me an op-portunity. "Lieutenant, would it compromise the scene in any way if I were to take a look inside?"

"No, Judge, not at all. I was just going in myself."

At the front door he removed enough of the tape for us to get by, and opened the door with a set of keys that must have been found during the initial search of the house. He put on surgical gloves, the thin latex gloves cops wear to handle evidence or examine crime scenes, and reminded me not to touch anything.

I stood in the front hallway, staring at the living room and, beyond that, the dining alcove. I don't know what I expected to see. The home was a simple one, and DeeDee Barber had been a good housekeeper. Everything was as it had always been. I could imagine the father, mother, and son who had lived there. I could not imagine how, why, the father, mother, and son had died there.

Lt. Cabrera was waiting for me. I motioned for him to lead the way and followed him into the back of the house, the bedroom area. The boy's bedroom was as I had always seen it, except that the bedclothing and pillows had been removed for blood spatter pattern analysis. The rest of the room had been examined, but apparently nothing of any value to the investigation was found.

Ed and DeeDee's room was more of the same — unremarkable except that the bed had been stripped. Videotaping and instamatic photography have long since replaced the old-fashioned practice of chalk-marking the floor, and any videos and still photos that were needed had been taken hours ago. Ed's personal effects had been gone over, but little or nothing had been impounded.

"Did he leave a note?" They usually do. I knew all about that.

"No note. We looked."

I stood there, I suppose for several minutes, staring. I couldn't even say what I was staring at. I remember thinking that this was the last time I would ever step foot in this house, which then struck me as an odd thought. "All right, Lieutenant. Thank you for your time. I'll be going."

"I'll see you out, Judge." He walked me as far as the front door, and I think we shook hands. I assumed he was the lieutenant who had sent Det. Washington and his partner to my home early that morning, but I didn't ask. I didn't even ask him what he was doing at the Barber house.

* * *

When I got home Miriam was setting the dining room table. Most evenings we eat in the kitchen, but Friday night is different. Miriam was raised in an observant home, and insists that *Shabbat* be honored. The twins are still young enough to enjoy rituals they do not understand. Joel is a pre-teen, and therefore obliged to consider all traditions uncool.

I was in the fifth grade when we moved down to Miami Beach to get my mother and her asthma away from the northern winters. The first person I met was a girl in the fourth grade who lived three houses down from us. She decided the day after we met that we would get married when we grew up. She had skinny legs and curly hair, and eyes that were larger and even darker than mine. I thought she was very pretty. I still do.

Miriam has only happy memories of childhood. Her father and mother and two older sisters loved her and fussed over her. She had nice friends, she did well in school. My father, who had never been sick a day in his life, died in his sleep when I was ... well, when I was about the same age Joel is now. I suppose I had a happy childhood before my father's death; but the memories of that time, happy or sad, seem to have died with him. After he died we never seemed to have quite as much of anything as everyone else had of everything. When I was old enough I worked afternoons and weekends at Billy Eisenberg's store and spent most of the rest of my time studying and worrying about what the future held for me. I graduated second in a class of about 500 at Miami Beach High. Miriam insisted that we go to the prom. I would have spent the evening worrying about whether I would do well enough at college.

I didn't ask Miriam if she had said anything to the children about Ed. It would have been inappropriate to say much to Marc or Alicia, but I suspect she said something to Joel. He was unusually reserved during the evening. I think he wanted to show me that he was man enough to accept another man's death, and old enough to accept an older person's grief.

While I was washing up and changing I heard Billy ring the doorbell, and heard the twins race to answer it. Moments later the announcement came that dinner was ready. Miriam placed *Shabbat* candles in her grandmother's ornate candlesticks, lit them, then covered her eyes before reciting the prayer invoking the Sabbath and blessing its light. Ordinarily in Judaism a prayer is said before an act is done, but once the prayer for the Sabbath candles has been recited, Sabbath has begun and it is forbidden to kindle a fire. For this reason the custom has developed: First light the candles, then cover the eyes so as not to see their flame while the prayer is recited. Throughout, Alicia stands by her mother's side, mimicking her words and movements with such seriousness that I can hardly keep from laughing.

After the candles have been lit, I lead the children in the short prayers that thank God for bread and wine. Finally, I read to Miriam the blessing traditionally offered by a Jewish husband to his wife. It begins at Proverbs 31:10.

> *A woman of valour who can find?*
> *For her price is far above rubies.*
> *The heart of her husband doth safely trust in her,*
> *And he hath no lack of gain.*
> *She doeth him good and not evil*
> *All the days of her life.*

Here I skip ahead to verse 25. The intervening passages require a greater attention span than I can expect of my children.

> *Strength and dignity are her clothing;*
> *And she laugheth at the time to come.*
> *She openeth her mouth with wisdom;*
> *And the law of kindness is on her tongue.*
> *She looketh well to the ways of her household,*
> *And eateth not the bread of idleness,*
> *Her children rise up, and call her blessed;*
> *Her husband also, and he praiseth her:*
> *Many daughters have done valiantly,*
> *But thou excellest them all.*

I was a little surprised when, just as we were finishing dinner, Bagel came over and put his head in my lap. Bagel and I really don't have much use for each other. When the twins were born, Joel started misbehaving—"acting out," the doctor said—and someone suggested that we get a puppy so that he could have something of his own. I told Miriam that a mutt would take more of her time away from Joel, not less, but she thought it was a fine idea, and we took a ride over to the animal shelter. Miriam decided that this one particular pup was a beagle; Joel mispronounced beagle, called the doggy "bagel," and Miriam was delighted. It's been Bagel the beagle ever since.

My personal feeling is that Bagel is a cross between a beagle and a large throw-pillow, or maybe a small beanbag chair. He could frighten a burglar away by faking a heart attack, but not otherwise. I guess he's good for the kids, because no matter how much they tug his ears or toss him around, he never snaps. He never even moves. I asked Miriam once if the dog could be suffering from post-traumatic shock syndrome, but she said that wasn't one bit funny.

When we first brought Bagel home, he was supposed to be Joel's dog. He was Joel's dog for about ten minutes, and he's been Miriam's dog since then. As I said, he and I have little use for each other. I have nothing left to say to a dog that is already trained to go to the bathroom outside, and he has nothing left to say to a person who is already trained to pay for his dog food.

So it sticks in my mind that he came over to me that evening as I was sitting at the dinner table, closed his eyes, and put his head in my lap. "Miriam," I said, "the dog's going to throw up."

Miriam sat down in the chair next to mine and moved the dog's head from my lap to hers. She stroked its head and neck rhythmically, and it made the sort of purring noise I would have expected from a cat. The doorbell rang. I answered it, as I had a hundred years ago that very morning.

Miriam has never liked Jack Sheridan. As he stood on our doorstep, swaying like a slightly drunken palm tree, he wasn't a candidate to change her opinion. But there he was; so I invited him in. Miriam paroled the children from the table, and they disappeared.

"Well, Billy, how's business?" The four adults—Miriam and I, Jack, and Billy—wandered into the TV room. Jack had asked the question. He was duly informed that the *shmatte* business was not what it used to be.

" ... and how's your business?"

"The relentless pursuit of justice continues." Jack, too, had his canned answer. He turned to Miriam. "Sorry I missed dinner."

"Can I offer you anything now?"

"How about a bourbon?"

I was right. Today would not be the day for Miriam to improve her opinion of Blackjack Sheridan. I went to the liquor cabinet and got Jack his drink.

The four of us were ranged along an L-shaped couch. Billy sat opposite the television, which was turned off at that moment. Jack was in the crook of the L, slumped forward with his elbows on his knees, both hands wrapped around his glass. I sat at the end of the couch, my arm over Miriam's shoulders. And of course because Jack was there, Ed Barber was there, too. Ed and DeeDee were both there, and for the first time ever they were monopolizing the conversation. The rest of us couldn't seem to get a word in.

Billy jingled the change in his pocket. "So, Jack, how's business?" But he had asked that one already, so he asked, "How are the criminals these days?"

Jack didn't look up from his bourbon. "Innocent till proven indigent." Again the canned answer. He took a few swallows and sat back against the couch. "When Clark and I"—it was *Clahk and Ah*; liquor brought out the drawl—"were young prosecutors, it was all great fun. We saw law school classmates go with the big firms, start to make the big bucks, but it didn't matter. We were in trial, we were called to crime scenes at three o'clock in the morning, we were on the front page of the *Herald*. We would get around to making money, but right then we were lawyers, real goddamn lawyers. Then one day twenty years went by and it was too late to get a job with a big firm, or with any firm. Criminal law was all I knew. So every morning

I get up and go to court and punch 'em in the fist with my nose, and belt 'em in the knee with my balls."

Not even the blow-up in court that morning had made me realize how completely Ed's death had crushed Jack. Blackjack Sheridan was not a weepy drunk. I had never, till that moment, heard him wax nostalgic about any past he had ever known. Billy, jingling his pocket change, began telling some story about his traveling salesman days back when he brought the gospel of the Steinfeldt and Tinker EZ-fit Trouser Company to the dry-goods merchants and clothing retailers of the Midwest ... I didn't pay much attention. Jack's glass was empty. Miriam, without interrupting Billy, took the drink from Jack's hands, walked into the kitchen with it, left it in the sink. When she returned, Billy's story had drifted away into silence. When the silence became oppressive Jack began to fill it with his own reminiscences.

"Hey, Clark," he said, "you remember the time Judge Galena had that big, fat, albino-looking guy before him? It was on some nothing kind of case, but Galena looks down at him and says, 'Well, Slim, you better hope they never arrest the Pillsbury Dough Boy or the police will make you stand in the line-up.'" It was a specimen of cruelty, not of humor, but Jack was laughing out loud at the recollection. Strangely, I found myself giving in to laughter as well. "And the electric chair form? Remember Galena's electric chair form? He'd have some poor old black defendant in front of him on a bullshit case, lurking with intent to gawk or some such thing, and he'd say, 'Well, Willie, I'm looking at your record and I see here that I had you before me once and I gave you credit for time served, didn't I? Then I had you before me again and I suspended entry of sentence, didn't I? Then, let's see now, I had you before me one more time and I put you on probation, and I warned you, didn't I, I said I didn't want to see you in here again, didn't I?'" Jack provided a faithful rendition of Judge Galena's voice, his gestures, the grave, pompous shaking of the head. "Then the little pervert would look down at his clerk and say, 'This defendant leaves me no choice. Madam Clerk, hand me the electric chair form, please.' And the clerk would actually give Galena some piece of paper, and all the proceedings would come to a halt while he sat there for fifteen minutes pretending to be filling it out. Of course poor Willie would about shit himself."

Jack and I were rocking back and forth with laughter, screaming with laughter, crying with laughter. The story wasn't even funny. It was an appalling tale of judicial abuse and racism. I think back on it now and I can't find anything funny in it. I think back on it now and I'm ashamed to have laughed. But I laughed then. I laughed and I howled and I cried, not so much because the story was funny but because I needed, and Jack needed, to laugh and howl and cry. Miriam, I could see, was offended.

I got myself under control, and Jack did too. His laughter stopped; but it stopped just a few seconds before his crying did. He wiped his face furiously with his shirtsleeve, embarrassed and angry. When his self-control had returned to him, he looked up and said, "Goddamn good thing they made you a judge, Clark. You never could cross-examine for spit." He was smiling that old Blackjack Sheridan smile. I'll live forever, said that smile, and never again let anyone see a piece of my heart.

Miriam smiled too and started to explain how of course they made me a judge because of all my good qualities. She even said that I was "God-fearing," not the sort of compliment a man gets every day. Jack reached forward and picked up the family Bible from the coffee table. I had told Joel to return it to my study after I read to Miriam from Proverbs during dinner, but his pre-teen attention span had failed him somewhere along the way.

"I don't want a God-fearing judge," Jack said, "I want to try all my cases before atheists."

"And why is that?"

"Because a God-fearing judge is forgiven. When he sentences my client to die in the electric chair, he can sleep at nights, because he's forgiven. I want my client sentenced by a judge who knows that no one and nothing in this universe can forgive him. I want him to look in the mirror every morning and know that he and he alone must bear the cross for having sent some poor dumb sumbitch up to Starke to fry." He

thought for a minute, then held the Bible up. "Miriam, you remember the story about King Solomon and the two women ..."

Miriam remembered. "Both had infants. One child died,
and each mother claimed that the living child belonged to her,
and the dead child to the other woman."

Jack nodded. "First Kings, chapter three, verse sixteen."
Nothing about Jack surprises me, but Miriam looked like she'd
seen a fish ride a bicycle. "I'll bet your mama, or your Sunday
school teacher, told you that story showed what a wise old man
King Solomon was. Well it doesn't." He put the book back on
the coffee table. "The Bible says those two women were prostitutes. And you know what prostitutes don't want around the
house? Babies. Bad for business. Isn't that right, Clark?" I supposed it was right. "They couldn't kill both little babies. No,
that would be ham-handed murder. But maybe, if they were
clever about it, they could kill one. That would leave one
hooker to tend to customers while the other one was tending to
Junior." Jack yawned. "So that's what they did. Those two
women smothered one child to death, and then both went crying and sobbing to old King Solomon, each claiming the living
child was hers. Solomon may have known his way around the
Psalms and Proverbs, but he didn't know much about how
prostitutes have to live their lives. They made him think it was
a child custody case, and they got away with murder."

No one spoke for a long moment. I thought about asking
Jack what his point was, but then Jack stood, announced that he
had to be going, said his goodbyes. I walked him out to the car.

"You OK to drive home?"

"Sure." He smiled that Blackjack smile. I think he even
gave me a little wink. "Clark, there is something."

"What's that?"

He was suddenly serious. "That Linden kid, Clark. You've
got to let him out on bail. You've got to let him out, Clark."

"Go home, Jack." I turned and walked the length of the
driveway back to the house. I got as far as the door before I
heard his engine turn over. I leaned against the doorframe and
watched him drive away.

I was thinking about the first case I had ever worked with

Ed Barber, the case on which we met, back in my prosecutor days. A little girl had been abducted, a sweet-faced nine-year-old whom the papers referred to as "Baby Karen," and when her corpse was found the autopsy photos made strong men weak. The press and the community were up in arms like nothing Miami-Dade County had ever seen, and I was responsible for organizing the investigation with the various police agencies involved. One of the detectives in Ed's homicide squad was an old-timer named Sullivan. Sully was at the tail-end of a police career that went back to the days when there were separate lock-ups for white and "colored," when there was no ACLU in Florida, and when street justice was dispensed at the business end of a nightstick. He was a hulking old drunk from the bare-knuckle school of police work, and he had conceived the notion that a small-time pimp and part-time police snitch named Vega knew something about the Baby Karen kidnapping. He picked Vega up, took him into one of the interrogation rooms at the station, and soaked a towel in the sink. Then he tied knots in the towel, and the process of interrogation began. It was a one in a million accident that I learned what was going on. I was with Ed at the time. He tried to tell me to forget about it, that it was something I didn't need to know about. I didn't wait to debate the point. When I burst into the interrogation room Vega was slumped down in a folding chair, Sullivan was standing over him, the towel was flying and Vega's face looked like ground chuck.

For two or three long seconds Sullivan and I stood there eyeing each other. I heard someone walk in behind me and knew without looking that it was Ed. I wasn't going to give him a chance to choose up sides. "Detective Barber, I want this man"—I pointed to Vega without taking my eyes off Sullivan— "transported to Jackson Hospital immediately."

Sullivan loomed over me. His voice was whiskey growl, scarcely more than a whisper. "Go fuck yourself, or I'll do it for you."

I drew myself up to my full height, which brought me about even with Sully's neck. "Detective Sullivan, I will personally see you indicted for aggravated battery. If this man dies, make that murder one. And I'll have your badge."

I think it was the badge that did it. Sullivan was a short-timer, and he wasn't going to forfeit three decades worth of accrued retirement benefits because of a piece of shit named Vega. He turned his back on me, walked over to the sink, and slowly rinsed his face. Ed picked up Vega the way you pick up a child, and we walked out of the room together.

The ride over to the hospital—Ed driving, me riding shotgun, and Vega stretched out in the backseat—was just fifteen minutes or so, but there was time enough for the only angry conversation I ever had with Ed Barber.

Ed kept his eyes on the road, speaking to me without looking at me. "Nice bluff."

I knew what he was asking. I knew that he was entitled to an answer. "No bluff, Ed. Sullivan will be charged and prosecuted."

"Bullshit. You're bullshitting."

It wasn't a question, so I didn't answer. And I wasn't bullshitting. A few minutes passed. Ed started again.

"So what are you saying? That it's more important not to smack around a pimp than it is to catch the assholes who kidnapped Baby Karen?"

"There's a law against kidnapping. We're going to catch the assholes who did it and see them prosecuted. There's a law against pimping. If I catch Vega doing it, I'll see him prosecuted. And there's a law against beating a man half to death with a damp towel. I caught Sully doing it, and I'll see him prosecuted."

He turned to me. Ed wasn't much for shouting, but he was close to shouting now. "But he's a cop! He's a cop and you're a prosecutor! You're supposed to be on the same side!"

"The law is what matters."

"Fuck the law! What about justice? What about that?"

"The law is what we live by. Justice is what we live for." It was the law school answer, but it wasn't much of an answer. The law is what we live by. Sometimes justice is what we live without. *La ley es apenas la sombra de la justicia*, the Cubans say. The law is but the shadow of justice.

We rode in silence for a few minutes. Then Ed asked, "Did it ever cross your mind back there in the interrogation room that Sullivan was about this close"—he held his thumb and index finger so that they almost came together—"to working *you* over with that towel?"

I extended my arms toward Ed, hands open, palms down. At fifteen minute's remove from the police station, my hands were still trembling involuntarily. Ed started to laugh. He was not much of a laugher, but he laughed what for him was a good long laugh. "You're a tough little runt when you have to be, aren't you, Clark?" He laughed some more. "A tough little runt." We've been friends ever since.

Billy was in the TV room where I had left him, but his head had tipped back and he was snoring. Miriam was in the kitchen tidying up. When I got close enough to touch her I saw the tears.

"What is it?"

"Nothing. I was ... thinking about DeeDee." She was handing me the wineglasses, the ones that went on the high shelf she had trouble reaching. When the glasses were gone she put her arms around me, and her head on my shoulder. "Clark, that story Jack told about King Solomon and the two women—is it true?"

"I don't know. Anyone who could tell us for sure has been dead a long time."

We held each other close. When she spoke again, it was in a whisper. "Why? Why would Ed ever do such a thing?"

We stood there like that for a long time.

Chapter Two
Last Year

Jack leaned over the wooden railing of the balcony and considered carefully whether to puke on the bird of paradise flowers in the garden below. It was a straight shot, one floor down, a shot that he made with unerring accuracy most mornings.

Some of the flowers were in bloom. Green stems led up to a pod formed like a beak from which sprouted, feather shaped, orange and blue petals. The effect was of a long-stemmed pinwheel, multi-colored, exotic. Each stem was surrounded with a heavy growth of leaves, upturned to catch and hold the rain. Much experience had taught Jack that puke, descending rain-like from the balcony, would land heavily on the leaves and then trickle into the base of the plant. The automatic sprinklers were set to go on about half an hour after Jack customarily awoke. They would wash the puke into the soil, completing the process of re-cycling. Last night's drinking would become this morning's fertilizer, all a part of nature's plan to bring flowers into the world.

After due consideration, Jack concluded that he was insufficiently hung-over to do a really good job of puking. There would be other mornings.

The balcony was of wood, carefully stained and lacquered to resist the sun and humidity. It ran the length of one side of Jack's bedroom and overlooked the courtyard. The house itself was old by Miami standards. It was one of an ever-decreasing number of such homes along Bayshore Drive, homes that had zoning variances allowing them to be used as both a residence and an office. The house had belonged to a doctor who had lived and practiced medicine there for so long that he claimed to have treated Jack's granddaddy—Blackjack the Second—for cirrhosis of the liver. Now the second floor was Jack's residence and the ground floor was the Law Offices of John Wentworth Sheridan IV.

He stood on the balcony, naked but for his jockeys, sucking up the morning air. In an hour the air would be damp and hot, but in the early morning it was, briefly, light and cool. It was a shame, he thought, that morning came at such an inconvenient time.

He went back inside the house, showered, shaved, dressed. If he got down to the first floor kitchen not later than 8:30 or so he could be sure of making the coffee. This was important. The members of his office staff had many good qualities, but they could not make coffee for shit. They made what the Cubans call *agua sucia*, dirty water. The coffee he made was too strong for them, but it was right for him. It was thick and strong, and it settled the stomach, particularly after the morning's puke.

At 9:01 Edwina Reulbach would arrive. Edwina had come with the house. As a young girl she had served as a part-time bookkeeper to the old doctor. As an old woman she served as a part-time bookkeeper to Jack. Perhaps she had liked, approved of, even admired the doctor. She did not like, approve of, admire Jack. She was clean and expressionless and precise. She arrived every morning at 9:01 and left at 12:59. Clients who paid in cash were given receipts whether they wanted them or not. Miss Edwina then filled out a deposit slip and walked directly to the bank with the cash, because if she delayed in doing so Mr. Sheridan might help himself to some or all of the cash, thereby violating federal income tax law and, worse yet, unbalancing her bookkeeping. In her opinion, too much cash in his pockets only made Mr. Sheridan "nigger-rich." Jack kept her around to fend off the IRS. Besides, she worked cheap.

A client visiting the Law Offices of John Wentworth Sheridan IV entered through the front door into a lobby area that would have been a foyer if the house were a home. At the back of the lobby was a sliding glass window, and on the other side of the window sat Charlene "Charli" Murphy. Charli was as young as Edwina was old, as careless as Edwina was scrupulous, as complaisant as Edwina was severe. She worked from 9:00, or whenever she remembered to show up, until 5:00, or whenever she departed for night classes at Miami-Dade Community College. It was not certain what Charli was studying at Miami-Dade, but Jack doubted that it was brain surgery. When a client came in and whined for half an hour at a stretch about his legal problems Charli's blue eyes grew dark with compassion and her milky skin flushed to the roots of her red hair, and she promised that Mr. Sheridan would call just as soon as he got back from court. The client left, placated, and Jack was given a note saying that client so-and-so had stopped by, and that it was nothing urgent.

Behind Charli, in what would have been the living room, were filing cabinets, xerox machines, law office clutter. All the way back and to the left was a room that might have been a guest bedroom or study, but had been converted decades ago into a sanctuary for Edwina. It was a very small room, furnished with nothing more than Edwina's desk and chair, the office safe, and a few shelves on which Edwina kept her books and ledgers. A single window looked out on Bayshore Drive, and an orchid plant, a vanda, sat on the interior window ledge. Beyond Edwina's office was a half-bathroom used by Edwina and Charli but not by clients.

Off the living room to the right was the kitchen. The large room that would have been the dining room was in the front of the house to the right, and had been converted into Jack's office. The area between Charli's reception desk and Jack's office had been made up into a kind of anteroom in which Jack's personal secretary had her desk and effects; but for some weeks now Jack had been between secretaries, and this was becoming a problem.

When Edwina arrived Jack was leaning against the kitchen counter listening to the soothing gurgle of the coffee machine and inhaling the smell of coffee in the making. As was her custom, Edwina proceeded straight to her lair. Somewhere between the front door and her office she announced "Good morning" in her expressionless way to anyone who happened to be listening. Jack replied as was his custom: "Why, good morning, Miss Edwina. And how are you on this lovely morning?" It was a rhetorical question.

Still leaning against the counter, Jack was halfway through his first cup of coffee when Charli showed up. He heard her take the phones off answering service and scribble some messages. Then she wandered into the kitchen in search of caffeine.

The kitchen was the only room on the ground floor that had been remodeled since the doctor's time. Most of the back wall now consisted of a sliding glass door that opened on the courtyard and made the kitchen, in the morning, the brightest room in the house. Charli squinted, groped for coffee, then leaned against the counter opposite Jack.

"Do I have anything in court today?"

She shook her head without looking up from her cup. "I don't think so." Charli did not view it as a receptionist's job to keep track of Jack's court schedule. That was something his secretaries had always done, something a secretary should be doing now. She had been nagging him to hire a new one, and she would keep nagging.

He knew that, so he said, "I've got someone coming in about the secretary job this morning, right?"

Charli nodded. "Ten o'clock." She went to the sink and ran hot water into her coffee cup. The coffee was too strong. Jack always made it too strong.

He turned to walk toward his office. "Cousin in yet?," she asked.

"I don't know," he said. "I'll check."

Jack's office was the largest room in the house. The floor was the original wood. Overhead hung a small, ancient-looking chandelier that cast a dim yellow light on the rare occasions that Jack turned it on, and it too may have been part of the original interior design. To the right as one entered the room, in the wall facing Jack's desk, was a built-in fireplace, and over it a handsome wooden mantelpiece. The fireplace was never used, but three logs were stacked in it as if they might be lighted one day. Arrayed on the wall above the mantelpiece were the sort of trophies all lawyers have: diplomas, bar admissions, framed newspaper clippings from high-profile cases. On the floor in front of the fireplace was a throw rug, which was supposed to be very valuable. The rug was a gift from a client, a sort of going-away present from a grateful Colombian whom Jack had gotten out on bail and who then promptly fled the jurisdiction.

The walls behind Jack and to his right—to the left as one stood in the doorway—were given over to bookshelves, floor to ceiling. The shelves were filled with the numbered volumes of the Southern Reporters and Federal Reporters, law books that every practicing lawyer must own and update and for which there is never enough room. The wall to Jack's left was mostly windows, which looked out on Bayshore Drive. Beneath the windows was a sofa that had no business being in the office. It was large and worn and stained and ugly and cheap. On this particular morning, as on many mornings, the sofa was occupied by a prone form loosely covered with unfolded pages from one of last week's editions of the *Miami Herald*.

Jack kicked the sofa, kicked it hard. "Hey, Cousin," he said.

The form beneath the newspapers twitched once and grunted. Jack sat at his chair and put his coffee cup on his desk. "You want some coffee?"

The papers rustled as the figure beneath them shifted position slightly. A noise came from under the papers, the sound of a human voice, and it might have said, "Uh-huh."

"Charli," Jack called out to the kitchen, "bring Cousin a cup of coffee, will you?"

Charli brought in a large cup of black coffee, set it on the floor next to the sofa, and retreated to the doorway. A hand crept out from the papers, felt for the cup, and then hand and cup disappeared beneath the papers. There came a slurping sound, and a low moan of pain. Cousin sat up slowly and brushed away the papers.

A large wooden cabinet stood at the foot of the sofa near Jack's desk. Cousin found his way to it, opened it, took out a bottle. He sat on the arm of the sofa to steady himself, and poured from the bottle into his cup. The cup full, Cousin extended it toward Jack and Charli, muttered, "Here's to the one that got away," and drank.

Looking at Cousin was like looking at Jack in a bad funhouse mirror. The image of Jack was clear, but it was oddly, crazily distorted. Jack's tan gave him an outdoorsy, healthy look. Cousin's skin was sunburned in some places and cheesy-white in others, patchy and blotchy, like skin cancer waiting to happen. Jack's hair was full and straight, and it seemed that he needed to do no more than run his fingers through it to keep it in place. Cousin's hair was the same color and texture, but it grew in clumps, like weeds in an abandoned garden. His breath was bad, and there seemed always to be a thick film at the corners of his mouth.

They actually were related, Cousin and Jack, although the great-aunt who could explain precisely how they were related had died some years before and neither Jack nor Cousin gave a shit. Cousin had a name, of course, but that was something else that no one remembered or gave a shit about not remembering. Cousin had no address of his own, no worldly assets, but he had few if any expenses, either. He slept on Jack's boat or office sofa, and on those occasions when he took a shower he did that at Jack's office too. Jack picked up his bar tab, and food was not an issue because no one could ever recall seeing Cousin eat anything but bar nuts and bar pretzels.

Yet of all the people associated with Jack's law practice, Cousin was the most important. In the early years it was Cousin who had built Jack's practice; and even now, when Jack's reputation was enough to keep the customers coming, Cousin was invaluable. Cousin was a boat person. Not a sailor — Jack was a sailor — but a boat person. He was a member of a colony, a subculture, located in Miami and the Keys, a subculture as distinctive and cohesive as that of the Vietnamese boat people who lived as squatters in Hong Kong harbor. The South Florida boat people were to be found in marinas and docks from Miami to Key West, or on boats wandering the Florida Straits between here and the Bahamas. They talked with other boat people about boats, and they hung out with other boat people in boat people hangouts. If a boat person was in trouble — and boat people were always in trouble — he asked another boat person where to go for help. If the trouble was legal trouble and the boat person who was asked was Cousin, the place to go for help was the Law Offices of John Wentworth Sheridan IV. Legal trouble for boat people usually meant drugs, and drugs usually meant good-sized legal fees.

When he wasn't in the company of boat people, and sometimes when he was, Cousin was in bars. Cousin knew, made it his business to know, dozens of bartenders in Miami. He tipped them well—hell, it was Jack's money—and kept them well provided with Jack's business cards. Bartenders, like boat people, often knew folks with legal troubles that needed expensive solutions. Cousin knew bridgetenders, the men who operated the bridges along the Miami River that had to be raised to permit shipping to move up and down the river and lowered to permit auto traffic across the river. And because he knew bridgetenders, Cousin knew if a ship was attracting the attention of Customs or the Coast Guard, a ship that might be carrying illicit cargo, a ship whose captain and crew might soon be facing legal charges. Blackjack Sheridan was a good lawyer, perhaps a great lawyer, but Miami was full of good lawyers who couldn't pay the rent. It was Cousin who made Jack the good lawyer into Jack the rich lawyer. The sofa that was worn and stained and cheap would stay in Jack's office; love me, love my sofa.

Charli spoke, still leaning in the doorway. "You want to go upstairs and take a shower?" In response, Cousin spent a few seconds sniffing himself all over. The process disgusted Charli, and she was sorry she had asked. Whatever Cousin smelled— stale liquor stains, stale sweat stains, stale piss stains, and perhaps just a hint of salt sea air—he answered, "Maybe later."

Jack turned to Charli. "Why don't you go answer the phone, darlin'?"

"It's not ringing."

"Well, why wait till the last minute?"

Charli disappeared. Cousin, clutching his Irish coffee, eased himself back into the sofa. He took a few more swallows and eyed Jack over the rim of the cup. "What are you up to today?"

"It's an office day," said Jack, meaning that he had no court appearances scheduled. "I need the time to finish prepping the Menendez trial."

"I thought the prosecution was offering Menendez a sweetheart deal to testify against the co-defendant."

"They're offering."

"He's not accepting?"

Jack sighed. "The co-defendant is Tiburon Quintero. Menendez has a wife and three kids."

"What does Quintero have?"

"A Sears and Roebuck charge card. As long as they still sell chain saws at Sears, Menendez isn't taking the plea bargain."

Cousin slurped his coffee. "Need me to do anything?"

"Yeah. Menendez and his wife both have a bad case of bartender syndrome. Go see him, will you?"

Bartender syndrome had nothing to do with bars or booze. Bartender syndrome was a chronic affliction of criminal defendants, the symptom of which was confusing your lawyer with your bartender. Clients suffering from bartender syndrome called and visited the office constantly, not because they had something new to tell the lawyer, nor because the lawyer had sent for them, but simply because they wanted to share their cares and woes with their lawyer one more time. Jack knew, as every criminal lawyer knows, that putting up with a certain amount of bartender syndrome was part of the job. There was an extent to which Jack was willing to listen, expressing compassion, as the client whined for the eleventy-seventh time that it wasn't fair, that lots of guys got away with what he had done, that the cops were picking on him for no reason, that he had read in the paper about a guy who got straight probation for the same crime, and so on and on. The problem wasn't that Jack lacked compassion. In truth he had more compassion for his clients' problems than he would ever have admitted. But what Jack wanted—what every criminal lawyer wants—was to tell the client, "Would you kindly shut the fuck up so that I can spend my time *preparing* your case instead of wasting my time listening to you piss and moan about it?" Of course, that kind of response wouldn't do, particularly if the client still owed Jack money. So it was Cousin's chore, as far as possible, to insulate Jack from the acute sufferers of bartender syndrome. If the client was in jail—Menendez was in jail—Cousin would visit him. He would listen patiently to the same inane questions that the client had asked during the last visit, and he would provide the same answers, knowing that he would have to provide them again next visit. He would bring extra change to buy the client coffee or soda from the visitors'-room vending machines. He would reassure the client that Mr. Sheridan was the best damn lawyer in this man's town, and that no case in the office was so important to Mr. Sheridan as this one. He would promise to telephone Mrs. Menendez and explain it all to her, not mentioning pointedly that he had explained it all to her a dozen times already. He would, in short, play the part of a good bartender; who better to do so than Cousin? And when it was all over and the client was reassured, he would hand the client a stack of business cards that said John Wentworth Sheridan IV and remind the client that if he made any friends here in the joint who needed a good lawyer, he should be sure to hand them Mr. Sheridan's card. If any such friends were in the visitors' room at the time, Cousin would buy them a coffee or a soda too. Hell, might as well get some new business out of it.

Cousin spoke again. "You want me to try to talk him into taking the plea?"

Jack shook his head. It was a mistake to talk a client into, or out of, a plea bargain. Suppose Jack told the client not to take the plea, and the client took Jack's advice and went to trial, and Jack lost and the client got 15 years? Jack didn't want 15 years of phone calls and letters claiming that it was all Jack's fault, 15 years of a client telling everyone else in the prison system that Blackjack Sheridan sucked as a lawyer. And suppose Jack told the client to take the plea, and the client took Jack's advice and was out in six months or a year, and two weeks after that his body or the bodies of his wife and kids were found in the trunk of a car in the Everglades? Where criminal litigation was concerned, every choice was a gamble. Jack always told clients that there were only two things he could guarantee: That whatever the client decided, he, Blackjack Sheridan, would do the best he

could to protect the client's interests; and that after the case was
over, he, Blackjack Sheridan, would not be the one going to
prison.

"No," Jack said. "Just make sure he understands what his
options are."

Cousin roused himself from the sofa. He offered his toast
again — "Here's to the one that got away" — and drained the cup.
Then he wandered out of Jack's office. His jail visit would take
three or four hours. After that he would find his way to a marina or two, passing the time and listening to people's troubles
until the bars started to open. So many bars, so little time.
Along about the early morning hours he might end up on the
sofa in Jack's office. Or he might spend the night on someone's
boat, at home in the company of boat people, at home with the
movements and sounds of the sea.

As Cousin was leaving, Charli's voice came through the intercom to tell Jack that I was on the phone. Jack picked up.

"Clark, I was talking to the Pope on the other line, but when
I heard it was you I put him on hold. How the hell are you?"

I told him I was fine. We chatted only briefly, I not being
much of a telephone conversationalist. No, Jack said he wasn't
coming down to the courthouse today. That was too bad, I
said, I had thought we might have lunch. Another time, perhaps; it would be a busy office day and Jack would work
through lunch.

It was the only time I spoke to Jack that day, and we didn't
see each other. It was only later, after everything happened,
that I set about reconstructing the events of that day, set about
parsing out every small detail of what happened to Jack from
morning to night. It was then that I remembered our telephone
conversation. If I had known then what I know now, I could
have said ... what? What could I have said that would have
made any difference?

Jack hung up the phone and ran his eye over the papers
from the Menendez file, spread across his desk. These papers
would occupy his day; these papers and the matter of hiring a
new secretary. This was a matter of some delicacy. He had
been without one since Nikki walked out a month and a half

ago. She had been a good secretary. She typed and took short-hand rapidly and well, spoke English and Spanish fluently, handled client emergencies at all hours of day or night uncomplainingly. She had a husband and a young child, and had been working for him for almost three years when she came to him to say that she was too much in love with him to go on being his secretary. He went into Edwina's office and returned with a large check and a letter of recommendation addressed "To Whom it May Concern." Then he patted Nikki on the shoulder, told her that it was all right, that she was doing the right thing, and showed her out. That was six weeks or so ago.

He had felt sorry for Nikki, genuinely sorry. He did not love her, but he had never wanted to make her unhappy, and it pained him to have done so. He had no particular compunction about sleeping with married women, but it was his rule not to date his own secretary.

The angel on his right shoulder told him that this was a good rule, a very good rule. The devil on his left shoulder whispered that he was free, white, and over 21, and so were all the secretaries he had ever hired. If avoidance of sin was the issue here, what greater sin could there be than letting a willing woman go to waste? Still, the angel had a point: Where secretaries were concerned, keeping it strictly business was good for business. Besides, he couldn't see himself breaking Nikki's heart or ruining her marriage.

Charli's voice came through the intercom again. His ten o'clock appointment, Ms. Rodriguez, was here about the secretary job. Charli came down hard on that last part, *about the secretary job*. Without waiting to be told, Charli escorted Ms. Rodriguez back to Jack's office.

When Teresa Rodriguez walked through Jack's doorway, even the angel on Jack's right shoulder got a hard-on. Jack stood and tried to smile, but it wasn't the real good Blackjack smile. It was a quick smile, an almost embarrassed smile, a smile he had no time to prepare. He gestured toward a chair opposite his desk and sat when she did. He had the presence of mind to ask if she wanted some coffee and was about to ask "or anything else" when he remembered that it was ten o'clock in the morning and some people might not understand. She said that she had coffee already. She sat up very straight, but gracefully, not stiffly. She was smiling, smiling the way people smile when they have a secret and want you to guess it. But Jack had already guessed.

"We met last Christmas," he said, "at the office party at Williams, Santos, and Banks."

"You remember."

"Of course." Of course he remembered. He remembered the dark brown hair and the darker brown eyes. He remembered the perfect tan color of her flesh, so smooth and rich that it put him in mind of beaches and palm trees and seashells rocking helplessly in the shallow surf. He knew that if he closed his eyes he would remember the scent of her, but somehow he knew, too, that she would read his mind, that she would know why his eyes were closed and what he was recalling. She had worn a sleeveless dress at the Christmas party, because it drew attention to the golden skin of her arms and shoulders, and to the lissome movement of her body. She was wearing a sleeveless dress now but not, he thought, the same one. "How's my friend Raul Santos?"

"Just fine."

"You've been working there for some time."

"Six years."

"It's a fine law firm."

"Yes it is."

"But you're planning to leave?"

"I've already given notice."

"May I ask why?"

"I heard you were looking for a secretary."

Jack had been making a conscious effort to look at her face and not at her legs or tits. He had been smiling, smiling the good Blackjack smile, and his southern accent was in full bloom. He had unbuttoned his collar button and loosened his tie just slightly, affecting that studied carelessness that as a boy he had admired in photos of Robert Kennedy. He had been doing fine, just fine, until she said that she was leaving a good job at a good firm because she had heard that he, Blackjack Sheridan, was looking for a secretary. His lips started to form the word "why?" but he brought himself up. The question was full of danger. What if it resulted in an answer that made it impossible to hire her? The angel on his right shoulder wasn't the only one in the room with a hard-on.

"Did ... did you leave the firm on good terms?"

"Absolutely."

"Would you ... do you mind if I call over there to confirm that?" Shit, he thought, what if she said she minded, then what would he say or do?

"Not in the least."

He was smiling again. Not in the least, she had said, she didn't mind in the least if he called over there to confirm that. Maybe he would call and maybe he wouldn't.

"Sure you won't have some coffee?"

"All right then."

He had Charli bring coffee. They chatted casually for a few minutes, discussing the nature of his practice, lawyers they knew in common, that sort of thing. Working in a criminal practice would be different than what she was used to at Williams, Santos, and Banks, he explained. There were the midnight calls from jail, the emergency bond hearings, the trials that would tie him up for weeks and oblige her to manage on her own. She thought it sounded much more exciting than what she was used to. He thought she was probably right about that. They talked salary in a general way, nothing too specific but it didn't appear that there would be a problem on that score.

"Do you like animals? Have any pets?" he asked.

"Three cats that I'm madly in love with. Why, are you allergic? Is it a problem?"

"No problem." Then just for the sheer hell of it, he said, "You took a long chance quitting your job before you applied here." *Chay-ence*, two syllables in decent Southern. "Truth is, I've already interviewed several applicants. One was good, very good."

She leaned forward, coffee cup still in hand. "You could do better."

"And how could I do better?"

"You could do me." Without looking down at the cup, she took a long, slow sip. It was only after swallowing that she re-phrased it. "You could hire me."

He cleared his throat. Then he asked softly, "Coffee OK?"

"Yes."

"Not too strong?"

"I like it that way."

"Are you free for lunch?"

"Sorry," she said. She put her cup down gently and stood. "I've got to get a few things out of the way today, so I can start my new job tomorrow morning."

Charli saw her out, actually walking her through the foyer and out the front door. It was obvious even to Charli that this was Jack's new secretary, so she made a point of saying, as they parted, "I'm Charli."

"Hi, Charli. I'm Teresa."

"Teresa ... mind if I ask you something?"

"What?"

"Did he ask you if you had any pets?"

"Yes." She smiled. "Why, what does that mean?"

Charli's innocent little face was knotted with the perplexity of it all. "Edwina and I are trying to figure it out. Sometimes he asks that ... especially, you know, the pretty ones."

"Then ask him why." It was an approach not likely to occur to Charli, and beneath the dignity of Edwina. Meantime, Jack was sitting at his desk, leaning back, with one foot up. It would be a few minutes before he regained any interest in the picky-ass problems of his client Menendez.

* * *

We thought of it as our regular Saturday morning break-fast, but what with one thing and another we were seldom able to get together more than one Saturday a month, maybe two. With Ed it was a question of his work schedule. With Jack it was a question of his play schedule—if he spent Friday night with his girlfriend *du jour* he was a no-show on Saturday morning. I was the one with regular habits. Since law school days I had spent my Saturday mornings at the university law library, catching up on research and reading new cases. The Cuban coffee shop where we met was on the way to the law library, and I could be counted on to show up every Saturday morning.

The coffee shop was tiny. There were half-a-dozen tables arranged almost cheek to cheek, and along one wall a counter with eight or ten stools. The two paddle-fans that hung from the ceiling and rotated at different rates of speed made the ceiling itself seem low. The place gave the impression of a doll's house, owned and operated by down-on-their-luck dolls. There was never more than one waiter or waitress in attendance, and it seemed never to be the same person twice.

This particular coffee shop was located half a block off Southwest Eighth Street, *Calle Ocho*, the spinal column of the old Cuban neighborhood. In its heyday, Eighth Street and its cross-streets seemed somehow to embrace the entire Cuban population of Miami, with every landmark restaurant, every cigar factory. The years passed, the children of the immigrants achieved financial success and moved out of the old neighborhood. But many of the landmarks remained, Cuban restaurants and Cuban cigar factories now employing Salvadorans and Nicaraguans.

Ed arrived first that Saturday morning. He had observed over the years that this restaurant was never really crowded, but never entirely empty either, and so it was that Saturday. Three old Cuban men sat at a table, two playing dominoes while the third smoked and critiqued their play. A younger man sat at the counter with his back to Ed, sipping coffee and reading the Spanish-language edition of the *Miami Herald*. On a shelf on the wall, among glasses and cups of various sizes, a radio was loudly broadcasting a Spanish talk show. Ed tried briefly to follow the flow of the radio conversation. He had struggled, over the years, to learn some Spanish, but with only indifferent success. Spanish speakers who wanted him to understand them could make themselves understood, but Spanish speakers who wanted to leave him in complete confusion could do that, too.

He had been seated for only a moment when I joined him, and then a waiter appeared out of the kitchen. The waiter was a small man, very dark complected. He set down glasses of ice water and wiped his hands on his apron.

"*Cafe con leche,*" said Ed. "*Y pan cubano, bien planchado.*" Cafe con leche was coffee with heavy milk, what the French call "cafe au lait" or "white coffee." Pan cubano was French bread in the Cuban style, buttered and toasted in a press. "Bien planchado," Ed had said, well pressed; which meant that the bread would be crisp and chewy.

"*Lo mismo,*" I said, the same. Then we were pleased that we had ordered just like real Cubans.

The waiter made two trips to bring our breakfast. The bread came in baskets, and then the coffee in large cups. It was a meal in itself, the coffee, enough whole milk and caffeine and sugar to keep a body going for hours. Ed broke a piece of bread in half and soaked it in the coffee slowly. When it had absorbed all the rich coffee-milk it would hold without dissolving, he put it in his mouth. About then Jack wandered in.

He shook hands with Ed and me, exchanged greetings, then sat in silence and rubbed his eyes. When the waiter appeared, Jack ordered, in a deliberately un-Spanish accent, "Cafe Americano. Cafe gringo. American coffee." How did he take it, asked the waiter. "In a cup."

Jack went back to the business of rubbing his eyes, and his forehead. His coffee arrived burning hot, but he drank it anyway.

Ed and I knew that Jack had been in trial in federal court for the past three weeks on the Menendez case. He had gotten a verdict just Thursday, a bad verdict for his client.

Ed spoke about it. "Tough verdict, day before yesterday." Jack shrugged.

I tried. "Was there ever any defense in the case?"

Jack shrugged again. "Salty the Seaquarium Seal could have prosecuted and gotten a conviction. Hell, I told the sum-bitch to take the plea, I told him not to go to trial. They had him on videotape and there aren't a lot of ways to cross-examine a videotape. Then he insisted that I call his brother-in-law as a defense witness to say I don't know what, and the piece of shit spun me on the stand." A witness "spins" a lawyer when he gives the lawyer a different answer during trial than he had given in the lawyer's office before trial. About all a lawyer can do when a witness spins him is to try to look as if the disastrous, unexpected answer he got was the helpful, expected answer he had hoped for.

"How about the co-defendant?"

"Quintero? He went down too."

"Al Guerrero represented him?"

"Uh-huh."

"Good lawyer."

"Real good lawyer."

Jack went back to rubbing his eyes. Ed went back to dunking his bread. A few seconds passed in silence, and then Jack started to chuckle. He still had his head down and his hand over his eyes, and for just a split second Ed and I thought he might be crying, but he was chuckling. It wasn't much of a chuckle at first, but then he looked up, smiling, and got to laughing pretty good. Ed smiled back and asked him what the hell was so funny all of a sudden.

"Al Guerrero," he said. "Damn, he's a piece of work. You hear about the closing argument he made in our case?" We shook our heads, no. "Well, the prosecution's main witness against us was a *chivato*, a snitch, by the name of Solly Hofman. Hofman should be serving time till the next ice age, but the prosecution cut him a give-away-the-candy-store deal to testify against us. Al got up in closing," Jack chuckled again, "Al got up in closing and said, 'Ladies and Gentlemen of the Jury: Once upon a time, on one of those hot, sticky summer days we have here in Miami, the sewers started to back up. In fact the sewer right across the street from where we are now, the sewer line in front of the U.S. Attorney's Office, backed up entirely. And from out of that clogged sewer there oozed onto the street a thick, suppurating, stinking, viscous slime. And the slime bubbled and oozed its way, all green and smelly, down the street and up the stairs in front of the U.S. Attorney building. And this gray-green pus-like slime, stinking to high heaven, slithered its way right into the U.S. Attorney's Office. And there, ladies and gentlemen—miracle of miracles—the slime spoke! And it said, 'Hi, my name is Solly Hofman. Let's make a deal!'" Jack laughed out loud, a kid's laughter, loud and pure and silly. "God damn, it was all I could do not to piss in my pants. Didn't do us a bit of good, of course, the jury still slam-dunked us, but God damn." He laughed again, and the joy of his laughter was such that Ed and I laughed a little too.

"A federal judge let Al get away with an argument like that?" I had to ask.

Jack cocked his head to the side a little. "Yeah, he let Al Guerrero get away with it. He probably wouldn't have let half-a-dozen lawyers in this town get away with it. He sure as hell wouldn't have let any of the kids from the Federal Public Defender's Office get away with it. But Al is Al, and he gets away with things. Reputation is everything in this business." He winked at me. "Even in *federal* court."

"I guess that's why Al works so hard to cultivate his reputation," I said. Al, for all his good qualities, never met a TV camera he didn't fall in love with. Then again, Al Guerrero wasn't the only big-shot Miami criminal defense lawyer who worked hard at cultivating an image, a style of his own. Jack Sheridan wanted every judge and prosecutor in town to think of him as Blackjack Sheridan, who stumbled into court half-drunk or all hungover, shot from the hip—and still managed to pull off the winning defense. A judge had once said of him, "Jack Sheridan's a great lawyer, but he's no Jack Sheridan." The remark had been intended as a slight; but it proved the power of reputation, and it delighted Jack.

It did Ed and me good to see Jack laughing. Ed was quiet by nature, and like many cops had swallowed his emotions years ago. I, anxious and ambitious, found it difficult ever to relax. But the bond among the three of us was such that when Jack laughed, he laughed for all of us.

The sense of relaxation that came in the wake of the laughter lingered for ten minutes or so, and then it was time to leave. Inside his car, Jack put on his sunglasses and opened the sunroof. It was a beautiful morning, hot and clear, and he would have to waste it.

A law practice generates paper. Each client means one or more files, and each file means stacks and stacks of pleadings and documents. When a case was closed out, the files usually continued to sit in Jack's office for a few months, taking up space. But the space would be needed for new clients' files, so the old files would have to be shipped off to storage in a warehouse that Jack rented out in west Miami-Dade County. From time to time it would be necessary to pull out an old file from the warehouse and return it to the office. Even when it was necessary, Jack put it off as long as possible. A trip to the warehouse was time-consuming, and invariably the file in question would be at the bottom of some half-rotted cardboard box in the far corner of the storage shed. He had been putting a trip to the warehouse off for weeks, and he could put it off no longer. It was a beautiful morning, hot and clear, a morning that cried out for sails unfurled before a high wind. He would have to waste the morning.

He drove east on Eighth Street to Brickell Avenue, turned south on Brickell till it became Bayshore Drive, then south again toward his house. He had promised Teresa double-overtime if she came in for half a day and helped him retrieve the files from the warehouse. She had accepted eagerly. He had warned her that the warehouse was hot and dirty, and had told her to dress down. He wore a gray T-shirt that said, "University of Miami Hurricanes," jeans, and boat shoes.

He pulled into his driveway a few minutes early, but she was already there, outside her car and leaning against it. She appeared to have just come from working out. Her hair was pulled back, and she wore a sweatband. She had on a tanktop, athletic shorts, and a pair of running shoes. Her eyes were covered with a pair of large, unfashionable sunglasses.

He rolled his window down and smiled. "Is that how you're going?"

She smiled back. "You said I could dress down." She walked over to his open window and handed him a piece of paper. It was a list of the files they were retrieving, by client name and case number. "You forgot this." He stuffed the list in his pocket as she walked around to the passenger door and got in.

"A/C or windows and sunroof?"

"Windows and sunroof," she said. "I'm a little sweaty." Her tank top was a light color, a shade of pink like a hibiscus flower, but in front, down the middle, her sweat had darkened it to red. He realized he was staring, then turned to look out the rear window as he backed into the street.

Traffic was light and they were at the warehouse park in about twenty minutes. Jack punched his code number into a keypad and the heavy main gate rolled noisily aside. They drove slowly along a large driveway that ran the length of the facility. To their right were rows of storage sheds, like barracks, running as far as the eye could see. Jack proceeded past a dozen rows, made a right, went about halfway down the row and parked. He unlocked the corrugated metal door of his shed and rolled it up. Inside was a space about the size of a one-car garage. The shed was filled, nearly floor to ceiling and nearly wall to wall, with cardboard storage boxes. Each box was stuffed with closed files. A number of boxes, he couldn't say how many, were knocked over sideways, with papers spilling from one file to the next or falling to the ground. A couple of large, lazy palmetto bugs were waltzing dust bunnies across the floor.

Teresa got out of the car and stood next to him. "Ugh," she said, and made a face. She could feel the heat emanating from the still air inside the shed, and smell the dust and mold.

He nodded. "These files have nothing to do all day but dry up and turn to dust. During the rainy season, some rusty water is sure to leak through the roof, and then the boxes turn to pulp and smell of rot." He looked at her and smiled. "I know all the most romantic spots to take a lady." He tossed his sunglasses inside his car and started moving boxes.

Each box bore the names and case numbers of the client files it contained. The boxes, as far as Teresa could tell, were arranged in no particular order. Finding a given file was largely a matter of chance, and luck. Jack took the list out of his pocket. Re-arranging boxes from pile to pile as they went, they cleared a path toward the back of the shed. It was fifteen minutes of stacking and re-stacking, of shifting boxes from pile to pile, before they found a box containing two of the files they were looking for. Jack pulled them out, handed them to her, and motioned toward the car. She placed the files in the front seat and returned to the shed.

"Take your sunglasses off. How can you see in here?"

She shook her head. "I'm fine."

In the heat and dust of the shed the act of breathing seemed unnatural, and she had to think about each breath. They worked in silence for another ten minutes or so, Jack handing her boxes and she checking them for the files they wanted. The boxes now seemed heavier, much heavier, than when they had first arrived. Sweat ran down Jack's forehead and stung his eyes. He pulled off his T-shirt, balled it up, wiped his face with it. But the T-shirt was soaked through, too.

He turned to see how she was doing. Her back was to him, and she was bent forward from the waist, her hands resting on an open box as she checked the files inside the box. He squinted twice, three times, clearing the sweat from his field of vision. He ran his eyes up the back of her thighs to where they disappeared in her shorts. After a few seconds she stopped leafing through files. She straightened up slowly, gracefully, and turned to face him. He moved toward her, pressed her against a pile of boxes. She turned her face up toward his, and then just before their lips touched she whispered, "Are you going to mark me?"

His reply was a whisper too. "Just a little."

"Are you going to hurt me?"

"Just enough."

He pulled off her tank top. Her breasts weren't pale, as he had expected. They were the same golden shade as the rest of her skin. It took him a couple of seconds to realize that she sunbathed in the nude, and the thought made him crazier than he was. They made love sprawled across three or four filing boxes. It occurred to him later that the air that had been so heavy and acrid with dust and mold had become, in those minutes, sweet and salty with the scent and taste of her. It occurred to him later that cockroaches might have crawled back and forth across his ass. It occurred to him later that the shed door was open, and that anyone might have driven by or even walked in. But these were things that occurred to him later.

He couldn't say how long it lasted. Afterwards they lay there, realizing for the first time how uncomfortable they were lying on cardboard boxes. She brushed his lips with her fingers and said, "You taste like coffee."

"You taste like paradise," he said. It was a stupid thing to say, he thought. He never said things like that to women, he thought. And he blushed at the thought. Looking for something to drive away the sound of his words, he said, "You're a bad girl, but you're my bad girl now."

She hesitated, and then for the first time she removed her sunglasses. He saw, even in the semi-darkness of the storage shed, the black and blue marks. "It's not that simple," she told him.

Chapter Three
Monday

The clerk of the court raised the document to her eye level, announced "State of Florida vs. Rodriguez," and gave the case number. I turned to Eleanor Hibbard.

"Is the prosecution ready to proceed?"

Eleanor rose. "Ready for the State of Florida, Judge."

I looked at Jack. He stood up. "Defense?"

"Ready for trial, Your Honor."

The form of a criminal trial in the English-speaking world has been fixed since about the early fourteenth century. If we could call to life any of the great trial lawyers of the 1800s — Rufus Choate, say, or Abraham Lincoln — he would feel very much at home in a modern trial courtroom. Occasionally a lawyer will bring a laptop computer or an overhead projector to court, and then we are reminded that beyond the walls of the courtroom a brave new world of technology exists. Occasionally evidence will be admitted in the form of audio- or videotapes. But the form of the trial itself, the choreography of the criminal justice system, is as it has always been and, for all I know, will always be.

"The bailiff will please bring in the venire." At my cue, the bailiff stepped into the hallway to bring in the jury pool from which the jury will be chosen. At the beginning of each jury term in Miami-Dade County, the clerk's office sends out thousands of jury summonses, from lists obtained from the Department of Motor Vehicles and the voter registrations. Many of those summoned have legitimate excuses — a documented medical problem, perhaps, or a family hardship. Some simply throw the summons in the trash, too busy or self-important to do their duty as citizens. From those who show up, juries must be selected.

The lawyers and I have been given sheets listing each member of the jury pool by name and assigned number. The entry of a jury pool into the courtroom is an exercise in cocktail-party psychology: As the bailiff scurries about making sure that the jurors are seated in the gallery in numerical order, the lawyers scan for clues. That juror in the first row, is that the *Wall Street Journal* she has tucked under her arm? Then is she well-to-do, successful, conservative, convinced that those who find themselves in trouble brought trouble upon themselves—a perfect prosecution juror? Or did she, on her way up the ladder, have to overcome the prejudices of conservative businessmen against ambitious businesswomen, learning in the process a sympathy for the underdog, the disenfranchised, minorities in general—the perfect defense juror?

"Ladies and gentlemen, please make yourselves comfortable. My name is Clark N. Addison, and I am a judge of the circuit court of the eleventh judicial circuit in and for Miami-Dade County, Florida." I love this part, I admit it. For most of the trial, a judge must sit quietly as lawyers and witnesses drone on, muddying the issues and boring the jury. There isn't a judge in the courthouse who couldn't tell you the number of tiles in his courtroom ceiling, from side to side, from front to back, and diagonally. But the beginning of the trial belongs to me. I need the jurors to take the system seriously, and to understand the centrality of their own role in that system. And I need the jurors to like me. I do; I did when I was a trial lawyer, and this is as close as I get to being a trial lawyer again. Besides, I'm up for re-election in a few years, and jurors are voters.

"Let me give you an overview of how this trial will proceed. In a few minutes, I'm going to ask each of you a series of questions, after which I will permit the lawyers to ask questions of you as well. At the conclusion of this question period, we will choose six jurors and one alternate juror to try this case. Our questions are not intended to embarrass you. They are intended only to enable us to pick a fair and impartial jury.

Please answer all the questions truthfully and completely." The rustling in the seats has stopped. The faces in the gallery are pinched with concentration.

"Once a jury has been chosen, the prosecution will make an opening statement. The defense may make an opening statement if it wishes, but it need not do so. What the lawyers say in opening statement is not evidence; it is simply a summary of what the lawyers believe the evidence will show. Evidence will come in the form of sworn testimony from the witness stand"— here I gesture toward the witness stand—"and in the form of documents or other exhibits that I receive in evidence.

"At the conclusion of all the evidence, I will instruct the jury on the law applicable to this case, and then the jury will retire to consider its verdict. Please do not discuss the case, or form any fixed conclusions about it, until that time."

So much for the preliminaries. I had instructed my bailiff to bring in a jury pool of thirty, which we would winnow down to six sworn jurors and one alternate juror. Each must be questioned to determine his, or her, competence to serve on the jury. There are the general questions: What do you do for a living, what does your spouse do, what part of the county do you live in, how long have you lived there? There are questions relating to the case: Do you know either of the attorneys, or the defendant? Do you have any close friends or relatives working in the State Attorney's Office, the City of Miami Police Department, or for any criminal defense lawyer here in town? Have you ever served as a juror in a criminal case before? Or been a witness? Or a victim? Is there anything about this experience that would prevent you from being a fair and impartial juror in this case? And there are the legal questions: Do you understand that in our system of justice the defendant is presumed innocent? And that you must return a verdict of not guilty unless you find that his guilt has been established to the exclusion of reasonable doubt?

It is a tedious process. Apply for a credit card at Burdines Department Store and you will be permitted to provide personal information in discreet privacy. But show up for jury duty and you will be obliged to provide personal information in the formal setting of a courtroom, surrounded by dozens of strangers. It is an uncomfortable, awkward experience, and most jurors are grudging with their answers. Coaxing information from them takes time.

On that particular Monday morning, two members of the jury pool spoke no English at all and were dismissed. A third stated very emphatically that, although she felt that she could be a fair juror in another kind of case, she could not participate in a case in which the defendant was charged with a drug crime because of something that had happened to her son many years ago. I had the bailiff escort her to the central jury room for reassignment to another judge.

"Ladies and gentlemen, I will now permit the attorneys, starting with the prosecuting attorney, to ask you some additional questions. Please be as honest and forthcoming with them as you have been with me. Ms. Hibbard?"

Eleanor rose, walked to the podium, placed her legal pad there, paused. "Good morning, ladies and gentlemen. As you heard Judge Addison say, my name is Eleanor T. Hibbard, and I am an assistant state attorney. The defendant is charged with the crime of trafficking in cocaine, and I will be prosecuting him on behalf of the people of the State of Florida." During jury selection attorneys are to ask questions, not make speeches, but no judge is such a stickler as to deny a lawyer a sentence or two of introduction. Eleanor had used her introduction well, wrapping herself in the flag.

"During the course of this trial, I may call the following witnesses." She held up her note pad and read off the names of a couple of uniform cops, a detective from the narcotics bureau, and a chemist from the crime lab. "Does anyone know any of these witnesses?" There was no response. "Has anyone here ever had any problems with the City of Miami Police Department or any of its officers?" No takers.

Some lawyers like to move around the courtroom during jury selection, asking a few questions here and then a few over there. Eleanor stands at the podium. She does not wander around the courtroom. She does not need to. Her voice, her marvelous voice, will wander for her. She will cast her voice at a juror in the back row as an experienced fisherman casts his line. "Mr. Kramer." She had hooked a flounder, a large, casually-dressed man, sixtyish, balding, liver-spotted. She reeled slowly. "I'll bet at one time or another you've been stopped by a police officer for some minor traffic offense, illegal turn, speeding, something like that?"

"Um ... yes."

"Do you feel that you were treated fairly by the police?"

"I guess so."

"You understand that the police are just doing their job—a very important part of their job—when they insure that traffic laws are complied with?"

"Yeah."

"So you don't hold it against the men and women of the Miami Police Department that you were stopped for a minor traffic offense, do you?"

"No. No."

Now the Voice went up in volume slightly, no longer a line cast at a single fish but a net cast across the whole school. "Does everyone feel the same as Mr. Kramer—that being stopped for minor traffic offenses on occasion is the fair price we pay for the protection we enjoy from the Miami Police Department?" There were vigorous nods of agreement. "Is there anyone here who feels differently from Mr. Kramer?" No one felt differently from Mr. Kramer. Kramer, tense and suspicious when Eleanor was questioning him one-on-one, was sitting back in his seat, comfortable and relaxed. He was, after all, the standard by which all others were judged. Eleanor had made an ally.

"Ms. de la Torre." The Voice was directed at a very fashionable young woman in the second row, a seat or two in from the end. "You indicated, in response to Judge Addison's questions, that you are involved in the management of a family business. Did I get that down correctly in my notes?"

"Yes."

"Would it be fair to say that to run a small business nowadays, you have to be a pretty good judge of people?"

Ms. de la Torre was that rare juror, the one who enjoyed the give-and-take of jury selection, who felt not at all self-conscious

chatting about her business and personal life in front of a courtroom full of strangers. She smiled when she answered, "You
bet!"

Eleanor smiled back. "If you are chosen to this jury, will
you use that same good judgment and common sense in evalu-
ating the evidence that is presented in this trial?"

"Uh-huh. Sure."

"Can everyone do that?" Eleanor was speaking to the entire
group again. "Will everyone agree to use their good judgment
and common sense in this courtroom, just as you do in every-
day life?" Nods of agreement, leavened with some mumbled
uh-huhs. "Mr. LaSalle, you work as a medical technician at
Jackson Memorial, is that right?"

LaSalle had been caught flat-footed. He was a pleasant
young black man, and when I had been questioning him he betrayed the slight trace of an accent I thought might have come
from somewhere in the Caribbean. His attention had wandered
in the moment before Eleanor called on him, and now he was
stammering at a furious pace, trying to make some kind of answer to a question he had not heard.

Eleanor cut in, her voice effortlessly silencing his. "I've
heard that there's a saying in the medical profession: When you
hear hoofbeats, think horses, not zebras. Did I get that right?" I
have no idea whether Mr. LaSalle had ever heard that saying at
any time in his life, but if Eleanor T. Hibbard wanted to make
him the courtroom maven on principles of diagnosis, he would,
and did, fall all over himself agreeing with her. "I suppose
that's just another way of saying what Ms. de la Torre was talking about—the importance of using common sense. Is that the
idea?" Oh yes, agreed Mr. LaSalle, that was the idea, that was
absolutely the idea. "When you hear hoofbeats, think horses,
not zebras." Eleanor had repeated it to no one in particular, as
if she were just enjoying the sound of good common sense. Ms.
de la Torre was craning her neck, hoping to catch Eleanor's eye
and earn another chance to contribute, but Eleanor had moved
on.

"I want to talk for a minute about the crime itself." She was
speaking to the group as a whole. "A few minutes ago, a mem-

ber of the jury pool told us that she felt she couldn't be a fair and impartial juror on this particular case because the charge had to do with drugs, and Judge Addison permitted her to return to the central jury pool. I'm sure it was difficult for her to stand up and admit a thing like that, and I think it showed a lot of character on her part to do it...

Jack was on his feet. "If the Court please, I object to the speech-making. I think that ... " He was about to do some speech-making of his own, but I cut him off.

"Sustained. Questions only, please, Ms. Hibbard."

"Yes, Your Honor. The question I was about to ask was: Do we all agree that anyone who is so troubled by the nature of the charge itself—a charge of drug trafficking—that he or she cannot be fair, ought to be honest and say so?" Nods of agreement. "Mr. Wells, we all agree that drug trafficking is a reprehensible crime, don't we?"

He was a juror in the second row, small, middle-aged, soft-spoken. "Yes."

"You understand that what the jury in this case will be called upon to decide is not whether drug trafficking is a reprehensible crime, but whether this defendant"—she pointed, her arm extended to its full length—"is guilty of that reprehensible crime. You understand that, don't you?"

He pushed his glasses up to the bridge of his nose, from where they had slipped. "Yes, ma'am."

For the first time, Eleanor left the podium. She walked over to the man seated in the first seat of the first row, and she stood opposite him, as close to him as she could get. For a few seconds—and it seemed much longer—she was silent; and her silence filled the courtroom as surely as her voice had. When she spoke it was barely above a whisper. "Sir, if I prove to you beyond and to the exclusion of every reasonable doubt that this defendant"—again the arm stretched out to its full length—"is guilty of the crime with which he is charged, what will your verdict be?"

He needed a few seconds, but he got it right. "Um...if you prove...guilty. Then my verdict will be guilty."

She stepped to her left, opposite the man in the second

chair. "Sir, if I prove to you beyond and to the exclusion of every reasonable doubt that this defendant is guilty of the crime with which he is charged, what will your verdict be?"

"Guilty."

A step to the left, to face number three. Same question. Same answer. And so it went, through number 27, each and all, face to face, eye to eye, voice to voice, until the word "guilty" had been repeated 27 times. Eleanor turned to me and said, very formally, "Thank you, Your Honor. The State of Florida has no further questions." She returned to her seat.

I looked at the clock on the wall in the back of the courtroom, the clock to which my wristwatch is always synchronized. It is a big, beautiful old clock, prominently bearing the name and trademark of the Elgin Watch Company of Elgin, Illinois. One of the folks in the court administration office unearthed it during building renovations a few years ago, and thoughtfully remembered that Elgin, Illinois is the place where I was born and passed the first decade of my life. The principal landmark in Elgin, Illinois is—or was, when I was a kid—the Elgin clocktower, a monument to Midwestern reliability. A glance at the courtroom clock gives me both the time and a reminder of an earlier time, a safer time, a time before there were questions of life and death to answer. "Ladies and gentlemen, we will take a 15 minute recess. When we return the defense will have some questions for you." I stood, the bailiff called out "All rise," and I headed for my chambers.

A judge's chambers in the Metro-Justice Building consist of two rooms and a half-bath. (There are few perquisites associated with being a criminal court judge, but at least we do not have to use the courthouse's public restrooms.) The reception area houses my secretary, with her desk, phones, and word-processor; three very uninviting chairs; a Xerox machine so old it was probably built by Mr. Xerox himself as an 8th-grade science project; and a walk-in closet containing office supplies and a coffee machine. A corridor of some three or four paces'-length leads to my private office. I entered the reception area, picked up the morning's phone messages from Carmen, took two or three fast sips from her coffee cup—she started to protest, but I was drinking from the side that did not have her lipstick on it—and headed for my office.

Carmen Maria Aleman de Escobar is not a young woman. I am not sure that she ever was. She became my secretary when I was still in the State Attorney's Office, and has been with me ever since, following me to the bench when I became a judge. Her family had been visiting relatives in Union City, New Jersey, a heavily Cuban enclave, when word came that Castro had overthrown Batista and that they could never return. They settled in the New York area for a few years, then relocated to Miami, Cuba's branch office. She married and raised children. She divorced, and the children moved away. Unusually for a Cuban, she seemed to feel no great loss at the dissolution of the nuclear family. She is, after all these years, fiercely loyal to me; and she types so fast that the computer must get cramps. Her principal shortcoming, if she has one, is her sharp tongue and her shameless love of gossip, of "*chisme*." In this she is not alone. The Metro-Justice Building has always been a rumor-mill, and always will be. Most courthouses are that way.

I had scooped up my phone messages on the way back to my office and, having dropped my robe over the back of my chair, I was standing at the office window, folding and unfolding the message slips in my hand. I could see the cars in the parking lot baking in the heat of the mid-day Miami sun, but my mind was not on the cars or the parking lot or the sun. A single thought had occupied my attention through the weekend, and now it was back: I simply couldn't accept the idea that Ed Barber had left no note, no letter, no explanation of any kind. I knew that Ed wasn't Mr. Words. Just the opposite; he was one of the least talkative men I ever knew. When it came to writing, filling out the narrative portion of an offense incident report was heavy lifting for him. Lt. Cabrera had assured me that there was no suicide letter. But I couldn't stop believing that before this friend, this man I had known so well, had shot his wife and his child and himself he had left me some note, some communication, some clue, something. Maybe I didn't want to stop believing.

Over the weekend I had done some silly things. I went

through the mail we had received over the past few days to see
if anything could have been overlooked. I played back all the
messages on our telephone answering machine. Of course
there was nothing from or about Ed. I played them all back
again.

During the workweek Miriam chauffeurs the kids to school,
Hebrew school, ballgames (Joel), dance lessons (Alicia), karate
classes (Marc), so it's only fair that I do the weekend driving
duties. Saturday afternoon I had dropped Joel off at a friend's
house and found myself driving along Killian Parkway, not all
that far from the Barber house. For a quick second I actually
thought about stopping by for one last look. I no sooner had
the thought than I was annoyed by it. The police had been over
the house with more than their usual care. If there had been
anything to find they would have found it. Besides, I had no
key. The *Miami Herald* would have a picnic with a headline like
"*Judge Arrested Breaking into Double-Murder/Suicide House.*"

I glanced at my wristwatch. We were more than ten minutes into our 15-minute break. The thought of returning to the
bench brought my mind back to the here and now. In the reception area Carmen and Jack, who have shared a love-hate relationship since way back when, were exchanging a few pleasantries.

"What do *you* want, Sheridan?"

"Well just fine thank you, pretty lady. And you?" What
Jack wanted was to use Carmen's phone. He picked up the receiver and started to dial his office. As it rang, he leered at her
and asked, "And what do *you* want?"

"What do I want? I want Castro to get cancer of the balls. I
want the Marlins to win the pennant. And I want you to get off
my phone and out of my office so I can get some work done."

Jack covered the phone with his hand, leaned toward Carmen, and assumed a very conspiratorial air. "Has it ever occurred to you, Carmen, that you are a gay man trapped in a
woman's body?"

"*Fuck* ..."

"Yes, hello, this is Sheridan, what's going on at the office?
Uh-huh ... uh-huh ... no, that's all right, that can wait till I get

back. OK. OK. All right, I'll call at the next break." He cradled the receiver, called Carmen *"Corazon de melon"* in surprisingly good Spanish, winked at her, and walked out of the office. That was Blackjack Sheridan. I waited a few minutes, snuck past Carmen, and headed for the courtroom.

"Ladies and gentlemen, thank you for your promptness." I was back on the bench, and the members of the jury pool had indeed been prompt in returning from their morning break. "Counsel for the defense will have some questions for you. Mr. Sheridan?"

Jack stood, thanked me, and turned to face the 27 people seated in the gallery. He smiled that Blackjack smile. "Ladies and gentlemen, my name is Jack Sheridan. I'm a lawyer here in town. Been here all my life. But this is a special case for me," Jack walked over to his client, stood behind him as they faced the jury pool, placed hands on Rodriguez's shoulders, "because in this case I speak for my friend Felix Rodriguez. Anybody here know Felix?" No signs of life. "Let me introduce Felix's family." He gestured toward the back of the courtroom. "Teresa, would you and Felix junior stand, please?" Against the far wall, the woman responded to Jack's beckoning. She did not stand. She rose. She rose as heat rises off the Miami macadam in summer, shimmering and graceful. She rose as smoke rises from a fire, filling the senses. She was a classic Cuban beauty, dark-eyed and olive-skinned, and although Jack had told her to dress conservatively for court, nothing short of a chador would have masked the beautiful lines of her body. When Jack introduced her, the jurors turned, somewhat perfunctorily, to see who was being introduced. I saw Mr. Kramer do a double-take that would have done credit to a cartoon character. Next to her stood a small child. I can't recall what he looked like.

"Thank you, ma'am, you can have a seat. Does anyone know Mrs. Rodriguez or little Felix junior?" Faces spoke of envy, faces spoke of desire, faces spoke of admiration, but no voices spoke. Jack moved on with his questioning. Unlike Eleanor, he did not stand behind the podium. He stood in the middle of the courtroom. He used no notes, and his hands clutched no legal pad. He spoke informally, casually, as if to neighbors over the backyard fence. "Ladies and gentlemen, I want you to think back to that day, not too long ago, when you went to the mailbox and found that you had received a jury summons. How many were pleased to receive that summons, and have been looking forward to serving on a jury?" Groans, some chuckles, the rolling of eyes. In the front row a man started to raise his hand; then, realizing he was a minority of one, quickly put it down. Jack spoke to him. "That's all right, Mr. ... ?"

"Vazquez."

"Mr. Vazquez, have you been looking forward to serving on a jury?"

Vazquez was a little hesitant to admit it, but he did.

"I take it Mr. Vazquez, that you consider it a duty of citizenship to participate in the criminal justice system?"

Mr. Vazquez liked the way that sounded. "Yes, I do." Jack nodded, thanked Mr. Vazquez for sharing his thoughts. First chance he got, Jack would kick Mr. Vazquez off the jury. The last thing a defense attorney wants on his jury is a volunteer. A volunteer is a vigilante, is someone who came to court to serve as a citizen-soldier in the war on crime.

"You all heard Judge Addison say that we're interested in picking a jury that can be fair and impartial. We're not suggesting that anyone here is bigoted or prejudiced. When I was a boy, I had a newspaper route. One day as I was delivering papers on my bicycle, a neighbor-lady's beagle bit me. It wasn't much of a bite, hardly drew blood, but you know to this day I don't think I could be a fair and impartial juror in a case in which the defendant was a beagle." There were smiling faces in the gallery. "An English sheepdog, sure; a French poodle, no problem; even a German shepherd. But if Snoopy were the defendant, I just don't think I'd be the right juror." More smiling faces, a few laughs. The jurors were enjoying this, and so was Jack. I have no idea if Jack Sheridan had a newspaper route as a kid. I don't even know if he had a bicycle. But when he told that story it sounded so real, so much a part of him, that you had to wish it to be true if it wasn't. Eleanor sat stiffly in her seat. She could object, of course — technically, Jack should have confined himself to asking questions, not telling tales — but she knew the jury would never forgive her if she did. "So do you all understand that by our questioning we're just trying to find the fairest possible jury for this particular case?" Heads nodding; of course they understood. "And everyone sees how important it is for you to give complete and truthful answers to our questions?" Heads nodding; of course they saw. "And you all understand I don't mean to give any offense by the questions I ask?" Heads nodding; who could be offended by a former newspaper delivery-boy?

"Folks," — it was folks now, not ladies and gentlemen — "Judge Addison described for you the order in which a trial proceeds. You all understand, don't you, that the order in which a trial proceeds is fixed by law, and has been pretty much unchanged for centuries?" Jack's hands were upturned to show that the question was for the group, not any individual, and again there was the nodding and murmuring of general agreement. "You all understand that the order in which this trial is going to proceed is not something we made up special for this trial?" He smiled, to show that it was a silly question, and they smiled back. "So if I were to turn to Judge Addison and say, 'Well, now, Judge, I know how usually the prosecution gets to make opening statement before I do, and closing argument before I do, and so on, but this case is special and I sure would like to go first,' why, you know, Judge Addison would just tell me to sit down and behave myself. You all understand that, don't you?" More smiling and nodding. Jack spoke to a woman in the third row. "So ma'am, as you listen to the testimony of the prosecution's witnesses, will you keep reminding yourself that it just wouldn't be fair for you to form any conclusions until all the evidence and all the arguments have been heard?"

"Yes I will."

"And can everyone else promise to do that too?" Yes, they would do that too. "The prosecution has indicated that most if not all of their witnesses will be police officers. Of course we all have a lot of respect for police officers. But police officers are human and they can make mistakes." Jack addressed Mr.

Kramer. "Mr. Kramer, you believe that police officers are human and can make mistakes just like the rest of us, don't you?"

"Sure."

"So it won't offend you when I cross-examine the police
witnesses, will it?"

"No, no problem."

"You understand that it's my responsibility to point out any
little thing an officer might have overlooked or unintentionally
left out?"

"Uh-huh."

"You understand that by cross-examining these police officers, I'm not accusing them of lying?"

"Sure, no problem."

Jack surveyed the jury pool. "Everyone feel the same way
as Mr. Kramer?" Everyone did. "No one will be offended when
I carry out my responsibility of cross-examining police witnesses?" No one would. "Everyone understand that even the
best police officer could make a little mistake, and that it might
be important for me to bring out that mistake?" Everyone understood. "Judge Addison has mentioned to you, and will explain to you again during this trial, that the United States Constitution provides that a defendant in a criminal case need not
testify; and that if he chooses not to testify the jury must not
hold that against him nor take it as evidence of guilt." Jack
looked at Ms. de la Torre. For the questions he was about to
ask, he needed someone who would do more than merely give
assent to whatever suggestion was offered. He needed someone eager to speak up, someone who would use her own words
to help give the group a little refresher in seventh-grade civics.
"Ms. de la Torre, let me ask you this, ma'am: Does that principle of the United States Constitution make sense to you?"

"Yes. Sure."

"Well ma'am, why do you suppose it is that a person who is
innocent might chose not to testify in his own defense?"

"Well, because ..." The civics lesson was not forthcoming.
Ms. de la Torre was, for what was no doubt one of the only
such occasions in her life, at a loss for words. Like most laymen
and too many lawyers, she venerated the Constitution without

ever having given much thought as to what it said or what it meant. Her face darkened with frustration.

If he knew anything at all, John Wentworth Sheridan IV knew how to come to the aid of a lady in distress. He walked over to defense counsel table, shifted among some papers until he found one to his liking, and held it up. "Ms. de la Torre, about a century ago a very distinguished judge named Field sat on the U.S. Supreme Court. In a case called Wilson versus United States" — he turned to me and gave the citation — "149 U. S. 60 at page 66" — then turned back to Ms. de la Torre — "he wrote these words: 'It is not everyone who can safely venture on the witness stand though entirely innocent of the charge against him. Nervousness when facing others and attempting to explain offenses charged against him will often confuse and embarrass him to such a degree as to increase rather than remove prejudices against him. It is not everyone, however honest, who would, therefore, willingly be placed in the witness stand.' Ma'am, is that how you view this important constitutional principle too?"

Ms. de la Torre had been handed a cold beer on a hot day. "Yes. I really do."

"Ma'am, there's another very important constitutional principle Judge Addison will stress during this trial: The principle that for a juror to sit in judgment on Felix Rodriguez, that juror must presume — that means believe — that Mr. Rodriguez is innocent. Do you agree with me that any juror who does not believe that Mr. Rodriguez is innocent as he sits here now should say so and ask to be excused?"

"Yes. I really do."

"Please look at Mr. Rodriguez, ma'am." She did so, squinting with concentration or myopia or both. "Are you prepared to believe in his innocence as he sits here today?"

"Yes." She said it very solemnly.

"And if the prosecution fails to prove his guilt beyond and to the exclusion of all reasonable doubt, will you have the courage to return a verdict of not guilty?"

"Yes."

"And if, during the jury's deliberations, a fellow juror says to you, 'Well, Ms. de la Torre, there is some evidence against him, they proved him a little guilty, maybe we better convict him just to be on the safe side,' what will you say to that fellow juror?"

This time she was ready. "I would say that was wrong, that was against our responsibility as jurors. I would say we have to go by the Constitution."

"Even if that means acquitting a man against whom there is some evidence of guilt?"

"Yes. That's what makes America special."

Jack stood stock-still and sphinx-silent. The answer was perfect, better than perfect, and he wanted to freeze the moment, let the answer hover in the air, let the jurors soak in it, marinate in it. In the courtroom time can be made to move slowly, and silence is a powerful weapon.

Finally he spoke. "Ladies and gentlemen, this is a very important part of the trial. It is the only part in which you get to speak. Later on, during the examination of witnesses, you may be just bursting to say something or to ask some question and you won't be able to. So I want you to take a minute before I sit down and think if there is anything that has come to you, by way of a comment or by way of a question, that you would like to share with us now." Long seconds passed. No takers.

Jack returned to counsel table. "Thank you, Your Honor." He sat.

I had my eye on the courtroom clock. "Ladies and gentlemen, it is after one o'clock. The bailiff will now lead you down to the juror area of the cafeteria for lunch. Please be back in your same seats by 2:30. Thank you." I stood, the bailiff called all rise, and the courtroom emptied.

Back in chambers, I called Miriam. The mail had not yet arrived at the house, and there had been no out-of-the-ordinary phone calls. She didn't ask why I wanted to know. I suppose she knew why.

I opened a small brown paper bag on which Miriam had written in large block letters, "Dad" — Alicia and I had gotten each other's lunches once, which meant that I ended up eating fruit roll-ups and animal crackers — and took out my sandwich.

I was staring out the window, eating without tasting, when Carmen poked her head in to ask if I wanted a *cafecito*, a Cuban coffee, known everywhere but Miami and Havana as espresso. I shook my head no, then changed my mind.

She returned with two thimble-sized plastic cups, handed one to me, and had a seat in the one good chair opposite my desk. I sipped the thick, dark liquid. "Have we gotten the office mail yet today?"

She shook her head. "It usually comes about two or three." I knew that.

"Any ... any unusual calls or messages?"

"No. Why, are you expecting something in particular?"

I went back to staring out the window, but I answered her. "Ed. I keep expecting ... I keep expecting to hear from him. I keep thinking I'm going to get an explanation, a reason why. You know a man half your life, and you think ... ." I finished the coffee, turned to face Carmen. "Is everyone still talking about it?"

No, nobody was talking about it. Well, maybe a few of the lawyers who had stopped by chambers, and a couple of cops, most of the clerk's office, and a messenger from a delivery service. "And Anita from Que Será Será's chambers, she wanted to talk about it." The Honorable Kay Surrey is a good judge. She is intelligent, fair-minded, and experienced. She has a good judicial demeanor on the bench. But her name lends itself to Spanish-language parody, and for as long as anyone can remember she has been known around the Metro-Justice Building as Judge Que Será Será. "You know, Anita and Sheridan's secretary, that Rodriguez woman, used to work at the same law firm."

"What Rodriguez woman?"

"Sheridan's secretary. She was in court today with her husband."

"Her husband? Jack's client is his secretary's husband?"

"Sure." The phone rang in the outer office, and Carmen stood up. "How do you suppose a *comemierda* like Felix Rodriguez gets a bigshot lawyer like Sheridan?"

At 2:30 I was back on the bench. The members of the jury

pool filed in at the bailiff's signal and settled into their seats. "Ladies and gentlemen, thank you for your promptness. I hope you enjoyed your lunch. The attorneys and I will now confer at sidebar for a few minutes. Please bear with us." Eleanor, Jack, and the court reporter huddled with me next to the bench. We would pick six jurors and an alternate. I read the names and numbers of the members of the jury pool one at a time. Either side can ask that I dismiss a given juror for good cause. Apart from that, each lawyer has six "peremptory challenges" — the right to dismiss a juror for any reason, good or bad, other than racial or religious bigotry. The selection process is conducted in whispers so that the jurors do not hear what is said about them or who says it.

Jury selection concluded, Eleanor and Jack returned to their seats. "Ladies and gentlemen, I will now read the names of our chosen jurors. Kindly take a seat in the jury box as your name is called." I read off seven names. Kramer made the cut. De la Torre didn't. The chosen seven found their way without much enthusiasm to the jury box. There they were asked to stand and raise their right hands, and to swear "to well and truly try the case between the State of Florida and Felix Rodriguez and a true verdict render, according to the law and the evidence."

I looked in Eleanor's direction. "The prosecution will now proceed with its opening statement." Eleanor stood, walked to the podium, adjusted it to face the jury box.

"May it please the Court, and ladies and gentlemen of the jury. During jury selection, you indicated that you did not know Officer Roscoe Belmont of the City of Miami Police Department. You will meet him during the course of this trial. I will call him to the witness stand, and through his testimony I will prove to you that the defendant Rodriguez is guilty of the crime of trafficking in cocaine. During jury selection, you indicated that you did not know Detective Tom Rasmussen of the narcotics section of the City of Miami Police Department. You will meet him during the course of this trial. I will call him to the witness stand, and through his testimony I will prove to you that the defendant Rodriguez is guilty of the crime of trafficking in cocaine. During jury selection, you indicated that you did not know Paulina Ashland of the Metro-Dade Crime Laboratory. You will meet her during the course of this trial. I will call her to the witness stand, and through her testimony I will prove to you that the defendant Rodriguez is guilty of the crime of trafficking in cocaine." When the lawyering in my courtroom is bad, is boring, being a judge is a window into Hell. But when the lawyering is good, good the way Eleanor could be good, being a judge is the best ticket in town. I concentrated on maintaining my judge face: thoughtful, attentive, but always noncommittal.

"On the night in question, Officer Belmont was in uniform, driving a marked police cruiser on patrol in Coconut Grove. Just after midnight, as he headed south along Grand Avenue, he saw a Ford Taurus stopped along the side of Commodore Plaza. The car had its hood propped open, and the defendant Felix Rodriguez was looking at the engine. Officer Belmont pulled his police car over, got out, and walked over to the Ford to see if Mr. Rodriguez needed help, and to make sure that traffic was not obstructed.

"As Officer Belmont walked toward the front of the Ford, he glanced inside the passenger compartment and, on the driver's-side floorboard in the back, saw something that his years of police training and experience told him might be cocaine. He radioed for a detective from the narcotics bureau, and asked Mr. Rodriguez to have a seat in the back of his police car. Within minutes, Detective Rasmussen was on the scene. And what Officer Belmont suspected to be cocaine proved to be exactly that: More than half a kilo, more than 500 grams of 96 per cent pure cocaine. His cocaine"—Eleanor extended her arm to its full length, her index finger leveled at the defendant—"found in his possession in the back of his car."

She left the podium, walked the few steps to the clerk's desk, and asked very formally for the indictment. The clerk leafed through what appeared to be a compost-heap of papers and handed one to Eleanor. She returned to the podium and read aloud from the document, word for word, the richness of her voice giving a terrible force to the stale legalese. " ... in violation of Florida Statutes section 893.135, against the peace and

dignity of the State of Florida, and to the evil example of all others." She put the paper down and paused, making eye contact
with the jurors. "Ladies and gentlemen, at the conclusion of
this case I will return to ask you for the one verdict that law and
justice demand: a verdict of guilty as charged."

As Eleanor was taking her seat I turned to Jack. Ordinarily
I would have asked, "Does the defense wish to make an opening statement?" But Jack was already on his feet, already moving toward the jury, unwilling to grant them a moment to stew
in the mood created by the force of Eleanor's rhetoric.

"May it please this Honorable Court, and ladies and gentlemen of the jury. It has been said that circumstantial evidence is
the greatest engine ever invented for the conviction of the innocent. Let me explain what I mean by that. One day during
blueberry season, a woman spent all day baking blueberry pies.
She set them out on the window ledge to cool. When she was-
n't looking, her little boy snuck one of those pies and was finishing off the last bite of it when he heard his mother's footsteps. So quick as a wink ..."

Quick as a wink Eleanor was on her feet. "Judge, this is argument. It has nothing to do with the facts and it has no place
in opening statement. I object."

"Your Honor, this is an analogy that will help me to place
the facts of this case in context. I'm just about to get to the evidence itself." As Jack was responding, I snuck a peek at the jurors. The message on their faces was clear: Can we please hear
the end of the story?

"The objection is overruled. But please, Mr. Sheridan, let's
get to the evidence."

Jack smiled at the jury. "Well quick as a wink, that young
fellow grabbed the family cat, wiped the last of the blueberries
and piecrumbs all over her face, and then hid behind the nearest bush. The next thing he saw was that cat fleeing for her life,
with Momma and her broom in hot pursuit. And the thought
that crossed his mind at that moment was, "There goes poor
Kitty — another victim of circumstantial evidence." Jack paused
for a moment. The story wasn't all that funny, but his obvious
delight in telling it coaxed smiles and a few laughs from the

jury. The punch line had almost been obliterated by Jack's southern—*Theah goes poah Kitty*. The sight and smell of a jury inevitably rendered Jack's accent as thick as a puddle of tar.

Jack moved from the center of the courtroom to stand behind his client. As he had during jury selection, he placed both of his own hands on Rodriguez's shoulders. "It was a Saturday night, and Felix Rodriguez was on his way to a friend's house. He walked out of his house, hopped into his car, and drove off. No, he didn't look under the seat or inspect the back part of the car, he just turned the key and put it in gear and drove away like we all do. As it happens, his car had been sitting unlocked in his driveway all day." Jack moved from behind his client, walked slowly toward the jury, and stopped about half-a-dozen feet from the jury rail.

"Those of you who know the Coconut Grove area know that on a Saturday night it is one of the busiest and most heavily policed sections of town. Felix made no effort to travel by side streets. He drove on the major arterial streets. When his engine died, he managed to pull over to the side of the road. He opened the hood and tried to figure out what the problem was.

"The evidence will show that Felix was pulled over along the side of that busy street for a good ten to fifteen minutes before Officer Belmont happened by. During that period, Felix Rodriguez could easily have disposed of the cocaine that was later found in his back seat. He could easily have thrown his shirt or some other object over the cocaine to conceal it. He could have pushed the cocaine under the car seat, or secreted it in the trunk. He did none of these things. He did none of these things because he had no idea the cocaine was there. He did none of these things because he did not know, and to this day does not know, who put it there or how it got there.

"The prosecutor has told us that Officer Belmont will testify in this trial. We welcome the testimony of Officer Belmont. Officer Belmont will acknowledge that at no time did Felix Rodriguez try to steer him away from the car, or to deny him an opportunity to look inside the car. Officer Belmont will acknowledge that Felix Rodriguez seemed genuinely surprised when the cocaine was recovered from the back of his Ford. Officer Belmont will acknowledge that Mr. Rodriguez was completely cooperative with the police and answered all their questions. These are features of Officer Belmont's testimony that the prosecutor did not tell you about. But this is what the evidence will show.

"The prosecutor has told us that Detective Rasmussen and Criminalist Ashland will testify in this trial. We welcome the testimony of Detective Rasmussen and Criminalist Ashland. They will acknowledge that there is absolutely no evidence that Felix Rodriguez's fingerprints were ever on the wrapping in which the cocaine was found. This is a key feature, a critical feature of their testimony that the prosecutor did not tell you about. But this is what the evidence will show." Jack paused, just standing there with his hands in his pockets as if he were waiting for the next bus. Then he leaned toward the jurors as if he were about to impart some secret. Reflexively, they leaned toward him. "The reason there will be no evidence that Felix Rodriguez knew of the cocaine in his car is because he did not know of the cocaine in his car. He is really and truly innocent." Jack turned, walked slowly back to his chair, patted his client confidently on the arm, and had a seat.

I spoke. "Counsel, please approach." Jack and Eleanor came forward as the court reporter scurried into position to hear our bench conference. "Is the prosecution ready to call its first witness?"

For once the Voice was small and meek. "Judge, I really didn't think we'd get this far today. I told the officers to be here first thing tomorrow morning. I could try to get through to them and get them here in ... I don't know, maybe ..." She looked at her watch.

I looked at mine, and cut her off. "That's all right counsel, step back." She and Jack retreated to their places. I addressed the jury. "Ladies and gentlemen, as you can see it is after four o'clock. Ordinarily we would work for another hour, but we're going to recess a little early today. I have a short calendar tomorrow morning, so please be back not later than ten o'clock. Remember to discuss this case with no one, and to form no fixed opinion about it yet. Thank you for your service today. The bailiff will see you out." The lawyers stood at polite attention while the jurors shuffled out, then began to collect their files. "Mr. Sheridan." Jack looked up. "Can I see you in chambers on a matter not related to this case?"

"Certainly, Your Honor. If I can have just a moment to finish packing my trial bag?"

I gestured to indicate he could take his time. Jack and I try to make it an invariable rule not to discuss off the record any cases he has before me. I wanted the prosecution to know, and the court reporter to note, that the rule was being followed.

I bootlegged Jack past Carmen and into my office. After he made himself comfortable, seated with one leg hooked over the chair arm, he pulled out his flask. "As they say down at the bank, here's looking up your old assets," he offered, and took a glug of Old High-Test.

I waited for him to put the flask away. I was about to ask him if he had checked his mail, his phone, anything, for some message from Ed; but Carmen chose that moment to stalk into my office with the day's mail. She handed it to me, and as I leafed through it, she said to Jack, "I don't know why he"— meaning me—"keeps you around."

"Just fine, thank you for asking. And how is your day going?"

"*Tienes guayabitos en la azotea.*" You have little creatures in your attic. In English we say, "You have bats in your belfry."

He yawned and stretched. "Old Clark keeps me around because he's still hoping to learn how to cross-examine. You never could cross-examine for spit, could you, Clark?"

The mail was a disappointment. There was the usual correspondence, the usual pleadings and other legal documents, the usual form letters. Nothing, but nothing that could have been construed as from or about Ed. I went through it all again, doing ridiculous things like shaking the envelopes and holding the letters up to the light. Meantime, Jack took another swig, which set Carmen off again.

"Ugh, I don't know which is worse, you or your scumclot clients." Carmen presumed all defendants innocent except those who felt it necessary to hire someone as cagey as Jack. He held the flask her way. "I take it that means you don't want a sip?" She made a face. "As for my clients, Carmen honey, they are not scumclots so long as they observe Sheridan's Three Rules." He ticked them off on his fingers. "One, pay me the money you owe me; two, don't lie to me; and three, pay me the money you owe me."

All of this left Carmen underwhelmed. She turned to me and asked, "Judge, can I leave 15 minutes early? I have to take Lucky to the vet."

Jack couldn't pass it up. "New boyfriend, Carmen?"

"*Fuck ...* "

I interrupted. "No problem." It was 4:30 anyway. "Go ahead and leave now, you'll beat the traffic."

She turned to go. Jack spoke to her back. "Carmen, sugar, you take care now, y'heah?"

We sat in silence for a few minutes after she left. "With twenty-twenty hindsight ...," I began, and then I stopped. If we had said or done something we could have said or done, should have said or done, would Ed still be alive today? I didn't bother to ask the question aloud. It was, I knew, a question that had no answer. And Jack would trash the question; he would tell me something like twenty-twenty hindsight is what you get when a stripper with forty-inch hips turns around and touches her toes.

"Clark?"

"Yeah."

He shifted in his seat. "Look, I know you don't like to do this, but I need to talk to you about bail for that Linden kid I represent." He looked at me, his expression asking for permission to go on. He didn't get it. "Clark ..." And then he gave up. I would not let him step across that line, and he knew it, and I was angry that he had tried, and he knew it. He shifted in his seat again, and then he got up and left.

* * *

Late summer days are long in the subtropics, and if you want to see the stars —the fat, heavy ones that drip starlight over the Miami night—you have to wait. But the wait is worth it. It was worth it that evening. Miriam had gone to sleep, the kids had long since gone to sleep, and I sat on the patio with the barbecue a few feet behind me and the sky just beyond arm's-reach above me.

The coming of autumn will bring the snowbirds. Retirees will come from the big cities of the North, filling the condos of Key Biscayne and Miami Beach, complaining that the winters are not so warm as when they first started visiting here. Canadians will come, settling in Hollywood and Hallandale, eager to play in the ocean on winter days when no self-respecting Floridian would think of it. Tourists will come, if they have any money left after stopping in Orlando to see Mickey Mouse and Shamu the Killer Whale. And drifters will come. They will come because they have no place else to go, and because sleeping in the shade under the I-395 overpass is better than shivering in the steam that rises from a sewer in New York.

Glen Hundley was a drifter. If he was from anywhere, he was from Indiana. He had a small-time record there, vagrancy, trespass, things like that. The worst thing they ever caught him for was a gas-station stick-up, but that just means that most of the time they didn't catch him.

We caught him. We caught him for what he did to Baby Karen. We caught him, and we convicted him, and we sent him to death row. Jack and Ed and I did that. We did that a long time ago.

Ed is—was—a big man. As a youngster he had been a Golden Gloves boxing champ, and he had the cauliflower ears and banged-up, receding hairline to prove it. His hands were too big even for a man his size. More than once I saw him crush a walnut between his thumb and forefinger. When he spoke his face betrayed little expression; the expression was in his voice. It was a husky, earthy voice, a sound like the texture of a burlap bag.

After the incident with Detective Sullivan and Vargas, Ed did all witness interrogations in the Baby Karen case personally.

Interrogations were a specialty of Ed's. More often then not he would send out for pizza and when it was delivered, have someone take a Polaroid of himself offering a slice to the delighted suspect. Confession usually occurred between slice one and slice two. When the defense attorney protested at trial that the confession had been beaten out of his client, the Polaroid was produced in evidence.

Ed was also the master of the "Xerox polygraph." This, as he explained it to me, was a method of interrogation to be employed only on the very gullible—a category that included, fortunately, most of the dopers, hookers, pimps, drifters, and street people scooped up by the police for routine interrogation. Ed would take a piece of blank paper, write the word "LIE!" on it, place it face-down on the glass of the stationhouse Xerox machine, and close the cover over it. Then he would bring the person to be interrogated into the Xerox room and explain that the device before him was the latest model polygraph—a foolproof lie-detecting machine. In solemn tones, he would direct the poor soul to place his, or her, hand on the machine. "Do you know who killed Cock Robin?" "Um ... no ... I don't." The machine would hum, a piece of paper would fall into the paper-sorter, and Ed would hold it up slowly to the interrogee. "See what it says? You're lying!"

It was Ed who interrogated Glen Hundley. We had plenty of evidence to prove the crime, but without a confession we had almost nothing to show that it was Hundley who did it. Hundley was a skinny, pale-faced kid in his mid-twenties, with coal-black eyes and a rough stubble of beard. He had little schooling, but he was a graduate of many a police grilling. His defense to being interrogated was to re-invent himself suddenly and frequently. One minute he was angry, screaming, cursing. The next he would clam up, seeming almost catatonic. Later he would be courteous, deferential, cooperative. Through all his moods Ed stuck with him, quiet but firm. Ed went a night and a day without sleep, but in the end Hundley confessed.

We were taking no chances with Hundley. We got him on the morning calendar for a first appearance hearing without any delay. New cases are assigned to the different judges by blind rotation, and that morning blind justice gave us Judge Ogden Galena.

Judge Galena's friends, if he had any, called him "Auggie." Everyone else called him Your Honor to his face, and behind his back "Big Chief Tuck-a-buck-away" because when it came to a dollar he was as tight as a clam with a cramp. Jack usually called him something like "the perverted dwarf," but only when no one but Ed and me was listening. I never met anyone who could remember a time when Judge Galena wasn't on the bench. Some of us thought that the first thing Ponce de Leon did when he got to Florida was make Auggie Galena a circuit judge. He wasn't much to look at. He was a tiny man, much shorter even than I, but with a large, bony jaw and long bony fingers he would never grow into. He had one leg shorter than the other, so that he walked with the rolling, bow-legged gait of a sailor just ashore, or a cowboy just off his horse. In private conversation he was vulgar, sexist, given to the recital of an unending supply of filthy limericks. On the bench he kept his mouth shut; he had always been a judge, he had no way to make a living if he weren't a judge, if the *Miami Herald* heard any of his trashy remarks he wouldn't be a judge any more, and he knew it. He made a great pretense of speaking French fluently — he never announced a recess, always a *"pause-cafe"* — but I always suspected it was a few phrases learned by rote with a lot of double-talk thrown in. Some judges, proud of their scholarship, write lengthy opinions supporting their rulings. Galena never wrote any opinions — Jack referred to this as "save-a-tree jurisprudence" — and his rulings consisted of "sustained" or "overruled." He believed, probably correctly, that the less a judge said and did the less the court of appeals would have to overturn. He almost always ruled in favor of the prosecution, because he believed, probably correctly, that no one ever lost an election for being tough on crime. For all of it, he had a trial instinct, a certain cunning that enabled him to find his way out of the trial jungle safely without being able to read the map or compass.

The corrections officers brought Hundley into the courtroom in handcuffs and leg shackles. I had hoped that the press hadn't learned what was going on, so that we could get Hundley in and out of court quickly and quietly, but there were cameras and microphones as thick as mosquitos after summer rain.   The good news was that with so many journalists present Galena wouldn't recite his favorite limerick, the one that began "There once was a man from Nantucket."

Galena managed to get through the first appearance hearing without much trouble. He informed Hundley of his rights, denied bail, and announced that he would be appointing Robert Sunday to represent the defendant.   After Hundley was dragged back to his holding cell the press left the courtroom and milled around in the hallway. I snuck out through the judge's chambers, leaving Jack to answer reporters' questions in the corridor.

Ten years or so ago, Bobby Sunday was in the twilight of a good, not great, career. He worked hard, he cared about his clients, he fought for them in court by day and visited them in jail by night. He had always made a living but had never gotten rich. He had had some good verdicts, but had never gotten famous. He was not brilliant, but he was dogged and competent. The pressure of trying so many cases for so many years had worn him down, but had not knocked him out. There was no prospect of Glen Hundley being acquitted. There was no money to be made, no glory to be earned by representing him. No lawyer would want the representation. Bobby Sunday would take it. He would take it because he still believed, after all these years, that the most wretched among us was entitled to the best defense the law allows. He would take it because he knew that if he did not take it, someone not nearly as conscientious would be made to take it. He would take it because he and Judge Galena had been trading favors for decades, and Judge Galena would ask him to take it as a favor. It wasn't that Auggie Galena was concerned about Glen Hundley's rights. It wasn't that at all. Galena wanted to be the judge who would sentence Glen Hundley to die in the electric chair, but to do that he would have to make sure Hundley got a fair trial, a trial that would stand up on appeal. Bobby Sunday was Auggie Galena's insurance policy.   Bobby Sunday would make sure Glen

Hundley got a fair trial, and then Auggie Galena could electrocute him.

Bobby Sunday—it seems odd to think of an older man as "Bobby," but I never heard anyone call Bobby Sunday "Robert" except when court was in session—was taller than average and heavy-set. He had been an athlete as a youngster, but year by year the bunched muscle had turned to loose flesh, and the taut skin had given way to make room for it. He was so bull-necked that his head seemed to sit directly on his torso. His hair, slicked back and brilliantly shiny, was and always would be the ebony black of cheap dye or shoe polish. In the courtroom his eyes, face, hands, body, were full of animation. Outside the courtroom he was so quiet and expressionless that you could stand next to him on the courthouse elevator or in the cafeteria line and not even realize that he was there.

In due course Bobby filed a motion to suppress Glen Hundley's confession. A motion to suppress asks a judge to rule that certain evidence is inadmissible, because it was got at illegally or because it would be unfair to use it at trial. When a motion to suppress is filed, the judge conducts a hearing and makes a ruling. If he grants the motion, the jury never hears about the confession, never even knows it existed. If he denies the motion, the confession is introduced as evidence at trial just like any other evidence.

I wrote a lengthy legal memorandum in opposition to Bobby's motion and sent it to Judge Galena. It wasn't that we were really worried that Galena would grant the motion. We just wanted to make sure we gave him a good record for the court of appeals. Jack, Ed and I spent days, nights, and weekends working on the presentation we would make at the hearing. Jack would handle most of the witness examinations. I would make sure all the legal bases were covered. Ed, of course, was our star witness.

The morning of the hearing the courtroom was again swamped with reporters. After the case was called, Galena asked the attorneys on the case—Bobby, Jack, and me—to approach the bench. He was partial to bench conferences because they were off the record, which meant he could always deny that he said whatever it was he said. We exchanged some pleasantries, and he asked us if we had heard the limerick about the girl from Madras. I started to tell him that we had, but it was too late. "There once was a girl from Madras," he intoned, and we got to hear all about her again. Apparently she had the most beautiful ass. It was not pink, as you might think, but was gray, had long ears, and ate grass. When he got done laughing, he asked, "Now, fellows, how long is this hearing going to take?"

I looked at Jack, and at Bobby. "We should be able to finish sometime early tomorrow, Judge."

"We should be able to finish today. Some of your newer judges are as slow as sludge, but I see no reason we shouldn't finish this up today."

Then why bother to ask? "We'll make every effort, Your Honor."

He barked a name at the court clerk that wasn't hers, but she turned around anyway. "Let me see the file in this case." She was a young woman with a very athletic figure that Galena made a point of describing, in a mutter just loud enough for her to hear, as "nothing but gristle and gravy." He leafed casually through the file that she handed him as we returned to our places at counsel table. Jack was working hard to keep from laughing, and as we sat, Ed leaned over and asked him what was so funny.

"The perverted dwarf is sitting on a phone book," he whispered to Ed, fighting the chuckles that wanted out. "The press is here, and he wants to sit tall in the saddle."

Galena was speaking. "The court has read with care the written submissions of both parties." He had glanced at them. "Let me say that both sides have done very fine work in their written pleadings." The court of appeals, in affirming his ruling, would be able to comment that Judge Galena had been scrupulously even-handed and courteous to all attorneys. "Is the prosecution ready to proceed?"

Jack had regained his self-possession. "We are, Your Honor."

"Please call your first witness."

"The State of Florida calls Detective Edward Barber."

I watched Ed take the oath and have a seat in the witness box. There is an instant, when a witness first takes the stand, in which he seems a stranger to you. He could be your father, your brother, your best friend. It doesn't matter. In that instant, it is as if you are looking at him for the first time. You see a man every day for years, and then when he takes the witness stand you see a defect in his physical appearance or manner of expressing himself that you have never seen before. I looked at Ed; and although, for that fleeting second, I saw a stranger, still I saw no defect of appearance or expression.

Ed stated his name and identified himself as a Metro-Dade homicide detective. Jack took the notebook that I had helped him prepare and walked to the podium. When a jury is present, Jack works without notes or a podium. There must be no barriers between him and the jury. But today there was no jury. Our only audience would be Judge Galena; Judge Galena and the moving tape of paper on which the court reporter was typing symbols which would one day be transcribed into words and read by the court of appeals.

"And are you the lead detective in a case captioned 'State of Florida vs. Hundley,' also known as the 'Baby Karen' case?"

"Yes, sir."

"In the course of your investigation of that case, did you have occasion to come in contact with the defendant, Glen Hundley?"

"I did."

"Do you see him present in the courtroom today?"

Bobby stood up. "Your Honor, there is no jury present. For purposes of this hearing only, we stipulate to the identity of the defendant."

"Yes, there is no jury present. Let's move along, Mr. Sheridan." His Honor had spoken, and Jack nodded.

"When did you first come in contact with the defendant Hundley?"

Ed gave a date and time, sometime during evening hours. He had met Hundley at the police station, where Hundley was being held in the "interview room."

"Did you speak to the defendant Hundley?"

"Yes, sir."

"And what was your purpose in speaking to him?"

We had gone over the wording of this answer with care. "To see if he would speak to me voluntarily and of his own free will about the Baby Karen case." I had pointed out during our preparation that "voluntarily" and "of his own free will" meant the same thing, but Jack and Ed were taking no chances.

"When you first entered the interview room, Detective Barber, how did the defendant Hundley appear to you?"

"He was dressed in his own clothing, a tee-shirt and jeans. He was seated, and had handcuffs on."

"Were his hands cuffed behind him or in front of him?"

"In front of him."

"Did you leave the handcuffs on him?"

"No, sir. I arranged to have them removed."

"Were you armed?"

"No, sir."

"Were you in police uniform?"

"No, sir. I was dressed as I am today." We had asked Ed to wear the same clothes to the hearing that he had worn when he interrogated Hundley.

"And for the record, Detective, how are you dressed today?"

"I'm wearing a *guayabera* and wash pants." Ed was not Cuban, but he had picked up the habit of wearing *guayaberas*, lightweight cotton overshirts worn loose and not tucked into the pants. He owned, as far as I knew, one suit. It was dark blue, and he saved it for jury trials. I think he had two ties.

"What did you say to the defendant Hundley when you first came in contact with him?"

"I showed the subject"—police officers do not interrogate people, they interrogate subjects—"my badge, and identified myself to him. I asked him when he had last slept, and if he felt alert."

"And what did he say?"

"He said he had slept the night before, and that he was OK."

"Did he appear to be alert and responsive to your questions?"

"Yes, sir."

Out of the corner of my eye I glanced at Hundley. He had pushed his chair away from the table before him, and was slumped down with his forearms on his thighs, staring at the floor between his feet. Bobby Sunday had notepads, papers, lawbooks, spread out on the table in front of him. From time to time, he would furiously re-arrange these props, as if the outcome of the case depended entirely on the order in which things were piled before him. I never saw him take a note or refer to a book.

"What else did you ask him?"

"I asked if he wanted to go to the men's room. He said he was OK. I asked if he wanted some coffee or soda. He asked for coffee and I got him some. I asked if he wanted something to eat."

Judge Galena thought this would be a brilliant time to interrupt with a witty remark. "Pizza, detective?"

Ed grinned, a somewhat embarrassed grin. "No, Your Honor. He said he wanted a Wendy's bacon cheeseburger and a frosty."

Jack jumped back in. "And did you arrange to get him his burger?"

"Two."

"You indicated, detective," Jack continued, "that it was your intention to determine if the defendant Hundley would speak to you voluntarily and of his own free will about the Baby Karen case. Did he speak to you?"

"Yes, sir."

"Freely and voluntarily?"

"Yes, sir."

"Did you threaten him in any way?"

"No, sir."

"Did you promise him anything in exchange for speaking to you?"

"No, sir."

Jack had a document marked as evidence by the clerk of the court, and presented it to Ed. "Can you tell the Court what this is, detective?"

"Yes, sir. This is a rights waiver form."

"And what is a rights waiver form?"

A rights waiver form, Ed explained, is a standard form used by police to assure that a subject understands his constitutional rights and is waiving them of his own free will. It lists the various *Miranda* warnings—the right to remain silent, the right to an attorney even if the subject cannot afford an attorney—and asks, after each, "Do you understand this right?" The subject writes "yes" and his initials next to each question. At the bottom of the page, the form asks, "Knowing and understanding your rights, do you still wish to talk to me?" Again the subject writes "yes," and then signs. At least two officers witness the signing and date the form. Jack had Ed explain how he and another officer had reviewed the form carefully with Hundley, then had witnessed Hundley initial and sign the form. When Ed concluded his explanation, Jack offered the form in evidence. Galena received it without even looking at Bobby.

Jack and Ed worked well together, and they had developed a nice rhythm through the preliminary questioning. Now it was time for the payoff. Jack picked up a stack of papers. The papers were ordinary lined notebook pages, the kind the kids use in school. There were eight pages, stapled together at the upper left-hand corner. Jack had them marked as a single exhibit by the clerk, and then showed them to Ed.

"Do you recognize this exhibit, Detective Barber?"

"Yes, sir. I do."

"What do you recognize it as being?"

"This is the confession that Mr. Hundley wrote."

"Did he write it in his own hand?"

"Yes, sir."

"Did he number the pages consecutively?"

"Yes, sir."

"Did he sign and date it at the end?"

"Yes, sir."

"Did you sign as a witness?"

"Yes, sir."

"And was this done by the defendant Hundley freely and

voluntarily, after he signed the rights waiver form?"

"Yes, sir. It was."

Jack offered the exhibit in evidence. He handed it to the clerk, who handed it the judge. Auggie Galena wasn't much for reading, but he read all eight pages right then and there. He read all eight pages and the lawyers, the court personnel, and the press sat and watched him read. He wasn't just turning the pages, either. I could tell from his face that he was actually subjecting himself to the details laid out in those eight pages. I knew what he was reading. I had read it myself. I knew that when he was done reading, nothing on earth would keep us from convicting Glen Hundley.

It took him, I suppose, ten minutes or so to work his way through those papers. The courtroom was so silent that when he turned a page it sounded like thunder. Ed sat stock-still in the witness chair, looking at nothing in particular. Jack stood stock-still behind the podium, following Galena's reading, watching his eyes move, watching his face squint and pucker as he stared through a window into Hell. I sat stock-still at counsel table, afraid to move my chair or shift my position because of the noise it would make. But within my fear was a kernel of happiness, a happiness that came from knowing that the system worked, that Jack and Ed and I had made it work.

It was our first big win together. A few years later Judge Galena died in his sleep and I was named to his place on the circuit court. Jack gave a beautiful speech at my investiture. I had asked Ed to speak, too, on behalf of the Metro-Dade police department, but he turned me down. He took me out for a drink, though, and gave me a lecture on not catching a case of "robitis," inflammation of the judicial robe. A judge, he told me, should be someone who's perfect or someone who knows he isn't. Remember that, he said.

* * *

It was quiet on the patio; quiet as it had been that day in Judge Galena's court. I looked down at my wrist, but I had taken my watch off before dinner. The lights were off in all the neighbors' houses. I looked up at the sky. The new moon was smiling a Cheshire-cat's smile, all smile and no cat. I stood and stretched, and I could almost touch the stars. Almost, but not quite.

Chapter Four
Tuesday

"Please state your name, Officer, and tell us how you are employed."

Roscoe Belmont was a cop who looked like a cop. He was a black man, no more than medium height but square-shouldered and square-jawed. Like many of the City of Miami police, he was a weightlifter, and what he lacked in height he made up for in breadth and depth.

"Roscoe Belmont, City of Miami Police Department, presently assigned to the Uniform Patrol Division."

"And how long have you been in the Uniform Patrol Division?"

"Four years."

At the beginning of her direct examination, Eleanor had moved the podium alongside the jury rail. Belmont would tend naturally to turn toward Eleanor when he answered her questions, and she had positioned herself so that when he faced her, Belmont would be facing the jurors as well.

"Directing your attention to"—she glanced at her notes and gave the date of the crime—"I ask if you were on duty at or slightly after midnight."

"Yes, ma'am."

"Was your attention drawn to anything unusual?"

"Yes, ma'am."

"What was that?"

He shifted in his seat. "I was on routine patrol, traveling at that time along Grand Avenue in Coconut Grove. I observed a vehicle"—in the history of the world, no cop has ever seen a car, he has always observed a vehicle—"pulled over to the side of the road along Commodore Plaza. The vehicle was a Ford Taurus." He gave the license plate number military style, using the phonetic alphabet, A-alpha, B-bravo, C-charlie, D-delta. "I observed that the hood of the vehicle was in the open position, indicating that the vehicle was stalled."

"What if anything did you do?"

"I pulled my marked police vehicle in behind the stalled vehicle."

"And then?"

"I exited my police vehicle and approached the stalled Ford Taurus."

"As you approached the stalled Ford Taurus, was your attention drawn to anything?"

"Yes, ma'am."

"What was that?"

"As I walked from the back of the vehicle toward the hood, I happened to look inside the passenger compartment. On the driver's side floorboard in the back seat I saw what appeared to be a plastic package containing white or light-colored powder."

Eleanor left the podium and walked over to the counsel table on which her papers and files lay. Reaching under the table, she produced a package which she then presented to the clerk of the court. "Your Honor, I ask that this be marked the State of Florida's Exhibit A for identification." I directed that the exhibit be marked. "For the record, I am now showing State's Exhibit A to counsel for the defense." She started to walk toward Jack, but with a gesture and a shake of the head he indicated that the formality of showing him the exhibit could be dispensed with. She reversed course and approached the witness. "Officer, I show you what has been marked as State's Exhibit A for identification and ask if you recognize it."

It was a clear plastic package, larger than a grapefruit but smaller than a football, shaped like a very soft rectangle. A piece of gray duct tape ran the length of one side and held the plastic in place. Inside was a white powder that could have been baby powder or sugar but it wasn't. Belmont studied the duct tape. "Yes ma'am."

"How do you recognize it?"

"It has my initials and the date here." He pointed to a marking on the duct tape. "I placed them there when I impounded this evidence."

"Thank you, officer." Eleanor took Exhibit A back from the witness and returned it to the clerk. Then she resumed her place at the podium. "What do you recognize that exhibit as being?"

"It's what I saw on the floorboard in the back of the Ford Taurus."

"Officer Belmont, as part of your police training, are you taught to recognize narcotics and other controlled substances?"

"Yes, ma'am."

"And in your years on the City of Miami Police Department, including your four years in the Uniform Patrol Division, have you had occasion to impound narcotic drugs, including cocaine?"

"Yes, ma'am."

"On how many occasions, would you say?"

"I don't know, ma'am. Hundreds."

"Hundreds?"

"I would say so, yes, ma'am."

"Well, Officer Belmont, based on your training and experience, when you saw that package"—she pointed toward the clerk's desk—"on the floor in the back seat of the Ford Taurus in Coconut Grove on a Saturday night, what if anything did you suspect it to be?"

"Cocaine."

Eleanor paused for a moment. "At the time you made these observations, Officer, was there anyone present who appeared to be the owner or driver of the Ford Taurus?"

"Yes, ma'am. There was a gentleman standing by the open hood of the car, by the engine."

She stepped back slightly from the podium, and the Voice went up in volume, becoming a public address system. "Now I want you to look around this courtroom, Officer Belmont, and tell us if you see the man who was standing at the front of the car in which you saw the suspected cocaine."

It is a ritual. In every trial, one or more eyewitnesses will be invited, with as much flourish as the prosecutor can muster, to look around this courtroom and tell us if you see the man who ... . Does it prove anything? Is any witness really likely to point the finger of guilt at the black-robed judge, the uniformed bailiff, or juror number five? There are only two persons seated at defense counsel table, and one of them, to judge by his suit, his trial bag, and his law books, is a lawyer. A blind man could pick out the defendant with his cane. It is a ritual, nothing more. But trials are rituals, and the votaries—the judges, lawyers, and cops—must play their parts.

Officer Roscoe Belmont knew his part. He spent a long minute looking around the courtroom before pointing at Rodriguez. "There. The gentleman seated there, next to Mr. Sheridan."

"Your Honor," the Voice was full and rich and formal, "may the record reflect that the witness has identified the defendant, Felix Rodriguez?" I stated solemnly that the record would so reflect. The ritual was complete.

"Officer Belmont, what if anything did you say to the defendant?"

"I asked him for his driver's license, vehicle registration, and proof of insurance. I also asked him what the problem was."

"How did he respond?"

"He produced a valid Florida driver's license from his wallet. He produced registration and proof of insurance from the glove box of the vehicle. And he told me that he had been driving for about ten minutes when the car just died."

"Did you ask him about the suspected cocaine in the back seat?"

"Not at that time, no, ma'am."

"What did you do?"

"I asked him if he would please have a seat in the back of my police cruiser while I called dispatch."

"And did you call dispatch?"

"Yes, ma'am."

"Did you take the suspected cocaine, State's Exhibit A, into custody?"

"Not at that time, ma'am. Not till Detective Rasmussen arrived."

Eleanor took a moment to study her legal pad. Satisfied that she had left nothing out, she looked up at me and said, "Thank you, Your Honor. I have no further questions of this witness."

Like most attorneys, Blackjack Sheridan made it his business to sit quietly during the other side's examination, staring off into space, looking vaguely thoughtful but entirely unconcerned. He sat back in his chair, his legs crossed, his body motionless but for the occasional, the very occasional, jotting of a note on his legal pad with a plain yellow number two pencil.

Sheridan made a study in contrast with the client sitting next to him. Rodriguez was a hen on a hot quilt. He shifted in his seat, then shifted again. He bounced his leg nervously. He picked energetically at a pock-mark on his face until Jack tapped his hand with the number two pencil. He worked his lips as if he were chewing on a toothpick or playing with a cigarette. He might have made a nice-looking man — dark hair and eyes, athletic build — but he gave the impression that if he had something to say to you he would grab your lapels to get your attention and then deliver saliva at close range.

"Does the defense have any questions of this witness?"

Jack took his time getting to his feet. "Good ... ." He looked at the clock in the back of the courtroom. We had started late, and it was past eleven. "... morning, Officer Belmont."

"Good morning, Mr. Sheridan."

"I don't get out much anymore, but if I remember correctly from my younger days, Coconut Grove is a pretty busy place on a Saturday night. Is that still so?" Jack got out a lot more than he stayed in, but it was the witness, not Jack, who was under oath.

"Yes, sir."

"Lots of pedestrians?"

"Yes, sir."

"Bright lights and fast cars? Well, lots of cars, anyway?"

"Yes, sir."

"I suppose it's possible you might have driven by a stalled car pulled over to the side of the road and never even taken notice of it, isn't it, Officer?"

"It's possible, yes, sir."

"But one of the reasons you stopped for this particular stalled car is because Mr. Rodriguez flagged you down, isn't that right, Officer?"

Belmont took a moment to choose his words. "I wouldn't say he flagged me down, sir. He did appear to ... to wave, or beckon as I drove by."

Jack had asked his first series of questions standing at counsel table. He took a few steps into the well of the court, a few steps closer to the witness. "Beckoned, then." Jack was happy with the choice of words: "beckoned" was proper Southern. "At the time Mr. Rodriguez beckoned you, you were in your marked police cruiser, isn't that right, Officer?"

"Yes, sir."

"And at the time Mr. Rodriguez beckoned you, you were dressed in your City of Miami police uniform as you are now, isn't that right?"

"Yes, sir."

"So there can be no doubt that at the time Mr. Rodriguez beckoned you, he was beckoning a City of Miami police officer? No doubt about that?"

"No doubt, no, sir."

"I want to be clear on this point, Officer. A man with cocaine in plain view in the back seat of his vehicle flagged down a police officer in a marked police car, is that what happened?"

"If you put it that way, sir."

"I put it that way because that's what happened, isn't it, Officer?"

"Yes, sir."

"Officer Belmont, in your four years as a uniform patrol officer, have you ever"—*evah*—"been beckoned, flagged down, waved over by a driver who had narcotics in plain view in his vehicle?" Eleanor objected. I sustained. Jack took a few easy strides into the well of the courtroom, a few strides closer to the witness. "When you first approached Mr. Rodriguez, Officer, did he make any effort to get you to leave?"

"No, sir."

"Did he say to you, 'Officer Belmont, I really don't need any help here and I'm not blocking traffic, so no need for you to hang around'?"

"No, sir."

"Did he make any effort to prevent you from looking into the back seat of his car?"

"No, sir."

"In your experience, Officer, the presence of a police officer makes some people nervous, isn't that so?"

"Sometimes."

"But Mr. Rodriguez didn't seem particularly nervous to have you around, did he?" Out of the corner of my eye I snuck a glance at the defendant. If he didn't seem particularly nervous at the time of his arrest, he was vibrating like a tuning-fork now.

"I couldn't say if he was feeling nervous or not, sir."

"Did he start to sweat profusely?"

"Not that I noticed, sir."

"Did he seem shaky and jittery?"

"No, sir."

"Did he exhibit any other physical symptoms of nervousness?"

"Not that I recall, sir."

"So when I asked you, Officer, if Mr. Rodriguez seemed particularly nervous at the time you came in contact with him, the truthful answer is no, he didn't seem nervous. That is the truthful answer, isn't it, Officer?"

"Yes, sir."

"And when you asked him to have a seat in the back of your police car, he was cooperative, wasn't he?"

"Yes, sir."

"In fact he was cooperative and courteous with you at all times, wasn't he?"

"Yes, sir."

Jack had moved to within three or four feet of the witness stand. "And in all the time you were in his presence, Mr. Rodriguez never once said or did anything to indicate that he knew there was cocaine in the back seat of his car, did he?"

Eleanor objected, on the grounds that the question called for speculation and improper opinion testimony. I hesitated for just a second, then overruled.

"I don't know what he knew, sir."

Belmont was ducking the question. Jack wouldn't let him. "Officer, you filed an offense incident report, a police report, in connection with this matter, didn't you?"

"Yes, sir."

"And you have been trained by the City of Miami Police Department in the proper manner to fill out police reports, haven't you?"

"Yes, sir."

"And you understand that it is an extremely important part of your job to fill police reports out accurately and completely, isn't that correct?"

"Yes, sir."

"So you always make every effort to fill out your reports accurately and completely, don't you, Officer?"

"Yes, sir."

"And you did so in this case, didn't you, Officer?"

"Yes, sir."

"Did you note anywhere in your police report in this case, Officer, anything that Mr. Rodriguez said or did that would indicate that he knew he had cocaine in the back seat of his car?"

"No, sir."

"Because the truth is, Officer, that Mr. Rodriguez never said or did anything that would indicate that he knew he had cocaine in his car, did he, Officer?"

Belmont spent a few seconds searching for a back door and not finding one. "No, sir."

"Thank you, Officer. We appreciate your honesty. No further questions."

Jack had a seat. Eleanor spent a few minutes on redirect, focusing on the physical evidence: It was Rodriguez's car, so it was Rodriguez's dope. The witness was dismissed a few minutes before noon, and I summoned both attorneys to the bench.

"Ms. Hibbard, if your next witness will be very brief we'll hear him now. Otherwise we'll recess for lunch now so that the witness's testimony isn't broken up."

Jack jumped in. "Your Honor, if the Court would consider recessing this trial now, there's another matter we can take up out of the hearing of the jury that will require Ms. Hibbard's presence."

"What other matter, counselor?"

"Judge, I represent a young man named Linden. When you set bail in his case last week you ordered that he not be released unless we made a showing as to the source of the bail money. The family has raised the required amount, and they're very eager to see the boy released."

I looked at Eleanor. "Is there any reason we shouldn't hear Mr. Sheridan on his application now?" She couldn't think of one, and neither could I. I dismissed the jury for lunch with my usual speech about not discussing the case or forming any fixed opinions. The corrections officers brought Linden into the courtroom, and the clerk recited his name and case number for the record. I invited Jack to proceed.

"Your Honor, we're prepared to post the bail set by the court. The funds are being provided by Mrs. Vera Shields, a long-time family friend and neighbor. At this time I call Mrs. Shields."

A slight woman, about five feet tall, stepped forward from the gallery. She looked to be in her eighties. She wore a simple cotton dress with a small floral pattern, a dress that ran from her neck to her ankles, and her only other items of clothing were a pair of new Nike sneakers worn over white cotton athletic socks. There was no jewelry on her hands or around her neck, but an imitation tortoise-shell comb held her short gray hair in place. Her face, leathery and heavily lined, spoke of a lifetime in the Florida sun. Her gait was deliberate and her stride short, and I expected to hear from her that slow and slurred speech that betrays senescence. But her voice, when she took the oath and gave her name and address, was lively and energetic.

"And how long have you known the defendant Linden?"

"Since he was a boy, off and on."

"Do you know his family?"

"Known his momma for many years. We're neighbors."

Jack was enjoying himself. His witness's answers were brief and to the point. She kept her voice up. And only an ogre would cross-examine this little old lady. "Are you willing to put up his bail?"

"Yes, sir."

"Do you understand that if he fails to show up to court, you could lose all the money you put up as bail?"

"He'll be here. He's not going anywhere."

Jack was struggling not to chuckle. "You understand that the amount of the bail is $2,500?"

"Yes, sir."

"You have that money?"

"Have it here with me." She patted a small handbag she was clutching.

"I have to ask, ma'am, where you got that money from."

"Had it in the house, in mason jars and the mattress. Don't trust banks."

"And how did you come to have it in the house? Where did you get it?"

"Saved it over the years."

"Thank you, Mrs. Shields." Jack was well pleased. He looked at me and raised his eyebrows. I turned to Eleanor and asked if the prosecution had any questions.

"Mrs. Shields, I take it you are retired, is that so?"

"Yes, ma'am."

"You're a senior citizen?" Eleanor smiled. Perhaps she thought the question would help her make friends with the witness. She was wrong.

"I'm an old lady," Mrs. Shields snapped. "If you call old people 'seniors,' do you call dead people 'graduates'?" Jack didn't even try to hold the laugh in; he rocked back and forth and roared, smacking his thigh again and again.

Eleanor had asked what she thought was an innocuous question and had gotten her shins barked. But she was too good a lawyer to let it throw her. "Mrs. Shields, you've known the defendant and his family for many years?"

"Yes, ma'am."

"And you're willing to trust the defendant with $2,500 of your life savings?"

"Yes, ma'am."

"You must feel close to the defendant?"

"Pretty close, I guess."

"You must have felt very concerned when he was arrested?"

"Uh, yes."

"When was that?"

"When was what?"

"When was the defendant arrested?"

Mrs. Shields was stuck. She looked quickly at Jack, who had better sense than to try to help her out. She looked back at Eleanor, and muttered slowly "When was ... "

" ... the defendant arrested. Yes, ma'am, that is my question."

No answer.

"Was it last week? Last month? Last year?

No answer.

"If we were to check the jail records, would they indicate that you have been to see him in jail last week? Last month? Last ... "

Jack was on his feet. "Objection! Your Honor, I object! Argumentative! The prosecutor isn't even giving the witness a chance to answer! She's just harassing this ... this little old lady!" As an expression of his righteous indignation—and few lawyers were better than John Wentworth Sheridan IV in the expression of righteous indignation—Jack had marched up to the witness stand and placed his hand on Mrs. Shields's shoulder. He lowered his voice. "And I have another objection. This line of questioning is irrelevant. The only purpose of this hearing is to determine whether there is any reason the court should not accept the proffered bail money. There is no such reason, and the prosecutor's questions point to no such reason."

Eleanor was eager to respond, but Jack had a point. "Ms. Hibbard," I asked, "does the State of Florida have reason to object to the court's accepting Mrs. Shields's funds in payment of bail?"

"Your Honor, my concern is this: If this witness has been less than candid with the court about her relationship with the defendant, she may have been less than candid with the court about the source of her money."

Jack was eager to respond, but this time Eleanor had a point. It was time for me to rule. "I'm going to accept the money offered in payment of bail. The State Attorney's Office is free to look into Mrs. Shields's financial affairs through ordinary investigative channels. If anything comes to light that suggests that these funds are tainted, feel free to put this matter back on the calendar. I won't hesitate to impose sanctions and, if appropriate, revoke bail."

While I spoke, Jack continued to stand next to Mrs. Shields, patting her on the shoulder and making there-there noises. After I ruled, he escorted her out of the courtroom. I gave Linden the usual speech, explaining the conditions of bail to him and reminding him that if he failed to abide by them he could find himself back on the inside looking out. Then the corrections officers led him away to be released, and I announced the lunch recess.

Back in chambers, Carmen told me to phone Miriam. Apparently Alicia was sick and had to come home from school. I got Miriam on the line and was told that no, it was nothing serious, the same cold and sore throat that all the kids at the elementary school had. I was about to ask if we had received any mail or phone calls that could have anything to do with Ed when Alicia picked up the extension phone.

"Hi, Daddy." A cute, sad, stuffy little voice.

"Hi, Sweetheart. Are you sick, you poor thing?"

"Uh-huh."

"Well, you stay in bed and drink lots of juice and I know you'll be well in no time, OK? Love you." She clicked off. Poor kid; she had been hoping for expressions of sympathy and promises of surprise gifts, and all she got was fatherly advice about juice.

Miriam spoke. "Clark, you forgot your lunch again today."

I did? "Um, no, actually I was thinking about going down

to the cafeteria for lunch today. They have the macaroni and cheese on Wednesday."

"Today's Tuesday."

"Tuesday. That's what I meant.

"Clark?"

"Yes, dear."

"You don't like macaroni and cheese."

It occurred to me that I would ask about mail and phone messages another time. "I have to go now, Miriam. Love you." She told me she loved me too and hung up.

Over at the federal courthouse there is a private dining area where the federal judges eat lunch on white linen and china. I have never seen this myself, but I've heard it said several times and I have no reason to doubt it. Those federal judges don't know what they're missing. They don't have lunch in the cafeteria at the Metro-Justice Building.

In the cafeteria at the Metro-Justice Building all men are created equal. Robeless judges in shirtsleeves stand in the same cafeteria line with jurors, witnesses, even defendants. We huddle around small, coffee-stained tables with lawyers and cops who have appeared before us in the morning and will appear before us again in the afternoon. The too-much noise and too-little elbow room provide merciful distractions from the flavor, aroma, and appearance of the food.

The unwritten rules that govern social interaction in the cafeteria are as rigid and complex as those that govern a herd of walrus during mating season. I stood in the cafeteria line behind two attorneys, courthouse regulars, who were honoring the rule that teaches: Thou shalt complain.

"What is it with this line? I saw a glacier move faster than this."

"A glacier? I closed on my house faster than this."

"My wife gave birth faster than this."

"You know why they keep us waiting, don't you? They want to give the coffee a chance to ferment."

A lawyer who complains about the cafeteria lines, the demise of the law, the ingratitude of his clients, the weather, the Marlins in the summer, the Dolphins in the winter, and business—above all business—is a lawyer to be trusted. Never trust a lawyer with nothing to complain about.

Jack and his client's wife, Mrs. Rodriguez, were seated against the far wall at a table about the size of a washcloth. Miriam and I have been dating since forever, and married since I was in law school, so I can't pretend to be a ladies' man—that's Jack's department—but you couldn't miss Teresa Rodriguez. At a table a few feet over from where Jack sat four cops were having coffee. Actually they were pretending to have coffee, and trying not to form a drool puddle as they ogled Mrs. Rodriguez.

Her hair was dark; not black, but a rich, chocolate color. It fell in thick waves to her shoulders. She had high cheekbones, but the skin of her face was soft and full, not taut. Her skin had a kind of lustre to it. I had a sense, across a crowded room, that it gave off a warmth greater than, different from, the warmth of ordinary skin. When she spoke Jack leaned toward her, his face only inches from hers. I suppose he was straining to hear her over the racket in the cafeteria, but it seemed from a distance that he was drawn to that warmth of hers. You wonder why a woman like that would stick by a character like Felix Rodriguez. You wonder why, but you see it all the time.

Clients are funny people. They tell you they want the truth, but the truth is they don't. The truth is, no lawyer—not even one as good as Blackjack Sheridan—can tell you how a trial is going. The truth is, no lawyer knows what a jury will do. The truth is, no lawyer can guarantee or predict a verdict. All a lawyer can do is his best. So the lawyer tells that to the client, and to the client's family. He explains it in soothing tones, strokes the client's hand as Jack was doing to Mrs. Rodriguez. And then the client, or the client's wife, or the client's mother looks up with big sad eyes and says: But they won't convict, will they? You're sure of an acquittal, aren't you?

We are taught as children to tell the truth even when the truth hurts. Young lawyers, fresh from law school, cling doggedly to this rule in their dealings with clients. They tell clients frankly that the chances of acquittal are slim, that we should prepare for the worst. As the years pass they learn that all too often hope is all a lawyer can offer his client; and that false hope is better than no hope at all. Better to commiserate with the client once at the end of trial than every day during the trial.

I tried, for a minute, to imagine what Jack must have been telling his client's wife. Contrary to the impression you get from watching the eleven o'clock news, most criminal defendants are convicted, and most of them serve an appropriate prison term. When a Felix Rodriguez is caught with the drugs in his car, the chances of acquittal are slim. I watched Jack talking, gesturing; these were things he was certainly not telling Teresa Rodriguez.

Perhaps he was reminding her that jury selection had gone well. Some trial lawyers will tell you that picking a jury is the most important part of the whole trial. Get the right jury and you'll get the right verdict. Of course no lawyer knows if he picked the right jury until the verdict is returned, and even then the jurors don't tell you why they did what they did. Judge Galena used to tell young lawyers that trying cases to juries is like screwing: You can talk about it, you can read about it, if you're so inclined you can watch other people do it—but until you've done it a few times yourself you don't have any idea what's going on. Like a lot of the things Judge Galena said, it was crude but it was true.

Jack had stopped talking. Mrs. Rodriguez was looking down at the tabletop, taking out her worry or annoyance by crumpling a paper napkin. Jack reached over and stroked her arm soothingly.

"Hiya, Judge. What'll it be?" Staring at Jack and Mrs. Rodriguez I had shuffled slowly to the front of the line. Across the counter from me a kid who looked to be turning 14 was asking for my order.

"I'll have the special."

He stared at me blankly. "What special?"

"The Tuesday special."

The kid disappeared into the kitchen, where I heard him ask somebody named Herb if they had a Tuesday special. He returned with a toothpick in his mouth and asked, "The soup and sandwich special or the hotplate special?"

"What's the hotplate special?"

By way of answer he pointed at the contents of a plate sitting under a heating lamp behind him and to the right. The contents were brown and red and runny, but the runny part seemed about to clot.

"I'll have the soup and sandwich special." I paid the kid and moved down to the end of the counter. When I picked up my food I did not sit with Jack and Mrs. Rodriguez. It would have been a violation of the unwritten code: Thou shalt not talk to a lawyer when he is talking to his client or his client's family.

I found a seat at a tiny, rickety table and was checking my soup for life forms when a voice called my name softly. I looked up to see Al Guerrero.

Al has any case half-won the minute he walks in the courtroom. He is tall and handsome, but it is an ordinary-guy kind of handsome, the kind of handsome that Jimmy Stewart and Gary Cooper and Henry Fonda made movie careers out of. His looks never seem to change much as the years go by. He probably didn't look too young when he was young, and he doesn't look too old now that he's getting old. His hair is appropriately gray around the temples, but still thick and full, worn longish in back. Out of the courtroom he has a casual, man-of-the-people style. His collar button was undone and the knot of his necktie pulled down. His suitcoat was thrown over his shoulder.

"Well, well. What brings a big-shot federal lawyer like Al Guerrero to the Metro-Justice Building?" I asked, as I gestured toward a vacant chair. "Slumming?"

Al, grinning as always, took a seat. So did the chubby law clerk who was carrying his own briefcase, Al's, and some files. "I can't spend all my time down at the guilty factory." The guilty factory is federal court. Al looked at my lunch as if it had just been offered in evidence. Then he fished a few bills out of his pocket. "Ernie," he said to the law clerk, "get us something to eat, but not the soup."

Ernie took the cash. "You want the special?"

"What's the special?" Al asked.

I volunteered an answer. "I think they're calling it 'Chicken Hindenburg'."

Ernie was headed toward the cafeteria line. Al called over his shoulder, "Just coffee for me, Ern."

When I was starting out in the law Al Guerrero was already the stuff of legend. There are a million Al Guerrero stories, most of them told by Al Guerrero; and as Al never tires of saying, "All of my stories are true—especially the ones I make up." Years ago I asked Al how he got into the trial lawyer business. He told me that when he was a kid his family lived in New York, and Al made a little money selling flowers on Broadway when the theaters were letting out. "I'd see a young couple, maybe they just got pinned or it's a prom date, and I'd say, 'Hey, Mister, buy your wife a flower?' Then I'd see some old couple, tourists who came to the Big Apple to celebrate their fortieth anniversary and I'd say, 'Hey, Mister, buy a flower for your girlfriend?' I almost put all the other flower vendors out of business. And that," said Al, "is when I knew I was going to be a trial lawyer." I had started to ask him if that was a true story, but I knew what the answer would be.

Al is an old-time true believer. The defense of persons accused of crime is not merely his job, it is his faith. A couple of years ago I gave Al a lift to some bar association luncheon, and we had to stop on the way for gasoline. I pulled into the self-serve lane, hopped out, and started to pump my gas. Al got out and walked around to my side of the car. Over in the garage bay an attendant kept looking at Al with that don't-I-know-you-from-somewhere look. After a while curiosity got the better of him and he walked over to us. He was Pakistani, and he spoke with a strong accent. He and Al struck up a conversation—Al will make friends with a cigar store Indian if there's no one else around—and they figured out that he recognized Al from photos that had recently appeared in the *Miami Herald* because of some big case Al was trying. Then, in a very off-hand way, the guy said something like, "Really, I think the criminals have more rights than the rest of us."

For just a second I froze. I was waiting for Al to go ballistic, to hit the guy with a windshield wiper and tell him to drag ass back to Trashcanistan. Instead Al did what Al does best: He cross-examined.

"You know," Al said, speaking quietly but getting right into the guy's face, "that's just what I'd expect a criminal to say. I'll bet you've committed some crimes."

The guy tried smiling at Al, as if it were a joke. Then he saw in Al's eyes that it was no joke. "What do you mean, crimes? I commit no crimes."

"Oh sure," Al nodded as if he'd heard it all before. "Isn't that typical. You criminals are all alike. You're the first ones to say you're for law and order, but when it comes to your own crimes you won't own up to what you've done. Give me one good reason why the police shouldn't take you down to head-quarters for a little interrogation."

"What?"

"That's right. If you're as innocent as you pretend then you've got nothing to hide. You aren't afraid of the police, are you?"

If he wasn't, he was getting there. "Well, I ... no, I am not afraid, but ..."

Al was right on top of the guy now. "Then give me one reason—one good reason—why the police shouldn't find out just how innocent you really are at the end of a tire iron. Give me one reason they shouldn't do that."

"They cannot do that! They cannot! I have ... I have ..."

I saw Al's right arm headed toward the guy, and for a split-second I thought I was going to be a witness to an aggravated assault. But Al's hand came to rest on the poor Pakistani's left shoulder in a very comforting kind of way; and when he spoke, Al's voice was soft and soothing. "Go ahead. Say it. What do you have?"

"I have ... rights."

Al nodded. "Yep, you have rights. You, and me, and every-one who passes through this gas station. We all have the same rights." For the next ten or fifteen minutes, as the attendant lis-tened slack-jawed and goop-eyed, Al gave a short course in civ-ics as only Al could. I knew we'd be late to the bar luncheon, but I knew that nothing short of nuclear power would make Al Guerrero finish until he was finished. He was doing what he did best and cared about most, preaching the Constitution and the Bill of Rights and the precious, precious freedoms that make America America. He was doing what he always did and what he always wanted to do. Whether there happened to be a court-house handy at the time he was doing it was really beside the point.

I was brought back to the here and now by the re-appearance of Ernie, carrying a tray laden with spoils from the cafeteria line. Al received a small coffee, sugar, no cream. For himself, Ernie had only two bags of bar-b-que flavor chips; a large, moist serving of the Chicken Hindenburg; and a diet soda. Ernie did his impression of a trash-masher while Al and I kibbitzed over our coffee.

"Does my old saddle-buddy Blackjack Sheridan have a case in front of you, Judge?" Al asked, briskly stirring sugar into his coffee.

"Sure does."

"Heck of a lawyer. What kind of case?"

"Coke."

"Ah," Al grimaced. "Tough to win." He took a swallow of coffee, then started looking around for another packet of sugar. "Jack and I had co-defendants in a federal case last year. He did a beautiful jury selection. They just loved him. There's nothing as important as jury selection. With the right jury all things are possible."

"You guys get acquittals?"

"Acquittal? What's an acquittal?" Al tried hard to chuckle at his own joke. "Heck, you're not a lawyer in federal court anymore, you're a tackling dummy. You just sit next to your client and try to look pretty while he rides that guilty train down the guilty track to Guiltyville."

It was time for Ernie to contribute to the conversation: "I'm going to get some more diet soda. Anybody want anything?"

We passed. Al looked out the window as he sipped his cof-fee. "Pretty town."

"What?"

"Pretty town. Miami. It's a beautiful city. Folks come here from all over the world to make money, but they treat Miami like a toilet—go there, do your business, and leave. It's a beautiful city." Whether it was to his friends, his adopted hometown, or his professional calling, loyalty was one of Al Guerrero's best features.

Ernie returned, bearing a small diet soda and two packages of Twinkies. I ended up throwing away part of my sandwich and most of my soup, and I went back up to chambers.

Eleanor opened the afternoon session by putting Detective Rasmussen on the stand and moving him rapidly through his testimony. He identified himself as a detective in the narcotics section of the Miami Police Department, and explained that he had been dispatched to the scene in response to a call from a uniform patrol officer.

"And when you arrived at the scene, Detective, what if anything did you find?"

"Officer Belmont had a suspect in the back seat of his police cruiser."

"Do you see that suspect present in court today?"

Again the ritual. Again the finger of accusation was leveled at Rodriguez.

"Did you have any conversation with the defendant, Detective?"

"Yes, ma'am."

"Tell us about it."

"I explained to the suspect that I was a detective, and asked his permission to look inside his vehicle. I explained to him that he didn't have to let me."

"And what was his response?"

"He gave his consent."

Eleanor walked to the clerk's desk, picked up the plastic package, and presented it to the witness. "Detective, I show you what has previously been marked for identification as the State of Florida's Exhibit A, and I ask if you have ever seen this before."

Rasmussen did not look like a narc. He looked like a librarian. He was a small man with a big man's ears and nose. He was balding, almost completely bald. His glasses were thick. He wore a rumpled, dark, button-down shirt that had seen many washings but few ironings, and he wore it buttoned almost all the way up, even in Miami summer. When Eleanor showed him the exhibit he hunched forward to examine it, his furrowed forehead furrowing all the more and his thick glasses creeping down his large nose. He studied the duct tape along the exhibit as if he were deciphering hieroglyphics.

"Yes, ma'am."

"And what do you recognize this as being?"

"This is the package I found on the floor in the back seat of the defendant's car. I directed Officer Belmont to impound it, and to put his initials on it," he reached into his shirt pocket — did he have a pocket protector? — took out a pencil, and pointed to Belmont's scribbling on the duct tape, "here."

"What did you do next?"

"I returned to Officer Belmont's car, informed Mr. Rodriguez that he was under arrest, and read him his *Miranda* rights." For the benefit of the jury, Eleanor had Rasmussen recite the *Miranda* warnings just as he had given them to Rodriguez. He read them off a card in his wallet.

"Did you then ask the defendant Rodriguez if he understood his rights?"

"Yes, ma'am. And he acknowledged that he did."

"Did he then answer questions for you of his own free will?"

"Yes, ma'am."

"What did you ask him, and what did he tell you?"

"I asked him where he got the cocaine from. He said he had never seen it before in his life. He said he was driving to a party at some lady-friend's house when his car just died."

"What did you do with him at that point?"

"He was transported downtown for processing."

"And Exhibit A?"

"Was routed to the crime lab for analysis."

"Your witness, Mr. Sheridan."

Jack walked over to the clerk's desk and, for the first time, laid hands on the cocaine. Hand, actually; he picked it up in his right hand and asked, "Detective Rasmussen, you found this on the floor in the back seat of Mr. Rodriguez's car?"

"Yes, sir."

"It wasn't under the seat, was it?"

"No, sir."

"It wasn't under a floor mat, was it?"

"No, sir."

"It certainly wasn't hidden in the glove box?"

"No, sir."

"In fact, it wasn't hidden at all, was it, Detective?"

"It was lying on the floor in the back seat, sir."

Jack nodded at the answer and set the cocaine down. "Detective Rasmussen, do you remember what the interior of Mr. Rodriguez's car looked like?"

Rasmussen looked up, and his librarian face puckered with the effort of recollection. "Um ... generally, yes."

"It was pretty messy, wasn't it?"

"Yes, sir."

"You remember seeing things like food wrappers, laundry, beach towels in the car?"

"I think so."

"But the food wrappers hadn't been used to cover the package of cocaine, had they?"

"No, sir."

"And the laundry hadn't been used to cover the package of cocaine, had it?"

"No, sir."

"And the beach towel hadn't been used to cover the package of cocaine, had it?"

"No, sir."

"You're aware that Mr. Rodriguez had been stalled for about ten to fifteen minutes before Officer Belmont showed up?"

"I don't know how long he was there."

"Plenty of time to cover up the cocaine?"

"Like I say, Mr. Sheridan, I don't know how long he was there before Officer Belmont showed up."

"Can we agree, Detective, that Mr. Rodriguez was cooperative with you at all times?"

"Yes, sir. He was."

"He didn't have to give you permission to look in his car,

but he did?"

"Yes, sir."

"He didn't have to waive his rights and answer your questions, but he did?"

"Yes, sir."

"And he told you, very frankly, that he had no idea how that cocaine," Jack pointed at it, "got in his car?"

"That's what he said." Rasmussen put a little body English on the word *said*; Rodriguez said it, but Rasmussen didn't believe it.

"Of course, there's a way to find out if he was telling the truth, isn't there, Detective?" Rasmussen, unsure of what Jack was getting at, didn't answer right away. Jack posed another question without waiting. "In the course of your police work, Detective, you have become familiar with fingerprints, haven't you?"

"Yes, sir."

"You know that every person has a unique fingerprint, by which he or she can be identified?"

"Yes, sir."

"Of course, it isn't always possible to recover fingerprints from every crime scene, is it, Detective?"

"No, sir."

"Because some surfaces don't pick up fingerprints very well, do they?"

"No, sir." Rasmussen saw where this was headed, but there wasn't much he could do about it.

Jack held up the end of his own necktie. "For example, Detective, it would be very difficult to recover a fingerprint from a piece of cloth like this, wouldn't it?"

"Yes, sir."

"But something like glass or Saran Wrap would be an ideal surface to recover fingerprints from, isn't that right?"

"As far as I know, yes sir."

Jack held up the cocaine, held it up high. "This is wrapped in a Saran Wrap-like substance, isn't it, Detective?"

"It appears to be."

"So it might well be possible to recover fingerprints from

this wrapping?"

"I don't know, sir." Rasmussen hesitated. He didn't want to give away anything he didn't have to, but he didn't want the jury to think he was shading the truth. "It ... it might."

"And if Felix Rodriguez's fingerprints were on this wrapping, then we would know he was lying to you when he said he had never seen this cocaine before, wouldn't we?"

"Yes, sir."

Jack walked over to the witness and handed him the cocaine. "Detective, did you request that the Metro-Dade crime lab check this wrapping for fingerprints?"

"No, sir."

"You know that the crime lab has the ability to do that?"

"I know they have a fingerprints section, yes sir."

"But you never requested that this package be tested for Felix Rodriguez's fingerprints?"

"No, sir."

"Because you know perfectly well that if this package had been examined for fingerprints, it would have proved that Felix Rodriguez had never touched this package in his life, isn't that right, Detective?"

Rasmussen said he didn't know any such thing, but he said it to Jack's back because Jack had already turned and headed for his seat. At almost the same moment Eleanor, who moves rapidly for a bulky person, was on her feet and beginning her redirect examination.

"Detective Rasmussen, why didn't you request that the crime lab test Exhibit A for fingerprints?"

"There wasn't any need to, ma'am."

She gestured toward the jury. "Tell the jurors why there wasn't any need to."

"We didn't need fingerprints to tell us whose cocaine it was. We found the cocaine in Mr. Rodriguez's car, in Mr. Rodriguez's custody." He looked at the defendant. "It was his cocaine."

Jack was on his feet objecting and moving to strike the answer. I sustained the objection and reminded the jury that it would be up to them, and no one but them, to decide at the close of the trial whether the prosecution had proved that Mr. Rodriguez was in knowing possession of the cocaine. Rasmussen left the courtroom and Eleanor called her last witness, Paulina Ashland.

Paulina Ashland is a criminalist in the controlled substances section of the Metro-Dade crime lab. She and perhaps half-a-dozen others like her spend all day every day testing suspected cocaine to see if it really is cocaine, and testing suspected marijuana to see if it really is marijuana. It is very important work that must be almost as interesting as counting the tiles in the courtroom ceiling.

Periodically Ms. Ashland comes to court to testify in a case like this one. She has been before me many times, and her testimony is always the same. It begins with a recitation of her credentials, after which I will make a finding on the record that she is an expert in the analysis of controlled substances. Then she will state that she received such-and-such an item under case number so-and-so. She will explain that she tested the contents with a mass spectrometer, the workings of which she will describe, if the prosecutor permits, until I have silently re-counted all the ceiling tiles. She will then conclude that the suspected cocaine is in fact cocaine. The prosecutor will move that the exhibit previously marked for identification now be formally received in evidence. I grant the motion and ask the defense attorney if he has any cross-examination. The smart ones seldom do, and Jack is a smart one.

When Ashland left the courtroom, Eleanor announced that the State of Florida rested its case. I instructed the jury not to form any conclusions yet, and recessed for the day.

* * *

I think I've mentioned that Miriam and I got married while I was in law school. I tried to work part-time, and she had a job, but about the only thing we could afford in those days was poverty. Miriam was very pregnant by the time I graduated. I told her not to come to the graduation ceremony, she was uncomfortable enough without having to sit for three hours on a folding chair in the sweltering June heat, but I was the only *summa* in my graduating class and Miriam said she would come even if her water broke. Joel, whom we've always referred to as my graduation present, was born not long thereafter.

I had landed a job at the state attorney's office, where starting pay was all of nineteen thousand dollars for what turned out to be about a sixty hour week. After hours most of the young assistant state attorneys chased the Miami nightlife — Jack's legend on the bar scene was already taking shape — but I packed my trial bag and headed home to my wife and son. Jack dubbed me "Mr. Excitement." I tried to kid him back by telling him that most of the criminals he prosecuted in the daytime were guilty of about half of what he had done the night before. Of course Jack was right. I would have been as out of place as the Archbishop of Canterbury under the pastel neon lights of the South Beach club scene. Mr. Excitement.

Even now unless a trial runs very late I try to be home for dinner. I still bring work home, and after dinner I do my "homework" and help the children with theirs. That Tuesday night was no different, except that Alicia was let off the hook for her schoolwork because she was sick. I remember that Miriam was tired and we turned in before the 11:00 news.

I do not sleep well. That was a blessing when I was in law school and there was no time for sleep. It was a blessing, too, when the kids were little and I had to take my turns getting up to feed and change them. Now it is not a blessing. I wish I could sleep through the night. Miriam can.

At about 2:00 I realized I had been staring at the ceiling long enough to be annoyed about it. I slipped out of bed as quietly as I could, put on the ratty terrycloth robe that Miriam is always threatening to throw out, and wandered barefoot into the TV room. I sat on the couch in the darkness, sat where I sat the Friday night before when Uncle Billy and Jack had been here.

By day we choose what we remember, but by night the memories volunteer themselves. I was recalling, for reasons I did not immediately understand, a conversation Ed and Jack and I had many years ago, not long after the Hundley trial.

Jack hadn't owned a sailboat back then. With an assistant state attorney's salary, Jack owned his liquor on the installment plan and didn't own much else at all. But Jack was Jack, and he was friends with the dock masters at half-a-dozen private marinas. He always had the use of somebody's sailboat, and he was always after Ed and me to come along as crew.

Sailing is one of those things you love or you don't. Jack loves it. I don't. It was Miriam who usually encouraged me to go: It would get my nose out of the books, it would be fun for me, it would help me relax. Besides, she said, what's the point of living in Miami if you never go sailing? I don't know if Ed loved sailing or didn't, but more often than not he came along.

That time it was a Saturday, I think; a Saturday in springtime. Jack had sweet-talked his way into the use of a sailboat at Grove Isle, a ritzy tennis and yacht club a couple of miles south of downtown. Ed gave me a lift in that clunker he used to drive, and by the time we arrived Jack was already on board, tying and untying, folding and unfolding, lifting that barge and toting that bale. He had found, or talked somebody out of, a "Grove Isle Yacht Club" baseball cap, and underneath the shadow cast by its brim the Blackjack smile was beaming. Jack always said that sailing was the most fun you could have with your clothes on.

The boat had a little outboard motor that we used to get clear of the marina. When we reached the open waters of Biscayne Bay the wind picked up and Jack, grinning like a kid, shouted at no one in particular, "Make sail!" We loosed the mainsail — the jib was already unfurled — and the wind skipped us like a stone across the water. The sunlight was strong above us, and stronger still as it ricocheted off the shallow emerald waters of the bay.

"Make ready to come about!" Jack bellowed, laughing. Ed and I moved to the other side of the boat, the boom swung by, and we swooped across the shoulder of the wind. I looked back at the towers of Grove Isle, and they melted in the distance.

"Hey, Clark, you know how to navigate?"

"Sure. Moss grows on the north side of the tree, and outhouses are built with the door on the south side, so you triangulate the hypotenuse."

"Ed, come here and take the helm, and don't listen to anything Clark says." Jack handed off the tiller to Ed and went forward. He stood in the bow, holding on to a vane with one hand for balance, the wind flapping the loose tail of his T-shirt as if it were a small sail. I could only see the back of him, but I knew somehow that his mouth was wide open and his nostrils flared, swallowing the salt sea air hungrily. Facing the sea, he began to declaim at the top of his voice:

> *At Flores in the Azores Sir Richard Grenville lay,*
> *And a pinnace, like a fluttered bird, came flying from far away:*
> *"Spanish ships of war at sea! we have sighted fifty-three!"*
> *Then swore Lord Thomas Howard: "By God I am no coward;*
> *But I cannot meet them here, for my ships are out of gear,*
> *And the half my men are sick. I must fly, but follow quick.*
> *We are six ships of the line; can we fight with fifty-three?"*
> *Then spoke Sir Richard Grenville: "I know you are no coward;*
> *You fly them for a moment to fight with them again.*
> *But I've ninety men and more that are lying sick ashore.*
> *I should count myself the coward if I left them, my Lord Howard,*
> *To these Inquisition dogs and the devildoms of Spain."*

He got a lot of feeling into "Inquisition dogs and the devildoms of Spain." I think he would have gone on if his audience had been only the open sea and the ghost of Sir Richard Grenville. But he remembered us, Ed and me, and he turned and smiled. Not the real good Blackjack smile, just a little embarrassed sort of smile. "Hey, Clark," he pointed, "there's a cooler in the starboard lazarette." He pointed more insistently, directing me until I figured out what a starboard lazarette was and how to get the cooler out of it. Inside the cooler were beers on ice. Jack fished three out, tossed one to Ed and one to me. I looked at my watch. It was still morning. Jack, anticipating my thought, said "The sun's below the yardarm—*yahdahm*—somewhere" and took a long swallow.

Jack took the tiller from Ed and held it steadily as we streaked toward the Rickenbacker Causeway that links Key Bis-

cayne with the mainland. The wind was now behind us—
"abaft," Jack explained indulgently—and we positioned the two
sails at angles to each other, something Jack called "wing on
wing." With the wind behind us, the sound of the wind was all
around us. It was too much trouble to shout over it; we con-
versed by keeping our voices low and deep, and leaning toward
each other when we spoke.

Ed had picked up a line and was tying and untying knots,
practicing what he had learned as a Boy Scout long ago. He
tied and untied with a kind of rhythm, a steady cadence to
which the rope moved and turned in his fingers. The quick,
light movement of the boat and the steady beat of his handi-
work loosened Ed's tongue. He started to talk about a case he
had worked some years before, one Jack and I heard of but had
no involvement with. As I sit here in the darkness I can still
hear Ed's deep, husky voice under the rushing of the wind, and
see the rope dance and twist in his fingers.

An inmate had died in Dade County Jail. That in itself was
no problem. Most taxpayers figured a dead inmate meant a
savings to the county in room and board, and were glad of the
savings. It was the way he had died that was the problem. He
had died of a drug overdose. He had been in jail several
months awaiting trial, so the only way he could have died of a
drug overdose is if somebody smuggled drugs in to him, and
that isn't supposed to happen in Dade County Jail. That was the
problem.

The inmate's name, Ed recalled, was Levi Boone. Levi
Boone had not been a nice man. His rap sheet was in its sev-
enth edition. The charges against him at the time of his demise
were attempted murder and aggravated assault. There were
witnesses. There was a confession. There was ballistics evidence. He had no prospect of acquittal at trial—in such cases
Jack liked to say that the defense's only hope was to persuade
the jury that "death rays from the planet Viznar made him do
it"—and he was facing life imprisonment. If he could get drugs
in jail, he had no incentive not to enjoy them. He got cocaine,
and he enjoyed enough to blow his brains up.

Jack interrupted. Irony, he pointed out, sure is ironic.

I waved my hand at Jack, a shut-up wave. "How," I asked Ed, "did he get cocaine in the jail?"

Ed was releasing a half-hitch. "Getting small amounts in is no big deal. The inmates' girlfriends wrap the stuff in baggies and stuff the baggies up their ..." Ed gestured toward the crotch area. "That gets them past the guards. Inside the jail they go to the bathroom, remove the baggie, rinse it off in the sink, and put it in their mouth. When they kiss their boyfriends, the switch takes place. Of course, the inmate can't hold the baggie in his mouth, because he's going to be searched too. So he swallows it. Then he's got to hope the coke makes the ride through his guts without perforating the baggie, and that he can fish it out of the crapper without too much trouble."

I remembered that I hadn't taken any dramamine, and I was feeling a little seasick. Listening to Ed's story was like driving past a terrible car crash: You know you shouldn't slow down and look, you don't want to slow down and look ... but you can't take your eyes off it. There was something I had to ask.

"If you know all this, don't the jail guards know it too?"

Ed almost chuckled; almost, but not quite. "Sure they know. They don't care. Why should they? Stoned inmates don't riot."

"So is that how Boone died? Some woman brought him ... ?"

Ed cut me off. "I never knew for certain. They get small amounts of drugs that way. Larger amounts, like what probably killed Boone, they usually get from the guards."

From the guards? "From the guards?"

Ed nodded, tightening some kind of cloverleaf-looking knot. I looked back at the shore, and it seemed far away. The wind had grown tired, and now puffed at our sails lazily. Jack tacked and jibed a few times, then lost interest in the wind as it had lost interest in us. He took his shirt off, stretched out on the deck, and gave his full attention to consuming sunshine and beer.

"You remember any more of that poem?" Ed directed the question to Jack, who knit his brows slightly in thought.

"Not yet. I will in a few more beers."

It was true. That poem was the only one I had ever heard Jack recite, and stone cold sober he could seldom recite two lines of it. One night at a party I watched Jack drink shot after shot of tequila with salt and lime, and at the end of the evening he stood on the bar and delivered a poetic recitation that was downright thrilling. It was the same poem. I looked it up at the library, and I believe he got every word of it right.

The sun was high and strong, and I had a slight headache. I had eaten no breakfast. Sipping the beer I was holding would only make matters worse. I went below looking for water or Coca-Cola, found warm ginger ale, and settled for that.

Back on deck Ed had taken the tiller and was holding it steady, staring intently at the horizon. I followed the line of his gaze, but saw no fixed point on which he could focus. There was a cruise ship moving slowly in the distance. Otherwise, the ocean seemed deserted. Jack lay motionless on the deck, his T-shirt balled up under his head as a pillow. The empty beer cans he had lined up at his side rocked gradually with the motion of the boat.

The sails luffed in the still air. We could talk without shouting. "Ed, why would the jail guards provide the inmates with drugs?"

"For money."

"I know, but ... I mean, how much could the money be worth to them? If everyone knows what they're doing then they're going to get caught, and if they get caught they'll lose their jobs, go to prison themselves, ..." Jack chose that moment to struggle to his feet. His pale skin was pink with sunburn across the chest and shoulders. He managed to find one last beer among the cold water and ice chips in the cooler, popped it, took a long swallow. Then he motioned Ed away from the tiller and made some half-hearted efforts to find better winds. About half way through his beer, he held the can up as if he were making a toast, and gave us another verse:

Shall we fight or shall we fly?
Good Sir Richard tell us now,

For to fight is but to die!
There'll be little of us left by the time this sun be set.
And Sir Richard said again: "We be all good English men.
Let us fight these dogs of Seville, the children of the devil
For I never turned my back upon Don or devil yet."

We drifted along for a few more minutes when Ed looked up at me and said, "It isn't like that in real life."

"What isn't?"

"On TV and in the movies and in poems people commit crimes the way Captain Richard decided to go into battle in Jack's poem. They think about the consequences. They think about whether they'll get away with it or whether they'll get caught, and if they get caught what will happen to them. They weigh the pros and cons, and when they figure they've got more to lose by not doing the crime than by doing it, they commit the crime. It isn't like that in real life."

Jack and I were paying close attention. It wasn't just that Ed was doing more talking than he'd normally do in a month. The truth was Ed knew more about the criminal justice system than Jack and I did. We had college degrees and law school diplomas, and it said "Esquire" after our names, but Ed had been in the belly of the system longer than we had. When we were studying for college exams he was riding around in a patrol car, hoping the next motorist he pulled over for an expired tag didn't decide to shoot him. When we were listening to law professors and trying to stay awake he was staying awake nights, hunting missing witnesses in crack houses and whore houses and just plain houses. On those rare occasions when Ed got to lecturing I was reminded of an old Jewish saying Billy Eisenberg never tired of quoting: "Seek the company of those who are searching for the truth, and avoid the company of those who have found it." Ed was always searching for the next truth, and now he was telling us about the search.

"So you mean like a guy comes home and finds his wife in bed with his neighbor, so he picks up the lamp on the nightstand and caves their heads in?" It was Jack's question.

Ed shook his head, no. That wasn't what he meant.

"Everybody understands that guy didn't think before he acted."

I interrupted. "You mean the jail guards who smuggle drugs in to the inmates."

Ed nodded, yes. That was what he meant. "If they stopped and thought about it first, they wouldn't do it, would they? I mean, on the plus side, they get money, cash money. Everybody likes money, and somehow we like it better when it's secret money, money we don't have to tell the boss or the IRS or the wife that we got. But on the down side, the chance of getting caught is real high. Everyone knows that everyone's doing it, and the inmates will rat you out for a pack of cigarettes. If you get caught you lose your job even if you don't get convicted, and the IRS and the wife come and take the money away. If you get convicted you do a little time, and time in prison passes very slowly and painfully for a former jail guard." The way Ed used the word "painfully" we knew what he meant.

He wasn't finished. "If you laid it all out for a six- or seven-year-old kid—if you gave him the plusses and the minuses—he'd tell you in a minute not to do it. It isn't something you have to be real smart or real honest or real religious to figure out. Sometimes I think there must be some gland or something in our bodies that gives out a chemical that numbs our consciences, and that's how people commit crimes."

We had never heard Ed talk like that, Jack and I. We looked at each other, not sure if we didn't believe him or maybe didn't want to believe him. Ed saw the look. "Think of something bad you've done," he said. He directed the remark to Jack, then smiled. "Not you, Jack. That would be too easy. You, Clark. Think of something bad you did. Not a crime, I know you haven't done any crimes. Just something bad. Something that you were sorry for later, because you thought it was wrong. Can you think of something like that?"

"Well ... I ... "

"I'm not going to ask you what it is. Just yes or no: Can you think of something like that?"

Could I think of something like that? I suppose we all can. "I suppose we all can."

"That's right," Ed said. "We've all done things that we look back on as having been wrong when we did them. But the thing you did, whatever it was: You didn't have to do it to know that it was wrong. You knew it was wrong, and if you had thought about it you wouldn't have done it in the first place. You did it first, and thought about the wrongness of it afterward."

Jack wasn't particularly enjoying this. "Hell, Ed, we do shit all the time that we know is wrong. It's wrong to hurt some-one's feelings, even if he—or she—is a sumbitch. It's wrong to walk by a homeless person and not give them your loose change. It's wrong to throw a beer can in Biscayne Bay instead of recycling it." Jack punctuated this last observation by tossing his now-empty beer can over the lee side of the boat. It floated for a few seconds till it filled with seawater, then turned on end and headed for the bottom. "We can't make a big goddamn deal out of every little thing, or we'd never have time for the rest of our lives. That doesn't make us criminals. Here," he said, handing the tiller back to Ed. He walked to the bow part of the deck, balled his T-shirt up as a pillow again, turned his cap backwards, and flopped down on his stomach. But his eyes were open, looking at Ed, waiting for an answer.

"You're right, Jack. We can't make a big deal out of every little thing. We can't make every can of beer a moral cross-roads. So we learn to ignore the hundred little moral cross-roads that lie in our path every day, and then when the big one comes along, we do what we're used to doing. We ignore it." Ed dropped his voice a little. "That's how jail guards sell drugs to inmates."

Jack turned on his side, facing away from Ed. When the wind is still, you can feel the rocking of the boat more keenly, and I realized that for some time the motion had been annoying me. We had drifted closer to land, and far off to one side of us a speedboat pulled a waterskier.

"When I get rich," Jack said without moving a muscle, "I'm going to own a sailboat just like this one. And you know what I'm going to name it?"

I played the straight-man. "What?"

"I'm going to name it, 'The Way to Court.' Then, when cli-

ents call for an appointment on a nice day like this one, my secretaries won't have to say, 'He's out sailing and trying to get
laid just now.' They'll just say, 'I'm sorry, but Mr. Sheridan isn't
available. He's on 'The Way to Court' just now, and won't be
back to the office till late.' On the way to court, get it?"

"Got it."

Jack then treated us to a reprise of Sheridan's Pet Theory.
Since the dawn of human thought, he reflected gravely, man
has craved the answer to one question above all others. It was
not a question about life or death, about heaven or hell, about
money or power. The question was simply this: Is there a reliable way to tell whether a woman is willing to fuck you? The
man who could do that—the man who could cull the speckled
flock from the clean—would have happiness beyond riches, beyond power, beyond fame.

"Pets," I said, because I had heard this speech before.

"Think about it," Jack said. "Think about every woman you
ever knew who held a membership in Slut of the Month Club.
They all had cats or dogs or some damn thing, and they were
just crazy about little fluffy-wuffy or bowsy-wowsy." He
started telling the story about some woman he had known who
brought her three cats along when Jack took her sailing, and
about how she had flibbered his jib and hoisted his mizenmast.

I was still thinking about what Ed had said. I moved a little
closer to him. "If what you say is so, Ed, then ... then what separates people like us from the criminals, except opportunity?"

Ed had run out of answers, and out of words. His job, after
all, was to arrest people. Judging them was someone else's job,
and someone else's concern. He dropped the line he had been
knotting and leaned back, closing his eyes and turning his face
up to the sun. I had often heard Billy Eisenberg say that there
are two kinds of people in the world, Nixons and Kennedys.
They do pretty much the same things, but the Nixons always
get caught and never get forgiven while the Kennedys seldom
get caught and always get forgiven. The thing you need to
learn and never to forget, says Billy, is whether you're a Nixon
or a Kennedy. I would have liked to run Billy's theory past Ed,
but it was too late. The talkative spell was over. Ed was big

quiet Ed again.

"Hey, Jack," he said. "How does that poem end?"

Jack rolled over on his back, then propped himself up on his elbows. His lips moved silently for a minute while he found his place and his concentration. Then he cleared his throat and spoke:

> *And the stately Spanish men to their flagship bore him then*
> *Where they laid him by the mast, old Sir Richard caught at last,*
> *And they praised him to his face with their courtly foreign grace;*
> *But he rose upon their decks, and he cried:*
> *"I have fought for Queen and country like a faithful man and true*
> *I have only done my duty as a man is bound to do;*
> *With a joyful spirit I Sir Richard Grenville die!"*
> *And he fell upon their decks, and he died.*

Overhead somewhere a gull skreed, but I couldn't find it. The last ripple of the wake thrown off by the far-away speedboat thump-thumped against our hull. The air was still, hot, heavy.

"Good ending," Ed said.

* * *

By day we choose what we remember, but by night the memories volunteer themselves. I sat on the couch in the darkness, sat where I sat the Friday night before when Uncle Billy and Jack had been here and Jack had offered his own interpretation of the story of King Solomon and the two women.

For lack of anything else to do I went to the bookshelf, took down the Bible and, by the light of a reading lamp that wouldn't wake the house, found the Solomon story. "Then came there two women, that were harlots, unto the king, and stood before him." Was Jack right? Was it all a scam? Did two street-smart hookers get away with murder? Did they put it over on the wisest king and judge of Israel? Was Solomon just book-smart, a *summa cum laude* law grad with no insight into the minds and hearts of men and women? Would he have been out of place making the club scene on South Beach? King Excitement.

Jack had that insight. When we were prosecuting together he would turn to me in the middle of a defense witness's testimony and whisper furiously that the guy was lying about some small point, that he would rip the guy apart on that point in cross-examination. And he was always right. What did he see that I missed? How did he know?

I turned the pages restlessly. Second Samuel, chapter 11, verse 2: "And it came to pass at eventide, that David arose from off his bed, and walked upon the roof of the king's house; and from the roof he saw a woman bathing; and the woman was very beautiful to look upon." The story of David and Bathsheba, another Sunday-school favorite. David got Bathsheba's husband out of the way by having the army abandon him in battle. They would have loved David on South Beach.

I put out the light, walked the length of the house, shed the bathrobe, crawled back into bed. I could hear Miriam's rhythmic breathing. Even on the night after we learned about Ed — it was only last Friday; it was starting to seem like long ago — she had slept soundly.

I almost got to sleep. I remember feeling the warmth and calm that come in the instant before sleep. And in that instant the warmth became ice, and the calm became chaos, and I was sitting up in bed, sick. Not sick as Alicia was sick, not sick in body, but sick at heart. A virus of evil, of suspicion, had crept into my mind and was poisoning me with its toxin. It was ugly and filthy and vile, but I could not kill it, because it kept telling me that it was true. I went to the bathroom and ran the water, and whimpered for the ignorance, the precious, precious ignorance that had been mine only minutes before.

Chapter Five
Wednesday

"Your Honor, before the jury comes in there is a matter we need to address." Morning calendar had just concluded. Lawyers were gathering up their files and scattering to other courtrooms. Newly-arraigned defendants, officially welcomed to the system, were being marched back to lock-up. Jack was trying to make himself heard above the clamor.

"What matter, Mr. Sheridan?" I gestured for Jack and Eleanor to approach the bench.

"Your Honor, Mr. Rodriguez is considering taking the witness stand in his own defense. I need a ruling from this court as to priors, if any, that the prosecution can use for impeachment."

A criminal defendant has the right to choose to testify on his own behalf. A criminal defendant also has the right to choose not to testify on his own behalf, and if that is his choice the jury must not hold it against him. That is what the jury will be told. Maybe the jury will do as it is told and maybe it won't. Jack, who likes to say that he figures most jurors aren't any more crooked than he is, also figures that a defendant who doesn't testify will be viewed by the jurors as a defendant with something to hide. All other things being equal, Jack likes his clients to testify.

But all other things are never equal. A client may be too inarticulate to do himself anything but harm if he testifies. ("If you put that boy's brain in a jay bird's head," Jack had once said about a defendant, "the damn bird would fly backassward.") Another may be the sort who can't tell the truth even when it helps him to do so. Still another may have mannerisms so annoying that the jury will ignore what he says and convict him for how he says it. Many defendants are so thoroughly guilty that taking the stand would guarantee both a verdict of guilty and an added charge of perjury.

And there is another danger: Like any other witness, the defendant who testifies can be cross-examined about his prior convictions. Before any defendant decides to take a walk down Witness Street, his lawyer should tell him about the potholes; and for his lawyer to tell him about the potholes, his lawyer needs to know where the potholes are. Jack wanted to know where the potholes were. He wanted to know if the prosecution had any proof that Rodriguez had ever been convicted of a crime.

Eleanor went back to her file and pulled out some kind of computer run. "I show a domestic, about" she ran her finger along the page, "about ... a year and a half ago."

"How was it resolved?"

"Pretrial diversion."

The pretrial diversion program is a shortcut through the courts. The defendant is made to do things or to learn things intended to make him a better citizen. If he completes the program the charges are dropped. There is no conviction.

"Anything else?"

"Another domestic." Eleanor was studying the computer print-out. "I show it as still pending."

So Rodriguez had been arrested a second time for domestic violence. The charge was still festering somewhere in the system. Perhaps some day he would be acquitted. Perhaps some day he would be convicted. But he had not been convicted yet.

"Anything else?"

Eleanor looked up from the computer run. "No, Your Honor."

Then there was nothing to discuss. "I take it, then, that there is nothing to discuss?" Both attorneys shook their heads, no. Rodriguez was clearly no virgin, and maybe he was getting a better break than he deserved, but the law is clear: He could not be cross-examined about his previous criminal conduct, because it had not resulted in conviction.

"Are both parties ready to proceed?" Both parties were. "Then bring in the jury." All rose as the bailiff squired the jurors into their seats. I welcomed them back to the courtroom, hoped they had a restful night. "Does the defense wish to present a case?"

Jack was still standing. "We do, Your Honor."

"Call your first witness."

"I call Felix Rodriguez."

Jack had another pet theory: A defendant, particularly on the day he will testify, should appear in court in a dress shirt and tie but without a suitcoat. A suitcoat bespeaks power; a defendant should appear respectful, humble, powerless. Applied to Rodriguez, the theory had merit. He approached the witness stand uncertainly, and in his white dress shirt and dark tie he seemed youthful, almost lost. It occurred to me that he was the sort of man women want to mother. Perhaps that was the quality that had drawn Teresa Rodriguez to him.

"Mr. Rodriguez," Jack began, after his client had taken the oath, "you understand that the prosecution has charged you with the knowing and intentional possession of cocaine?"

"I understand that's what they've charged me with, yes sir."

"Please face the jury." Rodriguez complied, turning in his seat. "How do you answer that charge, guilty or not guilty?"

"Not guilty, sir."

"So help you God?"

"So help me God."

It was a good beginning. Too often defense attorneys start their clients off with biography: Were you born here in town? Did you marry your high school sweetheart? Did you work at the local widget factory till it closed? Such personal history is important—the lawyer needs the jury to like his client—but not important enough to put at the beginning of the defendant's testimony. What the jury needs to hear first is what Felix Rodriguez had told them first: I didn't do it.

"Thank you, Mr. Rodriguez. Now please tell us where you live." He gave an address in the Coconut Grove section of Miami. "Is that a house or an apartment?"

"It's, like, one of those little Bahamas-style bungalows." A small house.

"Do you own or rent that house?"

"I rent it."

"How long have you been living there?"

"Just a few months. Since my wife and I ... since we separated." He dropped his gaze, saddened or embarrassed to have to admit to the break-up of his marriage. A pained look came across the face of a juror, an older woman. Poor boy, said the look, poor boy.

"You live alone?"

He nodded, and answered quietly. "Alone."

"Do you own a car, Mr. Rodriguez?"

"Yes, sir."

"What car?" It was an old Ford Taurus. He gave the year, the color, the tag number. "And where do you keep your car?"

"In the driveway."

"Not in a garage?"

"No, sir. There's no garage. Just in the driveway."

"Is your property fenced in?"

"No, sir."

"Do you keep your car locked at all times?"

"Not really. No, sir."

Young lawyers are eager to learn cross-examination. During cross-examination, the lawyer is the star of the show. Older lawyers know that more trials are won on direct examination than on cross, and that more trials are lost on cross-examination than on direct. Good direct examination is the art that conceals art. The lawyer is not the star of the show. The lawyer must seem almost to disappear. The witness must seem almost to be telling his tale without being asked.

Yesterday, seated at counsel table, Felix Rodriguez was a jittery and annoying ne'er-do-well. Today, seated on the witness stand, he was a little lost lamb. His answers to Jack's questions were respectful and responsive. They told of a man down on his luck, who couldn't even afford to buy the thatched roof over his head. (So how could he be a drug dealer? Aren't all drug dealers rich?) They told of a man married to a beautiful woman and heartbroken because that marriage was coming to an end. And they told of innocence, sworn to before Almighty God. Maybe the jury would believe Felix Rodriguez's story and maybe they wouldn't. But it was good direct examination.

Now Jack was asking about the night of the arrest. "Where had you spent the evening?"

"At home. I was supposed to go to a friend's house, but I didn't leave home till late."

"How late?"

"It was ... at least eleven. Maybe later."

"And where was your car all evening?"

"Out front. In the driveway."

"Locked or unlocked?"

"Unlocked."

"Do you remember leaving your house and getting in your car?"

"Yes, sir."

"Did you examine the floorboard in the back seat when you got in the car?"

"No, sir. I just got in the car and went."

"Then what happened?"

"I drove along OK for a few minutes. I remember I was on Grand Avenue in heavy traffic when my car died."

"What did you do?"

"The usual stuff, you know, looked at the gauge to see if I was out of gas or if any of the warning lights were on. I kept trying to start the car again, and a couple of times it sounded like it was going to turn over, but it didn't. I got it off to the side of the road along Commodore Plaza. I turned off the engine and popped the hood."

Rodriguez was relaxing on the witness stand, speaking comfortably. Jack kept the questions coming at an even pace, looking for what some attorneys call the "Wimbledon Effect": Jurors' heads moving rhythmically back and forth from questioning lawyer to answering witness, as if they were watching a tennis match. "What is the area of Grand Avenue and Commodore Plaza like on a Saturday night around midnight?"

"It's like, you can hardly move. Cars are bumper to bumper, people are all over each other."

"Is the area well-lighted?"

"Yeah, real bright. People have drinks along the sidewalk."

"Do you remember when Officer Belmont drove by?"

"Yes, sir."

"How long had you been stopped along Commodore Plaza before Officer Belmont drove by?"

"About ... about ten or fifteen minutes."

"During that ten or fifteen minute period, what did you do?"

"Not much. I looked under the hood, but I couldn't see anything wrong."

"Did you touch or move anything within the passenger compartment of the car?"

"No, sir."

"Why not?"

"I didn't have any reason to."

Jack gestured toward the jury box. "Tell the folks what happened when Officer Belmont drove by."

Rodriguez did as he was told, turning to face the jurors. "He pulled his car in behind mine. He got out, he started to walk over to me. He looked inside my car for a minute, and then ... ."

Jack interrupted. "Did you say or do anything to try to stop him from looking inside your car?"

"No, sir."

"Why not?"

"I didn't have any reason to."

"All right. What happened after he looked inside your car?"

"He told me to sit in the back seat of his patrol car."

"Did you do that?"

"Yes, sir."

"Did he tell you why he wanted you to sit in the back seat of his patrol car?"

"No, sir. Well, he said something about it was a hot night and there was air conditioning in his car."

"Did you think that was really why he wanted you to sit in his patrol car?"

"I didn't know what to think."

"How long were you sitting in the back of Officer Belmont's police car before Detective Rasmussen arrived?"

"Not very long. Maybe ten minutes."

"What happened when Rasmussen got there?"

"Him and Officer Belmont asked if they could go into the back seat of my car. I told them sure. They fished around in the back of my car and pulled something out and showed it to me."

Jack walked over to the clerk's desk and picked up Exhibit A. He carried it over to the witness stand and held it within inches of Felix Rodriguez's face. "Is this what they showed you?"

Rodriguez looked at the cocaine, not at Jack. "I guess so."

"And what did you say when they showed this to you?"

"I told them I never seen that before in my life."

"Do you know how this got in the back seat of your car?"

"No, sir."

"Don't tell me." Jack pointed to the jury with his left hand, the hand not holding the package. "Tell them. Do you know how this got in your car?"

Rodriguez looked at the jurors, and they looked at him. "No, sir. I don't."

"So help you God?"

Rodriguez was still looking at the jury when he answered. "So help me God."

Blackjack Sheridan returned the cocaine to the custody of the clerk and then walked back to his seat as slowly and deliberately as his long bony legs would allow. As he did so, he said to Eleanor without bothering to look at her, "Your witness."

I looked at the Elgin clock, the big old clock on the back wall of the courtroom. Morning calendar had run late, and it was already past noon. "Ms. Hibbard, what's your pleasure? If your cross-examination will be lengthy, we can break for lunch now. That will afford you some additional time to prepare."

Eleanor was standing at attention. "I don't expect to be too long, Judge. If the court please, I'm prepared to proceed." A lioness was crouched to pounce and I had asked if she wouldn't just as soon put it off till later in the day.

"Certainly, Ms. Hibbard."

Eleanor walked to the clerk's desk, picked up the exhibit that Jack had set down only a moment before, and placed it on the rail of the witness box. She paused for a few long seconds. "That's cocaine, isn't it?" Her voice had a hard edge to it, but she had spoken softly, drawing the jurors in to her question.

"I guess so. If you say so, ma'am."

"You heard Criminalist Paulina Ashland testify that it was cocaine, didn't you?"

"Yes, ma'am."

"You heard her testify that it was just over half a kilo—about one pound—of cocaine, didn't you?"

"Yes, ma'am."

"About half a kilo of cocaine. Worth about ten or twelve thousand dollars, isn't it?"

"I don't know. If you say so, ma'am."

"And it was found in your car, wasn't it?" *Your* car, and the Voice clanged like the metallic slamming of the jailhouse door.

"Yes, ma'am."

"Did someone give you a twelve thousand dollar gift, Mr. Rodriguez?" Jack objected that the question was argumentative. I directed Eleanor to re-phrase it. "Do you know of any reason, Mr. Rodriguez, why anyone would give you something worth twelve thousand dollars?"

"No, ma'am."

"Did anyone owe you twelve thousand dollars at the time?"

"No, ma'am."

"Has it ever happened to you before, Mr. Rodriguez, that someone just *gave* you twelve thousand dollars worth of drugs?"

"No, ma'am."

"Or twelve thousand dollars in cash?"

"No, ma'am."

"Or twelve thousand dollars worth of anything else?"

"No, ma'am."

"But it's your testimony that on this occasion someone just gave you twelve thousand dollars worth of drugs, is that right?"

"I guess so. I don't know how it got in my car."

These questions had been posed in rapid-fire fashion. The Voice was a metronome, not loud but relentless in its beat, in its momentum, in its inexorable rhythm. But Rodriguez had withstood the frontal assault. His answers remained short and courteous, and he stuck to his story: I don't know how the cocaine got in my car. Eleanor repositioned herself by a few steps. A new line of questioning was coming. The rapid frontal assault would give way to the deliberate flanking maneuver.

"You've testified, Mr. Rodriguez, that you were arrested by Officer Belmont and Detective Rasmussen, is that right?"

"Yes, ma'am."

"And you knew that some day you would be going to trial on these charges, isn't that right?"

"Um ... yes, ma'am."

"And you knew that at that trial, you would be accused of the knowing and willful possession of this cocaine"—nodding at the exhibit, still sitting on the rail of the witness box—"isn't that right?"

"Yes, ma'am."

"But you knew that it wasn't your cocaine, that it was someone else's cocaine, is that the idea?"

"Yes, ma'am."

"And that someone else just planted this cocaine in your car as your car sat in your driveway, is that right?"

"I guess so."

"You testified that your driveway isn't walled in or fenced in, is that correct?"

"Yes, ma'am."

"So your car, as it sits in the driveway, is visible from the street, isn't it?"

"Yes, ma'am."

"And your car, as it sits in the driveway, is visible from the houses of your neighbors, isn't it?"

"I ... I guess so."

Eleanor picked up her legal pad and held it, and her pen, as if she were a secretary about to take shorthand dictation. "Mr. Rodriguez, I want you to help me make a list. Let's start with your across-the-street neighbors. The day after your arrest, did you call your across-the-street neighbors and say something like, 'I've been falsely accused of a crime and I was wondering if you happened to see anyone approach my car yesterday.' Did you have that conversation, or one like it, with your across-the-street neighbors on the day after your arrest?"

"Um ... no."

"How about the following day, Mr. Rodriguez. Did you have a conversation like that with your across-the-street neighbors the following day?"

"No, ma'am."

"I'm confused, Mr. Rodriguez. When was the first time that you called your across-the-street neighbors and asked them if they had seen anyone approach your car on the day that this cocaine was planted in it?"

"I ... I never did."

Eleanor appeared to write something in block letters on her legal pad. As she wrote, she muttered audibly, "Never called across-the-street neighbors." She looked up. "How about the neighbors to the right-hand side of your house. Ever try to ask them if they saw anyone approach your car that Saturday?"

"No."

"Or the neighbors to the left-hand side of your house?"

"No."

Eleanor repeated the writing-plus-mumbling routine. Then she asked, "So if I understand you correctly, Mr. Rodriguez, your testimony is as follows: You are falsely accused of the serious crime of knowing possession of cocaine; the cocaine was planted in your car at a time when the car was visible to anyone on or near the street; and you have made no efforts whatsoever—*no efforts whatsoever*—to find out if anyone knows anything about who planted the cocaine or when it was planted. Is that a fair summary of your testimony?"

Jack was on his feet objecting. The question was compound. The question was argumentative. The prosecutor was harassing the witness. He ran off a string of objections, not so much hoping he could find one I would grant as hoping that he could buy his client time to think of something intelligent to say. When Jack had run out of breath I turned to the witness.

"Mr. Rodriguez, do you understand the prosecutor's question?"

He thought of something intelligent to say. "No, sir. I don't."

I directed Eleanor to re-phrase the question. I could see her wheels turning for a moment. She knew she could break the question down into its component parts, asking each of a series of shorter questions in a way that would pass muster. But she knew, too, that she had made her point. Better to move on to another area of questioning than to risk diluting the good she had already done.

"I'll withdraw the question, Your Honor." She turned to the witness. "Mr. Rodriguez, let me ask you this: At the time your car broke down, you were on the way to a girlfriend's house, weren't you?"

"Uh ... yes."

"What were you planning to do there?"

"Do there ... ?"

"That is my question, Mr. Rodriguez. What were you planning to do at the home of your girlfriend?"

"I don't know. You know, just ... party."

"Party, Mr. Rodriguez? Is that your answer?"

"I ... I guess so."

Eleanor walked straight toward the witness box, picked up the cocaine, and extended it to Rodriguez as if she were handing it to him. "And at that sort of party, Mr. Rodriguez, do things go better with coke?"

Jack was on his feet again, barking every objection he could think of. I interrupted him to overrule, and directed the witness to answer the question.

Rodriguez was bouncing his leg in that jittery way again. "No," he said. Not, "No ma'am." Just a quiet little "no." Then his left hand crept up to the pock mark along his chin and he started to pick at it.

"And isn't it a fact, Mr. Rodriguez, that the reason you and your wife are divorcing ..." Eleanor never got to the far side of that sentence. If Jack had been barking before, he was howling now. I ordered both lawyers to sidebar.

Jack was beside himself. "I object! That was the most unprincipled, ..."

"Sustained."

" ... the most unprincipled, unethical ..."

"Your objection has been sustained, Mr. Sheridan. "

Jack was still sputtering. "I move for a mistrial! My client's fair trial rights have been irremediably compromised!"

"Your motion is denied, Mr. Sheridan." I shooed both lawyers away from the bench. When they were back at their places, I addressed the jury. "Ladies and gentlemen, the question the prosecutor started to ask was entirely improper. We are trying a criminal case, not a divorce case, and the relations between Mr. Rodriguez and his wife are not relevant to this criminal case. I am ordering that the prosecutor's last question be stricken from the record. Ms. Hibbard," I turned to Eleanor, "do you have any further questions?"

"No, Your Honor. Nothing further."

"Then we'll recess for lunch." I stood; the bailiff called all rise and escorted the jury out. In the heat of battle, even experienced lawyers are apt to step over the line. Eleanor was frustrated because the jury would never learn that Rodriguez had been twice charged with domestic violence. Jack had paraded the defendant's beautiful wife and innocent child before the jury at the outset of trial, giving the impression that the jurors would be doing a good deed if they returned Rodriguez to home and hearth. Frustration had prompted Eleanor to ask a forbidden question. But her sin was venial, not mortal. When I was first on the bench I would have reacted by holding a contempt hearing. Nowadays I react by breaking for lunch.

Back in chambers I found a call waiting for me from a gentleman who identified himself as Reverend Fullerton of the First Methodist Church of West Kendall. I remembered that DeeDee Barber had been active in some local church.

"What can I do for you, Reverend Fullerton?"

"I wanted to talk to you about the arrangements for tomorrow."

"Arrangements?"

"The funeral arrangements." Of course. The funeral arrangements. "I had a telephone conversation with a gentleman from the ... F.O.P.? Do I have that right? The F.O.P.?"

"The Fraternal Order of Police. Yes, that's correct."

"I don't mean to be judgmental, but he was ... well, he was unhelpful. He said there would be no official police representative present. He was quite terse. He did suggest, however, that you might wish to say a few words."

Ordinarily, the various police departments and police unions knock themselves out to insure that every cop has a decent burial. This case was different. Ed Barber had murdered his wife and murdered his child. And what was just as bad, maybe worse from the standpoint of his fellow cops, was that Ed had committed suicide. He hadn't died bravely in the line of duty. He hadn't died quietly in an honorable retirement. He had died as a coward dies, turning his service revolver to a use for which it was never intended. Ed Barber, my friend; Ed Barber, police officer; Ed Barber, murderer and suicide.

Reverend Fullerton must have known my thoughts. "His death was doubtful, and but that great command o'ersways the order, he should in ground unsanctified have lodged." He recited the line in his Sunday-morning pulpit voice.

"Hamlet?"

"Mm. Yes."

I sighed. "No, thank you, Reverend. I don't intend to make a speech."

"Just a short graveside ceremony, then? I don't expect there will be many in attendance."

"No," I said. "I don't expect there will." I hung up the phone and sat with my head in my hands for a few minutes.

A police officer is an ordinary man or woman who has been given the power of a demigod. A police officer can stop you as you walk along the sidewalk or drive down the street. He can enter your home by force. He can take you to the police station, keep you there for at least 24 hours, and ask you any questions he likes as many times as he likes in any kind of language he likes. At the police station he can beat the snot out of you, and if you make a complaint or file a lawsuit you will find that all the witnesses are cops who remember that you resisted arrest and attempted to escape and injured yourself when you slipped in the washroom. A police officer's friends are other police officers, and the rule by which he lives is that a cop protects another cop's back. A police officer believes that the world is divided into two classes of people: Us and Them. Whatever Us does to Them is all right, because Us could never get even for everything that Them has done to Us. A police officer believes that no society has ever existed, could ever exist, or will ever exist without police officers; and in this he is correct. The Greek gods could seldom resist the temptation to abuse their powers. Most cops do some of the time, and some cops do most of the time. Ed Barber was a good cop, the best I knew. In the police officer's world of Us and Them he had been one of Us. But in death he would be one of Them.

I got up and wandered out of chambers, headed nowhere in particular. I must have been looking down as I walked, because I remember squinting at the florescent glare off the cheap linoleum floor tiles in the corridor, and paying attention to the clack-clack noise that my dress shoes made. It was lunchtime, and the fourth floor was mostly empty. In the middle of the corridor is the elevator bank, and because an elevator door opened as I was passing, I got in.

The elevators in the Metro-Justice Building may be ugly and uncomfortable, but at least they're inefficient. I was watching the numbers count down from four, trying to add the force of my concentration to that of gravity and the team of hamsters that propels the elevator, when a voice behind me said, very softly, "Hi, Judge."

I turned. Standing behind me was a very old man. What was left of his hair protruded from the area above his ears like wings. The wings were wispy and unkempt, too stiff and dry to be combed into place, and they were dyed black. The hair was thin, and dried residue from the dye dotted the scalp around the hair like scattered pinpricks.

The small wings flanked a large and fleshy face. Pouches under the eyes rested upon heavy cheeks, which in turn cascaded into jowls; chins, three at least, perched almost directly on the chest, seemingly without a neck to make the connection. The knot of the necktie wouldn't be seen till the spring thaw.

The suitcoat and trousers were both blue, but of different shades. If they had matched once, they had faded at different rates. The zipper area of the trousers was sprinkled with small stains. I suspected an inside job.

It took me a few seconds to realize that what time and the criminal justice system had left of Bobby Sunday was standing on the elevator with me.

"Hello, Bobby. How are you?"

The elevator doors opened and we stepped into the first floor lobby. Here high ceilings keep florescent glare at a safe distance, and the windows that make up most of the wall around the main doors admit natural light. We walked over to an information kiosk in the center of the lobby area — abandoned during the lunch hour — and Bobby leaned against it. Bobby said he was fine, just fine.

"How about you, Judge? You still sitting in Judge Galena's courtroom?"

It had been my courtroom for some years now, but I understood that for Bobby it would always be Judge Galena's courtroom. Yes, I said, I was still sitting there.

We stood there the way you do when you're looking for some conversation to make. "Say, Bobby," I asked, "what the hell did Judge Galena do before he was a judge? I mean, did he ever practice law?"

Bobby shrugged. "I dunno."

"I thought you were his pal."

Bobby shook his head gently, so as not to knock himself over with his own jowls. "Not me. I mean, I appeared before him plenty of times. I gave money to his re-election campaign every time he ran because I knew what was good for me. But if he had pals I never knew who they were." I started to say something, but Bobby was parked in a cul-de-sac down memory lane. "I was always careful to laugh at his limericks. I remember, 'There once was a hooker named Alice, who'" Bobby paused for a moment. The details of Alice's adventures were lost in the mists of time. "'There once was a hooker named Alice, who ... something something something, ... They found ... something ... And her ass up a tree in Nogales.'" It was not a rendition of which Judge Galena would have been proud, but then again that didn't really matter anymore.

"Were you at his funeral?" The words were no sooner out of my mouth than I regretted them. It was a pointless question, a tactless, stupid question. What difference did it make if this living old man had attended the funeral of that dead old man? What difference did I expect it to make?

The question didn't seem to bother Bobby. "No," he said. And then, in that same expressionless way of his, he asked, "Were you?"

I shook my head. I had inherited Judge Ogden Galena's job and his courtroom, but I had not attended his funeral.

Bobby put a hand on my shoulder. "Don't give it a thought. In this business everybody dies alone."

In this business? In every business everybody dies alone. "In every business everybody dies alone."

Bobby tilted his head to the side very slightly, very slowly. "Yes," he allowed, "but in this business ... well, in this business everybody dies alone because in this business everybody lives alone." I thought I knew what he meant, but I wasn't sure. I was about to ask him, when he brightened up just a little and said, "You know, I tried a case with an Elvis defense in front of Judge Galena once."

The garden variety defenses to homicide are self-defense, alibi, mistaken identity (also known as SODDI—Some Other Dude Did It), maybe insanity, that sort of thing. The Elvis defense is a rare flower indeed. It asserts that the victim of the homicide is not really dead at all. The defense takes its name, obviously, from the King of Rock and Roll who, depending on whom you ask, is either dead or snacking at a Dunkin' Donuts in North Miami Beach. For the prosecution not to have a dead victim is uncommon. For the defense to assert that the missing victim is not dead is more uncommon still. It was part of the Metro-Justice Building lore that, many years ago, Bobby Sunday had successfully asserted an Elvis defense.

"I remember hearing that. How did you do it?"

Memory lane had turned into an eight-lane superhighway, and Bobby was driving with the top down and the wind in his ... well, scalp. It seems that some years ago—about the time the training wheels came off my first bicycle—a fellow named Hulbert came back from spending the day fishing to find his wife not home. Her car wasn't gone, and none of her things were missing, so Hulbert assumed she was visiting friends or some such thing, and didn't worry about it. In fact, he didn't worry about it for a couple of days, and even then made only the most perfunctory inquiries about his wife's whereabouts. The neighbors practically had to beg him to call the police. When the police showed up, the neighbors had no trouble remembering that the Hulberts had never gotten on all that well.

It turned out that, although Hulbert almost always took the same three or four friends out on the boat with him, he had been fishing alone on the day of his wife's disappearance. It turned out that Hulbert was having an affair with a woman—a young and pretty woman—at the office. It turned out that Hulbert had made some remarks to the effect that he really didn't ever expect to see his wife again. It turned out that Hulbert got indicted for murder.

Everyone who had anything to do with the case figured Hulbert had done it, but everyone also figured that the prosecutors faced an uphill battle. Their theory, of course, was that Hulbert had taken his wife out on the boat, given her a few taps, weighted her down with something heavy, and let the Gulf Stream do the rest. You'd have to ladle the Atlantic dry with a teaspoon to have any chance of finding a body, so the case was all circumstantial: the bitter marriage, the disappearance of the wife without a trace, Hulbert's tootsie on the side, the strange circumstance of his going fishing alone, his comments suggesting that he knew his wife would never turn up, and so on. They found some blood and hair samples on Hulbert's boat, but in those days before DNA testing that didn't prove much. It's common to find blood or tissue samples on a fishing boat.

Bobby went with the Elvis defense. He didn't just claim that his client didn't do it, he claimed that it wasn't done. To make an Elvis defense work, of course, all you need is for the courtroom doors to open at the most dramatic possible moment and for Mrs. Hulbert to walk into court.

"You didn't! You found the wife?"

Bobby shook his head, and even went to all the trouble of prying his cheeks apart with a little smile. "Not Hulbert's wife. But I found the next best thing."

"What?"

"Somebody else's wife."

Bobby's star witness was a Mrs. Medill. It turned out that her husband had disappeared the very day that Mrs. Hulbert had disappeared. It turned out that the Medills' marriage hadn't been going any better than the Hulberts.' It turned out that Mrs. Hulbert had bought her Ford at the dealership where Mr. Medill worked as a salesman, and it turned out that Mr. Medill had sold her that Ford. When Bobby showed Mrs. Medill a photo of Mrs. Hulbert and asked her if she had ever seen that woman before, Mrs. Medill didn't answer. She burst into tears. The prosecution didn't even bother cross-examining.

Bobby's closing argument must have been something to hear. He told the jury that he blamed Mr. Hulbert—yes, ladies and gentlemen of the jury, blamed him. Blamed him for his philandering ways. Blamed him for the thoughtlessness and inattention that drove his wife into the arms of another man. Bobby took some consolation in knowing—and you, members of the jury, may take some consolation in knowing—that Hulbert would have what was left of his bitter and empty life to nurse what was left of his bitter and empty heart. It was fit punishment for an adulterer, and Hulbert was an adulterer. But he was not a murderer. He was not a murderer because there had been no murder. Somewhere far beyond these courtroom walls, ladies and gentlemen, somewhere beyond the din of our voices, Mrs. Hulbert lives. She would spend what was left of her life nursing what was left of her own brave heart. And Bobby, for his part, wished her peace.

The prosecution argued like crazy that Mrs. Hulbert's affair with Medill simply meant more evidence of Hulbert's motive to murder, and that the disappearance of Medill himself was an irrelevant coincidence, but the jury had heard enough "what if?" and they acquitted. Bobby Sunday had asserted an Elvis defense and made it stick. How many guys could say that?

I took Bobby's pasty, fleshy hand and shook it. We stood there for a second or two, and then he scratched thoughtfully at a tuft of his hair, dislodging tiny flakes of dried dye like a shower of blue-black pixie dust. "What was it you asked me? Why Judge Galena became a judge? Come to think of it, I heard him say more than once that he became a judge because that way he wouldn't have to deal with judges."

No, I started to say, what I asked was what Judge Galena had done before he became a judge. But it didn't really matter. I had to get back to my desk, and I told Bobby so. He turned slowly, and headed off in the direction of county court, where misdemeanors and traffic infractions are handled. He had been a trial lawyer since before I was born, and now he was walking as fast as old shoes and older feet could take him to the trial of a dog bite or an illegal left turn. I rode the elevator to the fourth floor.

Back in chambers I took out my lunch, stared at it for a minute, pushed it aside. I touched the intercom button. "Carmen, a City of Miami narcotics detective named Rasmussen testified in the Rodriguez case yesterday. See if you can get him on the phone."

There was a moment of hesitation. Carmen knows what a fetish I make of being on time to every session of court. "Judge, by the time I get him on the phone and you talk to him, you'll be late getting back into the courtroom."

"Then I'll be late."

But I wasn't late. I was lucky. Rasmussen was in the stationhouse, not in the field, and Carmen had him on the phone in two minutes. "Detective Rasmussen? I was thinking about your testimony of yesterday. I was just wondering: Did anyone ever determine why it was that Mr. Rodriguez's car died? No? Well, where is the car now? So it hasn't been released yet? Would it be too much trouble for you to have it examined? No, no, nothing in particular, just my idle curiosity. Well thank you, I'll appreciate that. Yes, good bye, Detective."

My lunchbag was still sitting on my desk, and I stared at it for lack of anything else to stare at. But I wasn't hungry. I wasn't hungry at all.

There is no comfort in staring at a brown paper bag. Besides, it really was time to convene the afternoon session. I put on my robe, walked into the courtroom, heard the bailiff call all rise, had him bring the jury in. There is comfort in these things. There is for me, anyway.

"Mr. Sheridan, do you have any redirect of your witness?"

"Just briefly, Your Honor."

The lunch recess had given Rodriguez a chance to regain his composure. Jack took him back over familiar territory. He was sure he had no idea how the cocaine had gotten in his car. He had never asked the neighbors if they had seen anyone approach his car because it had simply never occurred to him to do so. He was not a drug user. He was not a drug dealer. He had given the police permission to search his car because he thought he had no reason not to. All these things he swore were true. He swore them without bouncing his knee, and without picking at his pockmark. He left the witness stand with the same little-boy-lost look he had brought to it.

"Do you wish to call any other witnesses, Mr. Sheridan?"

"No, Your Honor. The defense rests."

"Ms. Hibbard, does the prosecution wish to present any rebuttal?"

"No, thank you, Your Honor. We're prepared to proceed to closing argument."

The order in which lawyers make their closing arguments is fixed by statute. Because Jack had called no witnesses other than the defendant himself, he would speak first and last, sandwiching Eleanor's one closing argument between his two.

"Mr. Sheridan, are you prepared to make your summation?"

By way of answer Jack stood, walked to the center of the courtroom, faced the jury. "May it please the Court, and ladies and gentlemen of the jury. Felix Rodriguez is not charged with the possession of cocaine. As Judge Addison will explain to you, Felix Rodriguez is charged with the knowing and intentional possession of cocaine. The burden of proof is on the prosecution to establish beyond and to the exclusion of every reasonable doubt that Mr. Rodriguez knew the cocaine was in his possession, and that he intended to possess it. But Felix Rodriguez did not know that this cocaine"—Jack was pointing at the exhibit as it lay on the clerk's desk—"was in his car. And Felix Rodriguez did not intend to possess cocaine.

"Felix Rodriguez's car sat unlocked in his driveway all that Saturday afternoon. It sat unlocked in his driveway all that Saturday evening. It sat unlocked in his driveway till after midnight. Somehow, sometime, somebody put half a kilo of cocaine in that car. We don't know who did it and we don't know when and we don't know why. We probably never will."

Jack ran his fingers through his hair and took a few steps closer to the jury rail. It wasn't his way to bellow at the jury. Let Eleanor do that. Blackjack Sheridan was chatting with a half-dozen of his friends about a little misunderstanding, and misunderstandings were best set right without bellowing.

"Oh, we could guess. We could guess that somewhere out there is a doper who thought he saw a police car headed his way and threw his drugs into the nearest hiding place so they wouldn't be found on him, and that hiding place just happened to be Felix Rodriguez's car. We could guess that some drug dealer wanted to spite or cheat another by pretending to lose his cocaine, secretly intending to come back for it later. We could guess that a drug courier got his signals crossed and left his package in the wrong car. We could guess and guess and guess, and our guesses might be good or they might be bad. But Judge Addison will tell you that we are not here to guess." Here Jack did put a little urgency in his voice. "He will tell you that we are to decide this case on the evidence and nothing but the evidence.

"And what is the evidence in this case? A man intending to deliver a load of cocaine would likely keep to the back roads, staying away from cars, pedestrians, bright lights, and police patrols. But the evidence in this case is that Felix Rodriguez drove along Grand Avenue in Coconut Grove, one of the busiest and most heavily-policed areas in Miami. A man intending to deliver a load of cocaine would hide that cocaine in the trunk, or under the seat, or in a compartment in the door panels. But the evidence in this case is that the cocaine was found uncovered, unhidden, sitting pretty as you please on the floor in the back seat of Felix's car." Jack had finally called his client by his first name. Apparently Rodriguez was within the circle of friends, included in the little coffee-klatsch that Blackjack Sheridan was hosting over the jury rail.

"If a man knew he was delivering a load of cocaine and his car broke down, the first thing he would do would be to conceal that cocaine before the police showed up. But the evidence in this case is that Felix's car sat there for fifteen minutes or so before Officer Roscoe Belmont happened by, and Felix had done nothing to cover up or dispose of that cocaine. In fact Officer Belmont testified that Mr. Rodriguez beckoned him, actually beckoned to a passing marked patrol car.

"A man intending to deliver a load of cocaine would move heaven and earth to keep the police from looking inside his car where that cocaine was. But the evidence in this case is that Felix Rodriguez freely gave permission first to Officer Belmont and later to Detective Rasmussen to search his car." Jack walked over to the clerk's desk and picked up the package of cocaine with both hands. "A man intending to deliver a load of cocaine would have to touch that cocaine. And we know from the testimony of the prosecution's own witnesses that a plastic type of wrapping like this one would hold fingerprints very well. But the prosecution chose not to test this package for fingerprints. That was their choice. Because of their choice, they will never be able to claim that Felix Rodriguez's fingerprints are on this package. They will never be able to claim that Felix Rodriguez touched this package. They will never be able to claim that Felix Rodriguez was in knowing, intentional possession of this package. There will always be reasonable doubt. That is the evidence, the whole evidence, and nothing but the evidence."

Jack advanced toward the jury, still clutching Exhibit A in both hands. "And let's not hear"—let's not *heah*—"from the prosecution about the evils of Demon Cocaine. We all know that this is cocaine. There was never any issue in this trial about whether this is cocaine. We all know it was found in the back seat of Felix's car. There was never any issue in this trial about whether it was found in the back seat of Felix's car. The only issue in this trial—the only issue there ever was, the only issue there is, and the only issue there ever will be—is whether the prosecution can persuade you beyond all reasonable doubt that Felix knew this cocaine was in his car, and that he intended it to be there." Jack walked back to the clerk's desk, put the exhibit down, brushed his hands off on each other. Then he returned to the jurors, standing closer to them than he had before. He just stood there for a moment, his hands in his pockets, looking at each of the jurors in turn. "Ladies and gentlemen, you have heard me refer to that great constitutional principle that no American can be convicted while there remains the shadow of a reasonable doubt across his guilt. Some folks think that this principle exists to protect defendants, defendants like Felix Rodriguez. Those folks are wrong. This principle exists to protect jurors, jurors like you. It exists to protect you from the awful agony you would experience if a week, a month, or a year from now, you were to say to yourself, 'My God, what if I convicted an innocent man?' Don't let that happen to you a week from now. Don't let that happen to you a month from now. Don't let that happen to you a year from now. Find Felix Rodriguez not guilty right here and right now." Again he stood there, still and quiet, just looking at the jurors and letting them look back at him. Then Blackjack Sheridan turned and walked back to his seat.

Eleanor rose and waited for me to acknowledge her. "Ms. Hibbard, you may proceed with your closing argument."

She walked to the podium, swiveled it to face the jury, placed her legal pad on it. She nodded in my direction—"May it please the Court"—then turned to her true audience. "Ladies and gentlemen of the jury. Felix Rodriguez is a drug dealer who was caught red-handed. He was caught in possession of his own drugs, drugs he was transporting in his own car. His drugs, his car, his crime." As a church bell rings out tidings of death, so the Voice rang out tidings of guilt. His drugs, it clanged. His car, it clanged. His crime.

"What really happened on the night in question? We all know by now. We know because the evidence has told us. We know because our common sense has told us. Felix Rodriguez says he had a date with his girlfriend. It wasn't dinner at eight. It wasn't a nine o'clock movie. Felix Rodriguez waited until the dead of night for his date to begin. Then he and his cocaine went for a little ride.

"Somewhere in Coconut Grove his luck failed him. His car broke down. When the police showed up he made the best of a bad situation. He played it cool. He knew that if he tried to send the police on their way he would only attract their suspicion. So right then and there he began to lay the groundwork for the story he told you from that witness stand in this courtroom."

She walked over to the cocaine, picked it up, weighed it in her hand. "What story? The story that a pound of cocaine, twelve or fifteen thousand dollars worth of cocaine, just fell into his car from on high." She held the package above her head, arm extended. "It fell out of the sky and into the back seat of his car, like rain into an open convertible." She put it down again. "Ladies and gentlemen, even in Miami cocaine does not tumble out of the sky at random into the cars of innocent people. Cocaine is placed carefully, knowingly, and intentionally into cars by guilty people. Guilty people like Felix Rodriguez."

She moved to one side of the podium. "Mr. Sheridan tells us that his client must be innocent because a real drug dealer wouldn't transport his cocaine in the back seat of his car. Then in the same breath he tells us that someone else must have abandoned twelve, fifteen thousand dollars worth of cocaine without a struggle, without a reason, without an attempt to get it back." The Voice rose, and the courtroom walls struggled to contain it. "In this community men have killed for a few hundred dollars worth of this drug. In this community women have whored themselves for a few hundred dollars worth of this drug. In this community children have stolen for a few hundred dollars worth of this drug. But Mr. Sheridan tells you that it is reasonable to believe that someone simply walked away from twelve or fifteen thousand dollars worth of this drug. Mr. Sheridan tells you that someone simply made his client a gift of twelve or fifteen thousand dollars worth of this drug. And it is more reasonable to believe that, he tells you, than to believe the simple truth that this cocaine was found in his client's car because it is his client's cocaine."

She stood squarely behind the podium again, and brought the volume down. "Judge Addison will tell you in his instructions that a reasonable doubt is not a forced doubt, a speculative doubt, or an imaginary doubt. Such a doubt should not influence you to return a verdict of not guilty if you have an abiding conviction of guilt.

"If you have a reasonable doubt"—plenty of inflection on *reasonable*—"about the guilt of this man, then you must find him not guilty. You are honor-bound to find him not guilty. But remember that innocent is as innocent does. If an innocent man sincerely believed that drugs had been planted in his car as his car sat in his driveway in plain view of all the neighbors, he would have called the neighbors, visited the neighbors, sent his lawyer to interview the neighbors. He would have left no stone unturned, on the chance that maybe, maybe, someone would remember seeing something that would bring his innocence to light. But Felix Rodriguez did none of those things. He did none of those things because he knew there was no reason to do them. He did none of those things because he knew that there was nothing for his neighbors to have seen. He did none of those things because he knew exactly who put his cocaine in his car."

Slowly, slowly, she raised her arm to its full extension, her index finger aimed at the defendant. The Voice trumpeted its conclusion: "He did it! He did!"

After Eleanor scooped up her notes and regained her seat, Jack was entitled to a brief rebuttal argument. He went back to his theme, the inherent improbability of it all. It defied probability, he said, to believe that a drug dealer would carry his wares around like that. If the prosecution was to meet its burden of proof, it would need to produce the fingerprints it had been too lazy or careless to test for. As for the defendant, he had no burden of proof. It was not for him to prove his innocence by interviewing neighbors. It was for the prosecution to prove his guilt by evidence. The presumption of innocence.

The Constitution. Reasonable doubt. Thank you, folks. Thanks for Felix.

As the trial begins with me, so it ends with me. The last words the jurors will hear before they begin their deliberations are mine. I must instruct them, according to guidelines set down by the Supreme Court of Florida, on all the laws and rules they will need to know to return a fair verdict. I define the crime that the defendant is charged with committing. I inform them how to choose a foreman, and how to conduct their deliberations. I remind them that they must decide the case based only on the law and the evidence, not taking into account feelings of sympathy or anger. I tell them that we are all counting on them to follow the law and return a fair and just verdict. I wonder if they know just how true that is. I wonder if they know that every time a just and lawful verdict is returned in any courtroom anywhere in the United States, the jurors are putting a new coat of varnish on the Constitution.

Waiting out a jury verdict is an aspect of lawyering I do not miss. While a jury is out the judge goes into his chambers, has a cup of coffee, and catches up his paperwork. While a jury is out the lawyers chain-smoke, pace the hallway area around the bathrooms, and think about the new line of work they plan to go into starting tomorrow. What with one thing and another, the Rodriguez jury hadn't really begun its deliberations till nearly four o'clock, and I wasn't expecting a verdict by day's end. At a few minutes after five I was glancing at my watch, wondering how much more time to give them before I sent them home for the day.

Carmen's voice came over the intercom. "Detective Rasmussen on line two." I stared at the phone. I had kept the bad thoughts, the evil spirits of suspicion, out of my mind all day. I had exorcised them with the rhythm of routine. But now ... well, now it was time to answer the phone.

Yes, thank you for getting back to me so promptly, Detective. Uh-huh. Uh-huh. Sugar? Sugar in the gas tank. No, I didn't know it would. Really? I see. I see. Well thank you, Detective. Yes. Yes, goodbye.

I hung up the phone and swiveled my chair to face my one

window. At five o'clock the summer sun is still high in Miami. In the parking lot drivers started their cars, blasted the air conditioning, then waited outside the cars with the doors open until the heat dissipated. A lucky few, early comers, had parked in the shade of the massive banyan trees. The tabebuias gave beautiful flowers but little shade.

If Ed were here he would know what to do. If Ed were here he could explain it, put the pieces together so that it all made sense. If Ed were here we would talk it out and it would be all right. If Ed were here Ed wouldn't be dead.

Carmen was standing behind me. I can't say how long she had been there.

"Judge? Are you all right?" I did not turn. "I thought I heard ... I thought I heard ... crying. Are you OK?"

I did not turn, but I managed to speak. "Good night, Carmen. Have the bailiff send the jury home for the evening."

She paused. "Good night, Judge. See you tomorrow." I heard her heavy footsteps as she left.

I sat there for, oh, I don't know, ten or fifteen minutes, and then I picked up the phone. Jack would be on the way to his office or on the way to the bar, but I knew his cell phone number and I dialed it. On the second ring I heard Jack's voice, trying to sound like an answering machine. "You have reached the mobile law offices of John Wentworth Sheridan IV. If you are calling about a murder, press one now. If you are calling about a robbery, press two now. If ..."

"Jack?"

"Hello, Clark."

"Jack . . . we knew everything there was to know about Ed, didn't we?"

"Yes, Clark, we did. We knew everything there was to know."

I had to think about the next question. "And I know everything there is to know about you, don't I, Jack?"

He had to think about that one, too. "Well, sure you do, Clark."

Sure I did. "Goodbye, Jack. See you in court tomorrow."

"Clark, is there something ..."

No.   There wasn't something.   There was nothing.
"Goodbye, Jack. See you in court."

I picked up my briefcase, opened it wide. I tossed in a couple of new legal pads, my files in the Rodriguez and Linden cases, and a well-thumbed copy of *Hirsch's Florida Criminal Trial Procedure*. I do not sleep well. Tonight it would be just as well.

Chapter Six
Thursday

The dream came often when I was a teenager, less often as the years passed. I have not dreamed the dream in many years. Last night the dream came.

I am at a cemetery. A large group of mourners is gathered around a grave, a very large group. I don't know who the mourners are, but I sense that they are people I know. Their backs are to me. I walk toward them, but I do not get any closer. I walk faster, I run, but I cannot gain any ground. They are as far from me as when I first tried to approach them.

I try coming at them from a different angle. It does not help. Their backs are still turned toward me somehow. I am frustrated, exasperated, desperate. I start to cry, to run faster, but they remain as far from me as ever.

I see that the grave is open, that the casket has yet to be lowered, that there is no headstone. The mourners are all adults, older and somehow much larger than I. They are angry about something. I cannot get close enough to hear exactly what they are saying, but they are very angry. Their praying and mourning is like the buzzing of many bees. The buzzing is loud and then soft and then loud again. Each time it gets loud it frightens me. Each time it gets soft I know that it will only get loud again. I was taught in Hebrew school that the Jews were punished for murmuring angrily against Moses, and I did not know what it meant to murmur, but now I understand because I hear the sound of angry murmuring, like a hive of menacing bees. Frightened as I am, shaking and crying as I am, I am still trying to reach them, to tell them ... what? There is something I must tell them, some message they must hear. If only I can tell them, they will stop their angry buzzing. Everything will be silence, and I will not be afraid, if only I can tell them. But I can't.

We buried Ed Barber Thursday. We buried all three of them, Ed and DeeDee and Eddie Junior.

I say "we." It was Miriam and me, and three ladies from DeeDee's church who probably haven't missed a funeral since the days when the Dead Sea wasn't even sick. Reverend Fullerton conducted the service, and then two guys with shovels filled in the dirt. Ed had been a cop all his adult life, but no cops showed up. He had brought kids home to their mothers, kids who were injured or overdosed or just lost, but no mothers showed up. He had been officer of the month six times, had a dresser drawer full of commendations, but none of the brass who handed out the commendations showed up. I found out later—I didn't know it then—that Blackjack Sheridan had been sitting in the parking lot the whole time and couldn't, wouldn't, didn't get out of his car. I stood at the graveside in silence. The whole thing must have lasted fifteen minutes.

At one point during the short walk back to the parking lot from the graveside Reverend Fullerton put his hand on my shoulder. It was at that moment that I started to ask him why Ed ... why Ed did what he did. I didn't ask. It wasn't that I was afraid he wouldn't have an answer. It was that I was afraid his answer would be something like, "Isn't that really more your department, Judge? Isn't that the sort of thing you're supposed to know?" His, after all, was the kingdom of heaven. He would have looked at me with a face full of good intentions and asked me if I wasn't the one who was supposed to understand that sort of thing.

Afterwards, I dropped Miriam back at the house and headed downtown. The air in Miami is a petri dish, hot and thick, incubating every mold, germ, and spore that blows up from the Caribbean or down from the Everglades. By mid-morning the summer sun is bright enough to glaze a car's wind-shield like yellow jelly. It was still rush hour on U.S. 1. It is always rush hour on U.S. 1. Drivers inch along squinting through sunshine-lathered windshields, windows rolled up and air-conditioning huffing and puffing against the soupy air. Cut someone off in traffic and you can expect him to pull out a gun and shoot you, shoot your tires, and shoot your engine. Last week I saw a bumper sticker that said, "Keep honking, I'm reloading."

U.S. 1 begins down in the Florida Keys, stringing the tiny islands together like a necklace made of pebbles. Where it hits the mainland it runs north through groves of avocados, mangoes, and citrus. Redneck towns like Florida City, Homestead, and Perrine eventually give way to the more up-market South Miami and Coral Gables. Just before U.S. 1 grows up and becomes I-95, it passes through a part of the City of Miami called Coconut Grove. Coconut Grove wears many faces. One of its faces is black, and pinched with poverty. Some of Miami's worst and poorest neighborhoods are found here, and crack cocaine changes hands within sight of a local elementary school. One of its faces wears the well-kept look of old money. Some of Miami's most expensive homes line the waterfront here, and ancient banyan trees spread their limbs over churches in which William Jennings Bryan preached, hawked real estate, and dreamed of running for the Senate. One of its faces is young, wild, and fashionable. Next only to South Miami Beach, Coconut Grove is the Place to See and Be Seen on a Saturday night. Outdoor cafes line the sidewalks, serving trendy drinks to trendier drinkers. Well-draped pedestrians mob the streets, bringing auto traffic to an agonizing, horn-honking halt. It was through this Coconut Grove that Felix Rodriguez had tried — foolishly — to venture on the night of his arrest. The area is heavily patrolled. It was surprising that it took the police ten whole minutes to find him and his drugs.

Traffic lurched forward for a few blocks, then slowed again. I fiddled with the car radio. I didn't expect the Rodriguez jury to be out much longer. Jack had done his usual fine job, and if the charge had been anything but narcotics he might have had a chance. But the charge was narcotics, and that was all the jury would really need to hear. A robber, a burglar, even a murderer could rely on the presumption of innocence and demand that the jury acquit him if there was reasonable doubt as to his guilt. Not a drug dealer; a drug dealer was presumed guilty when the trial started, and would be found guilty when the trial ended. Juries have had it with drugs and drug dealers. Rodriguez should have gotten himself accused of a different crime.

The traffic light in the distance was green, but I wasn't moving much. Neither was the car in front of me, or the one in front of that, or the one in front of that, or the one in front of that. In the lane to my left a young woman in a Honda was putting on makeup as she crept along, and rocking out gently to whatever sounds were coming from her radio.

U.S. 1 had been laid out in simpler times, when Miami was a sleepy little town in Dixie. When my parents first brought us down to Miami from up north, a drive south on U.S. 1 meant a drive in the country. The area where Miriam and I live today was a U-Pick-'Em strawberry field when I was kid.

No American city has seen so much change in my lifetime as Miami. Baby boomers reached adulthood, looked for the sun, and swarmed to Miami. Cubans and South Americans came in their numbers, some rich, many desperately poor. The drug trade brought money and crime, and money and crime brought lawyers and businessmen. When I was a kid the tallest building in Miami was the little Flagler Street Courthouse, all of twenty-some stories high, with its pyramid roof a nesting ground for turkey vultures. During the 1980s the skyscrapers went up so fast, went broke so fast, and changed owners and names so fast that lawyers joked how in this town even the buildings have aliases.

I guess it all worked out pretty well for me. At the time I got out of law school the court system in Miami was growing like a fairytale beanstalk. There were so many crimes, so many cases, so many trials, that I was able to fly up the ladder. Then, at just the right time, a judgeship opened up and I grabbed it.

The way we pick judges in America is a funny way, if you think about it. A lawyer's job is to make the best case he can for his client. It isn't the lawyer's business to sit in judgment of his client. It isn't the lawyer's business to represent only those clients whom he finds to be morally worthy, or empathetic, or attractive. The most wretched among us is entitled to legal representation. The lawyer must suspend his own moral judgment in deference to his client's right to the effective assistance of legal counsel. To pass moral judgment on the client's cause is to be professionally unethical; the moral is unethical, and the ethical is immoral. So the lawyer sits in his office, day in and day out, building up a callus over his moral judgment so that he can do his professional duty to his clients. Pretty soon his moral judgment is just a memory, packed away in a footlocker in the garage where he put his recollections of the tooth fairy and Santa Claus. His moral muscles, paralyzed and flaccid from repression and lack of use, have atrophied to the point where he no longer misses them, or even thinks about them. He goes along like this for a decade or two, and then we promote him to judge. Having spent his professional life learning not to pass judgment, he is now in the full-time judgment business.

Many of my fellow judges tell me they had no trouble making the transition from lawyer to judge. They cannot always tell me why, or how. Oftentimes poor lawyers make good judges, and good lawyers poor judges. In theory, of course, a judge's job is simply to make sure that the law is followed to the letter, not to enforce his own notion of Justice, whatever that may be. It is a task requiring scholarship, not moral judgment. This theory works well enough for ordinary cases, but progress in the law comes when moral judgment is applied to hard cases, to cases that cannot be resolved because the legal result is not the just result. What does the judge do then?

I left that question where I found it, because I was pulling into the judge's parking lot at the Metro-Justice Building. Judge Surrey, knowing that I was attending a funeral, had been kind enough to cover my morning calendar for me, so I was free to work in my chambers until the Rodriguez jury returned a verdict. I was reading a habeas corpus petition from a defendant in an old case when Carmen, who had come to work sick, appeared in my office.

"Excuse me, Judge, but three attorneys say they need to see you."

"What is it?"

"It's Sammy the Weasel."

In the 1970s and 80s, the practice of criminal litigation in Miami was something out of Adventureland. The drugs were flowing. The money was flowing. Big-time narcotics dealers were thought of not as sociopathic criminals, not as modern-day Jack the Rippers, but as outlaw heroes, as modern-day Billy the Kids. Criminal lawyers cultivated a practice described not as "white-collar litigation" but as "white-powder litigation." And they cultivated an image. Al Guerrero had a Rolls-Royce. Ray Schwartz had a chauffeur-driven Rolls-Royce. Tad Small owned a yacht the size of some Caribbean islands, on which cocaine, beautiful hookers, and Dom Perignon were alleged to be perpetually available.

All of which brings me to Sammy the Weasel. Sammy the Weasel is, of course, not his real name. His real name will come to me in a moment. For as long as anyone can remember, he has been known around the courthouse as Sammy the Weasel. In the 1970s, the big criminal lawyers wore expensive cowboy boots. Sammy still does. In the 1970s, the big criminal lawyers wore open-neck sportshirts with heavy gold chains. Sammy still does. (A secretary once told me that Sammy blow-dries his chest hair. I don't want to know.) Sammy has a collection of Rolex watches for which he made a point of overpaying. His dark, wavy hair, graying at the temples, is carefully pomaded into place. The scent of a musk-based cologne, too-generously applied, enshrouds him. Add to all this a narrow, ferret-like face and shifty eyes, and the nickname "the Weasel" is here to stay.

In truth Sammy is not a bad lawyer. He lacks scholarship, and he can be as annoying as a rash, but his courtroom work is competent and his clients love him. He views all prosecutors, without exception, as the lowest form of vermin, and he does not hesitate to tell them so. As a result, it is a certainty that at some point in the pre-trial stages of a case in which Sammy is involved, there will be some kind of altercation that a judge will be called upon to resolve. If the case is one in my division, I am the judge who must resolve it.

"Send them in."

Sammy the Weasel came slithering in and helped himself to the one good chair opposite my desk. Apparently there was more than one defendant in whatever case they were litigating, because close behind Sammy was another defense attorney, Irving Park. Irv is a perfectly inoffensive lawyer with one enduring flaw. He feels that it is his constitutional obligation as a criminal lawyer to be colorful. Sammy the Weasel is colorful. Al Guerrero, Ray Schwartz, Tad Small, Blackjack Sheridan—all the big ones are colorful. They have a style, a cachet. Irving Park has no particular cachet. He was born to be bland. His efforts to make himself colorful, or what he thinks is colorful, are relentless. For a while, during his celebrated Hat Period, he had appeared in the courthouse wearing a cream-colored panama with a hatband that depicted green alligators, pink flamingoes, and other Florida post-card material. He went through a cigar phase, wandering the hallways of the Justice Building choking on expensive, oversized stogies. He gave it up when a cigar he mistakenly thought was unlit burst into flames in his briefcase. He did everything he could to develop a nickname. He tried to get people to call him Kid Park, Sonny Park, Doc Park. They called him Irving. He entered my office in that bland, inoffensive way of his and took a seat next to, and slightly behind, Sammy the Weasel.

Assistant State Attorney Grant Petrillo made a point of moving his chair to the opposite side of my desk from Sammy the Weasel. Grant was a likeable guy, easygoing, a former police officer who put himself through law school at night and became a prosecutor. Most defense attorneys look forward to working opposite Grant. Grant figures that everyone, even the defendant, is just fulfilling his role in the criminal justice system, and that in a jurisdiction as busy as ours no particular case is worth getting a heart attack over. There is, in any event, little chance of Grant Petrillo getting a heart attack, because he spends every spare minute swimming laps. He is only a few years younger than I, but he looks like an extra in a surfer-boy movie. I wondered what Sammy the Weasel could possibly have done to ruffle good old Grant's feathers. Then again, Sammy could ruffle the feathers of a plastic lawn flamingo.

Apparently the problem that brought the three lawyers to my chambers had arisen during a deposition. A deposition is the interview of a witness prior to trial, taken under oath and in a format more or less similar to examination at trial. Most states allow attorneys to take depositions in civil cases but not in criminal cases. If you are falsely accused of backing your car over my flower bed and I sue you for five hundred dollars, your lawyer can take depositions of the witnesses. If you are falsely accused of murder, your lawyer cannot take depositions of the witnesses — not in most jurisdictions, anyway. To our credit, Florida is one of only about a dozen states that authorizes the taking of depositions in criminal cases.

"It goes to the witness's credibility, Judge." Sammy the Weasel was explaining why he felt compelled to ask the witness a question to which Petrillo had taken apoplectic exception. "I have a right to test credibility."

"Credibility? Judge, Sammy the W ... Mr. Manheim" — yes, that was Sammy the Weasel's name, Samuel Manheim — "called the witness a ..." Grant used a word; a compound word, actually. "How is that testing credibility?"

"I didn't call him one," said Sammy, who seemed unable to understand so much ado about nothing. "I asked him if it wasn't true that he is one. And he is one, so I have every right to ask."

It took me a few moments after that to restore order. Grant Petrillo was so angry that his efforts to scream at Sammy the Weasel were drowned in the foam of his own spit. Sammy went on about prosecutors in general and Petrillo in particular for a good three minutes without drawing breath. Irv Park could think of nothing sufficiently colorful to say, but he did manage some very colorful hand gestures and facial expressions.

After the storm had passed I sustained Petrillo's objection to Sammy's question. The four of us spent about half an hour going over the topics that would likely come up during the remainder of the deposition and the language that would be used to frame questions about those topics. Then I told each of them what a fine lawyer he was and what a fine job he was doing for his case, and I sent them back to the playground to see if they could learn to share the toys this time.

Irv Park was halfway out the door when he stopped, rushed back, grabbed my hand and pumped it energetically. "Thanks, Judge," he said enthusiastically. "You know, you're just as smart as ..." The energetic handshaking stopped abruptly. The enthusiastic smile disappeared just as abruptly. His face fell. Poor guy; he couldn't think of a metaphor colorful enough to finish the sentence.

I went back to my desk and sat for a minute without moving, just listening for voices or steps in the corridor, satisfying myself that they were really gone. At the front of my desk sits a carved wooden nameplate, given to me by the Dade County Bar Association at the time I became a judge. Clark N. Addison, carved elaborately into a piece of Dade County pinewood. My parents, for reasons lost in the mists of family history, gave me a middle initial but no middle name to go with it. It has been a gag ever since I was a kid: What does the N. stand for? Nothing. Oh, N. for Nothing? No, it doesn't stand for anything.

On my side of the nameplate was a blotter, to the left and right of which were stacks of papers. I reached into my briefcase and pulled out another stack—the notes I had made last night—and set it in the middle of the blotter. In the old days, Jack and I and some of the other assistant state attorneys had prepared for trial by playing a game called "Dick Witness." "Dick" is not short for "Richard." One of us would take the role of a witness whom we expected to confront in the upcoming trial. The other would try to cross-examine. The one playing the witness was supposed to make the cross-examination as difficult as possible. He was to be balky, evasive, uncooperative, and a general pain. Hence the name "Dick Witness." (Jack invented the name, but it caught on quickly. Jack was the office Dick Witness champion.) The idea was that after a few rounds of Dick Witness, the real-life cross-examination, when it came, would seem easier.

I flipped through last night's notes, challenging myself to a game of one-man Dick Witness. But there was no point. I didn't want to play.

Billy Eisenberg called and Carmen put him through. "How's my favorite size 38 short?"

"Good, Uncle Billy. How's the *schmatte* business these days?"

"Ugh. The *schmatte* business isn't what it used to be." Then his voice became serious. "I wanted to check up on you, kiddo. How was the funeral?"

I took a page from his book and answered his question with a question. "You know what I liked about the clothing business, Billy?"

"This I got to hear."

"It left no unanswered questions."

He thought about that for a minute, and then asked an unanswered question. "So how was the funeral?"

"It was a funeral." He waited for me to say something else, but I didn't. Then I asked, "Billy ... how do you like living in Florida?"

"What?"

"How do you like living in Florida? I mean, do you miss living up north? Is it better here than there, or worse?"

I could feel him shrug the way he does, lots of eyebrows and not much shoulders. "I been living here twenty-five, almost thirty years. I don't know ... It's warm. It's warmer here than up north. I couldn't go back to the winters, not at my age, if that's what you mean. Hialeah's a gorgeous track, but they don't run there much anymore. Gulfstream is all right, just all right."

He was still thinking out loud, but I interrupted. "A lot of people die here, Billy. They don't tell you what they're really thinking, or what they really mean, and then one day they die."

"If they didn't die here, they'd die somewhere else, kiddo."

"Yeah. But they don't die somewhere else. They die here." Billy didn't say anything for a while and neither did I. "You coming to dinner tomorrow night?"

I could tell from his voice that he appreciated the change of subject. "Sure, you bet. And I've got something for you."

"Billy, look, if it's a hat, I ..."

"Try it, that's all, just try it. No charge. Just put it on. Wear it to one of those formal things you judges are always going to ..."

I had no idea what kind of formal things we judges were supposed to be going to, but I managed to squeeze a good-bye into his sales pitch and hung up the phone. Carmen came in with Cuban coffee, one for her and one for me. She sat down, took a few sips, and started coughing. It was a heavy, croupy cough.

"You should be home," I said.

She shook her head emphatically. "You can't give in to sickness. Once you start you never stop." Carmen normally wears pants to work, but today she had worn a dress and had made a special point of doing her hair just-so. She would show those germs that they couldn't get the better of Carmen Maria Aleman de Escobar. "We'll have a verdict by lunch?"

I sipped at my coffee. "Probably."

"Guilty?"

"Probably."

"Good." She tilted her head back to get the last drop of coffee from the thimble-size plastic cup.

"Why good?"

"Because he's a guilty dirtbag." This was not an invitation to discuss the evidence. Once Carmen decided a defendant was a guilty dirtbag, the evidence was beside the point.

I put my pencil down and rubbed my eyes for a minute. "You don't want to see your pal Blackjack Sheridan lose one, do you?"

That got me a little smile. "Sheridan will be fine with it. He knows his client's a guilty dirtbag. You know what he always says, that a truly innocent client is a lawyer's worst nightmare." It was true. Jack's job—any criminal lawyer's job—is to secure for his clients every right, every procedural protection that the law allows. If a given client was truly guilty, and Jack did everything he could for the guy, and the client still ended up going to prison ... well, Jack didn't tell him to commit the crime in the first place. But if a given client was truly innocent—not likely maybe, but it could happen—and the client still ended up going to prison, then it was Jack's fault and not the client's. An innocent client is indeed a lawyer's worst nightmare.

I picked up my pencil and went back to working on the file on top of the pile. Carmen had finished her coffee but seemed in no hurry to go. And then, after a few minutes of silence, she said the damnedest thing:

"Poor Sheridan."

"Poor Sheridan?" She nodded, and even sighed a little. "Why poor Sheridan? His client's a guilty dirtbag who deserves to be convicted, and Jack knows it and will be all right with it, remember?"

She shook her head like I didn't get it. "I don't mean poor Sheridan because he'll probably lose this trial. I mean poor Sheridan because he has no life. Your friend is lonely, Judge. Don't you see that?" I must have looked like I was going to say something, because she paused; but when I said nothing she went on. "He has that boat, he has money and the things money can buy, but he has no one to share it with. The girls he dates,"—she made a face—"the only thing he can share with them is what's in his pants, not what's in his heart. He had two real friends in the whole world, you and Ed, and now fifty percent of his friends are dead." She sighed again, a sigh of deep compassion. "*Pobrecito*." Then she stood up, reached across my desk, and patted me on the head, probably about the same way she pats her dog Lucky on the head. "You're lucky you got Miriam to take care of you. You certainly couldn't take care of yourself." She said it in the nicest way, and she meant it in the nicest way, and then she picked up our little plastic coffee cups and went back to her office. I would have given her an argument if I could have thought of one.

I opted instead for a quick stroll along the fourth floor corridor. There are courtrooms on the first five floors of the Metro-Justice Building, but the fourth floor is the floor of choice. This is so not because my courtroom and chambers happen to be on the fourth floor. This is so because of Shoe Shine Lady.

At the far end of the corridor—the end opposite from mine—Shoe Shine Lady plies her trade. She can be found there most weekdays, but not all; her schedule is her own, unknown and unknowable. When she is open for business, business is good. There will always be a backlog of two or three lawyers waiting for a shine, chatting with each other or on cell phones, uncharacteristically patient.

Shoe Shine Lady is tall and gangly. Her limbs are long, and there is an undefinable awkwardness about her movements, as if she were put together out of spare parts left over from other bodies. I suppose she is in her thirties, but I was never good at guessing women's ages. She is black by race but not by color; her skin is coffee-and-cream, except of course those parts of the hands and fingers perpetually blackened by shoe polish. She wears a smock, like an old bowling-league shirt, on the back of which a hand unskilled with needle and thread has embroidered the words, "Shoe Shine Lady." The bowling shirt is worn loose because Shoe Shine Lady has been, as Jack likes to put it, "blessed by the Tit Fairy."

She is from the islands somewhere—Haiti, I guess, or maybe Jamaica. The letter "r" falls off the ends of her words, and "th" becomes "d." When a customer shows up with a really unkempt, scuffed-up pair of shoes, she will work on one till it shines like new, then turn to the waiting onlookers and announce, "Dis"—pointing to the shiny shoe— "is you' brain. Dis"—pointing to the yet-to-be-shined shoe—"is you' brain on drugs. Any questions?"

There is a persistent rumor that Shoe Shine Lady got her start in the Metro-Justice Building as a defendant—that she was convicted of (depending on the version of the rumor that you hear) murder, or manslaughter, or something else. Of course Shoe Shine Lady does nothing to discourage this rumor; it's good for business. In any event, Shoe Shine Lady is none too talkative about herself, her background, her life. Ask her what her real first name is and she'll tell you, "Shoe."

I stood there watching Shoe Shine Lady's ministrations from a distance. Her customer was wearing tassled loafers, brown or cordovan but not black. She applied the polish with her bare hands, fingers moving back and forth from the polish tin to the shoeleather, back and forth rapidly. After a few minutes of this she took a brush in each hand, shining furiously from front to back. Sometimes, when the mood strikes her,

Shoe Shine Lady will flip the brushes in mid-shine, like an old-
time movie cowboy twirling his six-shooters. She will do this
without breaking rhythm, without interrupting the shining
process by more than a fraction of a second, and if onlookers
are not watching carefully they may miss the show. But today
Shoe Shine Lady was bent to her work, taking no time to show
off. When she put the brushes down she picked up a worn,
stained toothbrush and with it worked some polish into the
sides of the soles and the back of the heels.

I looked down at my shoes. I decided that they would wait,
and that I wouldn't, and I wandered back to chambers.

It was a few minutes before noon when we got the knock
on the juryroom door. The bailiff was handed a note, which I
read aloud in open court and made part of the court file. It said
simply, "We have a verdict. R. Kramer, Foreman."

There are lawyers who say they can predict the verdict the
minute the jurors walk back into the courtroom. They say that
if the jurors look at the defendant, actually make eye contact
with him, it's a "not guilty." They say no juror will convict a
man and look him in the eye. I don't know if I believe it. Now
that I'm a judge it really doesn't matter to me. As the Rodriguez
jurors shuffled to their places in the box, my eyes were wandering around the courtroom. Eleanor was neatening up her table,
stuffing papers in her briefcase. Rodriguez fidgeted. Jack was
slumped down in his chair, seeming to stare off into space. I
knew he was studying the jury out of the corner of his eye. The
visitors' gallery was all but empty. Alone in the back row of
dark fold-down chairs sat Teresa Rodriguez, a lily floating in a
dull brown pond.

When they were all seated I faced Mr. Kramer. "Mr. Foreman, do you have a verdict?"

He rose. They always know to rise. "We do, Your Honor."
He handed the folded form to the bailiff, who passed it along to
me. I unfolded it and read. It was duly filled out, signed, and
dated. There was nothing more for me to do. I handed it to the
clerk. "The clerk will publish the verdict," I announced.

The clerk stood, verdict form in hand. "In the case of the
State of Florida versus Felix Rodriguez, we the jury find the de-

fendant guilty as charged. So say we all. Signed, R. Kramer, Foreman."

"Ladies and gentlemen of the jury," I said, "thank you for your jury service. It has been a pleasure and a privilege for me to serve with you. The bailiff will now show you out." A few of them nodded at me unsmilingly as they exited. Eleanor, too much the professional to exult in a conviction, busied herself shuffling papers. Jack had his arm around Rodriguez's shoulder, whispering about the court of appeals. Rodriguez was docile, not even twitching, looking like he had been hit by a truck.

On the jury's verdict of guilty I find and adjudicate you guilty. That was my line. It was what every judge was supposed to say every time a guilty verdict was returned. I had said it to hundreds of convicted defendants. It was a matter of rote, a matter of routine. On the jury's verdict of guilty I find and adjudicate you guilty. As soon as I said it, the case would be over. As soon as I said it, I could stop worrying and stop caring. My suspicions would cease to have consequences. My unanswered questions would remain unanswered and, in time, cease to be questions. On the jury's verdict of guilty I find and adjudicate you guilty. Another defendant would be packed off to Florida State Prison at Starke for the minimum mandatory fifteen years. Florida State Prison is a window into Hell, but Felix Rodriguez probably deserved the view. On the jury's verdict of guilty I find and adjudicate you guilty. Just say it, damn it.

"The court will take a brief recess before proceeding in this matter." I stood to the bailiff's cry of "All rise," left the bench, and headed for chambers.

I am an occasional builder of paperclip chains. Sitting at my desk, about six paperclips into the chain I was working on, I heard Jack in the outer office. He exchanged terms of endearment with Carmen, used her phone for a minute, then wandered back to my office. I linked two or three more paperclips while he had a seat, made himself comfortable with one leg over the chair arm, and took a swallow from his silver flask. He started to put the flask away; I extended my hand for it.

His eyebrows arched. "You, Clark? I stopped offering fifteen years ago." I took a small sip straight from the flask. The liquor, bitter to the taste, burned on the way down. Then it pooled up in my stomach, trying to burn its way out.

I returned the flask to Jack. "Your client took it pretty well."

He shrugged. "It hasn't hit him yet."

"How about the wife?"

He shrugged again. I got up and went to the window. Rain had come suddenly, falling hard. When I was a kid up north the rain would move in gradually, settling itself in for a long stay. That kind of rain made people relax, the way a man re-laxes getting into a hot bath and knowing the bathwater will stay warm. Miami rain isn't like that. It comes on suddenly, then suddenly it stops. Miami rain makes you feel like a man getting into a hot bath and knowing the bathwater will turn cold any second. You can't let Miami rain fool you into relax-ing.

"You should have won it."

Behind me, I heard Jack. "How?"

The rain, torrential for a few seconds, was letting up. Water fell in heavy drops from the leaves of the tabebuia trees in the parking lot. The pink flowers were mostly gone, but the leaves remained.

I went back to my desk and sat. I looked down at my notes. "Mr. Sheridan," I began, "we've heard testimony during the course of this trial that your client's car broke down on the night of his arrest. Do you have any idea what caused your client's car to break down?"

Jack took his leg off the chair arm and sat up straight. He liked playing Dick Witness. He liked it because he always won. "No, sir. I have no idea."

"In the course of preparing for this trial, did you consider that question?"

"I'm sure I did."

"Did you ask your client, Mr. Rodriguez, if he had ever had trouble with that car before?"

"I don't recall asking him that specific question."

"Did you ask him generally if he knew of any reason why his car broke down?"

"He told me that when the car stopped he pulled over and raised the hood, but that he couldn't see anything wrong. Of course, he's not an auto mechanic."

"Did you arrange for the car to be examined by an auto mechanic while it was in police custody, in order to determine what caused it to stop?"

"No."

"So would it be fair to say, Mr. Sheridan, that you did nothing to determine what caused your client's car to stall on the night in question?"

"I asked Mr. Rodriguez himself if he knew what caused his car to stall. Other than that I did nothing."

I summoned Carmen on the intercom. She entered my office, glanced quickly at Jack, then at me. "Yes, Judge?"

"Carmen, did I speak on the telephone with a detective this week?"

"Yes."

"With which detective?"

"Rasmussen."

"What did he tell me?" There was no need to ask if Carmen knew. Of course she knew.

"You asked him to go to the police impound lot to try to figure out why Rodriguez's car died. He examined the car with the mechanic at the impound lot, and they found sugar in the gas tank. Regular table sugar, like you put in coffee. He said that sugar would clog up the gas line and stall the car."

"Anything else?"

She thought for a minute. "He said there was nothing else wrong with the car. He said that they checked for fingerprints around the gas cap, but they couldn't find any." She paused for a minute, then nodded to indicate that her report was complete. Unlike most gossips and busybodies, Carmen can always be counted on to get the facts right. I sent her back to her desk.

I turned to Jack. "Your defense in this case, Mr. Sheridan, was that Mr. Rodriguez did not know that the cocaine was in his car at all, is that correct?"

Jack took out the flask. He ran a finger along the engraved initials, then put the flask back in his jacket pocket. "That's right."

"And if his car had not broken down, he might never have learned of the presence of the cocaine there?"

"He might not have."

"And now it appears that sugar was placed in Mr. Rodriguez's gas tank?"

"So it appears." *It appeahs.*

"Had you known that, you could have argued to the jury that whoever put the sugar in the gas tank also put the cocaine in the car, couldn't you?"

"I guess I could have."

"In other words, you could have argued that your client was set up, couldn't you?"

Jack leaned his head back and stared off into space, the way he does in court when he's trying to pretend that a witness's testimony is boring him. Then he looked at me. "Goddamit, Clark, how was I supposed to know someone put sugar in the gas tank?"

"The same way I knew. You ask the detective."

"The damn detective didn't know till you asked him to check!" He stood and paced up and down a few steps. "I shouldn't be angry at you. Hell, you've saved my client's ass. I'll file a motion tomorrow to set aside the verdict." He stopped pacing, smiled that old Blackjack smile at me. "You were always a smart little bastard."

We looked at each other for a minute. Jack appeared ready to leave. "Sit down, Jack. We're not finished." He started to say something, but I said, "Sit down, Mr. Sheridan." He sat.

I looked at my notes and picked up where I had left off. "Mr. Sheridan, can you suggest any reason why you failed to look into the cause of Mr. Rodriguez's car breaking down?"

Jack answered very formally. "I've explained to Your Honor that it simply didn't occur to me to have the car examined. I will say in my own defense that I believe I did a more than competent job of presenting Mr. Rodriguez's case to the jury, based on the facts as I knew them."

"I agree, Mr. Sheridan" I said. "I think your trial performance in this case was a fine one. Perhaps the reason you neglected to look into the reason the car broke down was because of some particular stress you've been under lately?"

Jack fidgeted in his seat. "Well, ... yes, Your Honor is aware that I've recently experienced the death of a close friend."

"And was that the reason for your outburst in court last Friday?"

"I've already apologized to Your Honor for that. Let me say again that I'm very sorry."

"Apology accepted, Mr. Sheridan. My question was, is the recent death of your friend the reason you lost your self-control on one or more occasions"—I was thinking about Friday night at my house—"recently?"

"Yes, of course, Your Honor."

"And the reason you failed to look into the cause of the breakdown of your client's car in this case?"

"Yes, Your Honor."

"No other reason?"

Jack looked perplexed, or tried to. "What other reason is the court suggesting?"

I paused. That's how Jack would have done it. "Do I understand, Mr. Sheridan, that your client is the estranged husband of your secretary?"

He started to say something, stopped, and settled for, "Yes, Your Honor."

"They are divorcing?"

"Yes, sir, as far as I know."

"And we have learned during the course of this trial that on at least two occasions Mr. Rodriguez beat his wife, is that correct?"

It was a matter of public record, so Jack said, "Yes, sir."

"I suppose you have no way to know for certain if there were other beatings?"

He was a while answering that one. Finally he said, "I ..." That was as far as he got.

"You had your suspicions?"

"Yes, Your Honor."

"Of course even a divorce wouldn't guarantee an end to the beatings, would it, Mr. Sheridan?"

"Well, it ... it would ... no, not ..." His voice trailed off.

"Mr. Rodriguez would still have a right to visit his child from time to time, wouldn't he?"

"I suppose so."

"And those visitations could have turned into opportunities for violence?"

"Yes."

"And apart from his visitations, Mr. Rodriguez might simply make it his business to find his ex-wife, right?"

"I ... yes, Your Honor."

"Calling the police, or even getting an injunction, is no guarantee against an angry ex-husband, is it?"

Jack didn't answer that one. He didn't have to.

I hunched forward. "But if he could be put away somewhere, somewhere he couldn't escape from, somewhere he'd have to stay for fifteen long years ..."

Jack was on his feet. "No! If you're suggesting that Mrs. Rodriguez set her husband up, no, no, there is ... there is absolutely no basis for that suggestion!"

I sat very still at my desk, looking up at him. Being a criminal court judge in Miami is like being a lion tamer in the circus. The lion tamer's whip and chair, like the judge's robe and gavel, are props. It is the firm, quiet voice and the steady, fixed gaze that hold the beasts at bay. Let them smell your fear, or hear your voice tremble, and they'll eat you alive. "No, Mr. Sheridan," I said, "I am not suggesting that Mrs. Rodriguez set her husband up. I'm suggesting that you did."

I waited the several seconds it took for Jack to sit down. He held his head in one hand, his bony fingers rubbing his forehead.

I looked down at my notepad. I had written across the top of the page, "II Samuel 11:2." It was the story of King David, who so coveted Uriah's wife Bathsheba that he sent Uriah into the forefront of the battle and then had the army abandon him to die. "You represent a small-time doper named Linden. I don't believe he can pay your kind of legal fees. I think you made a deal with him: Free legal services in exchange for his dropping a little cocaine into Felix Rodriguez's car and a little sugar into Felix Rodriguez's gas tank. He delivered on his half of the deal. You had to deliver on yours.

"You were after me night and day to let Linden out on bail. You had to be. He was a ticking time bomb if you didn't get him out of jail. He had threatened you, told you he was thinking about going to the State Attorney's Office and offering to tell them everything. He'd promise to give them Blackjack Sheridan on a plate, on condition that all his pending charges be dismissed. That's a trade they'd make—once he told them what he knew about how the cocaine got into Felix Rodriguez's car.

"When you fell apart during the bail hearing last Friday I thought it was because of Ed. I'll give you the benefit of the doubt, Jack. Maybe it was partly because of Ed. Mostly it was because Linden was threatening you, threatening you right there in court.

"You had to do something. Linden's mother, Mrs. Halstead, told the truth when she testified that there was no chance she'd ever be able to come up with the bail money. So you came up with Vera Shields. That was smart, Jack. Vera Shields didn't know Linden well enough to pick him out of a one-man line-up, but she knew a good deal when she saw one. You put up Linden's bail money out of your own pocket, plus a little tip that Mrs. Shields earned just for some harmless perjury."

I stopped talking until Jack raised his head and looked up at me. "Linden's freedom should have bought his silence. Cash should have bought Vera Shields.' But it didn't. Shall I have Carmen come in and tell you about my telephone conversations with both of them?"

I have no idea, no idea, what I would have done if Jack had said yes. I had never spoken with Linden or Mrs. Shields, and Carmen would have no way to know what kind of bluff I was running. But sometimes in cross-examination you have to gamble on your own instincts. My friend Blackjack Sheridan had taught me that.

We stared at each other for a long second. Then Jack looked away, looked past me and out the window, looked past the parking lot and the trees, toward the western sky. He spoke with a great deal of self-possession when he said, "That won't be necessary."

I wanted to stop there. I wanted it to be over. But it wasn't over; not quite. "It was a perfect deal for everybody, wasn't it? You and Mrs. Rodriguez would live happily ever after. Linden would be out of jail, at least till the next time he got caught. Mrs. Shields would have a little something to put in her mattress. And society would be rid of a wife-beater. Even the crime was perfect. It had to be. You had to make a case that even you couldn't defend. You had to make Felix Rodriguez, your client, look so guilty that even the great Blackjack Sheridan couldn't get him acquitted. Am I correct, Mr. Sheridan?

He looked out the window. No answer.

"This court is waiting for an answer, Mr. Sheridan."

But I wasn't really waiting for an answer. We sat there in silence for a long minute, and then I leaned forward and asked, "What was it, Jack? After all those years of loving them and leaving them, did you find one you loved too much to leave?"

Now it was over. It was so over he could relax about it. He slid down in the chair and crooked a leg over the chair arm. When he spoke, it was slowly, thoughtfully, with his gaze still turned toward the window. "You know," he said," I'm fishing buddies with Raul Santos at Williams, Santos, and Banks, down on Brickell Avenue. They refer their criminal cases to me. Their corporate clients wouldn't want them getting their fingernails dirty handling criminal cases. She used to be a secretary there."

Jack was a good storyteller—most trial lawyers are—and now that the truth was out there was no reason he couldn't enjoy filling in the details. "Raul's firm throws a beautiful Christmas party every year, and I'm always invited. That's where I met her." He closed his eyes, relishing the memory. "They set up a bar in their conference room. I had just gotten a drink, and was looking out the window at Biscayne Bay, when Raul came over with Teresa on his arm and introduced me to her. 'This is my friend Jack Sheridan, the man to see if you're ever in trouble.'" Jack opened his eyes. "Raul introduces me to everyone that way. Anyway, Raul walked away to visit with other guests, and she and I stood there by the window. I don't remember what we talked about. I don't even remember what she was wearing. I remember that the irises of her eyes seemed to get larger and darker as we spoke, and at one point I actually put my hand on the bay window to steady my balance because I felt ..." he looked at me, trying to make me understand it: "I felt that I was going to fall into her eyes.

"After a couple of minutes she said she had to go mingle with the others. As she turned to go I held her arm. She smiled at me. 'Trouble,' she said. 'I'll call you if I'm ever ...' I interrupted. 'In it?' She looked at my hand on her arm. 'Looking for it.' A few months later I was looking for a new secretary and she walked in the door.

"I broke a lot of rules in my time, Clark, you know that. But I never broke the rule that says you stand up for your client. I never sold a client out for money, or for spite, or for anything under the canopy of heaven. Not until I did it for her sake. I would have done that and more to keep her."

Jack took the flask out and drained it. I wanted to ask him to go on. Was it her idea to frame her husband? Had she put Jack up to it? Or was it Jack's idea from the start? And if it was, had he told her about it, or kept it from her? But there was no point in asking. Either way, Jack would swear to me that she wasn't in on it, that it was his plan and that she was blissfully ignorant. Either way, I would suspect him of lying; and I didn't need to hear my friend Jack Sheridan lie to me again.

Jack put the flask away and stood. "Well, Clark," he said matter-of-factly, "what happens now?"

I swiveled my chair around slowly, my back to him. That was the question, wasn't it: What happens now? "You're going to have that motion to set aside the verdict filed and heard tomorrow morning. Attach an affidavit from Rasmussen, explaining about the sugar in the gas tank. On the basis of Rasmussen's affidavit, I will grant the motion and order a new trial. I will then recuse myself from any further proceedings in this matter. I haven't decided what my reason for getting off the case will be, but I'll come up with one. The case will go to another judge and another prosecutor. Maybe the state attorney's office will re-prosecute and maybe they won't. That's your problem, and Rodriguez's. If anybody asks me what I know about this case, I'll tell them. If no one asks me, there'll be nothing to tell."

A few minutes went by in silence, and then I heard the sound of Jack leaving the office. Abruptly, the sound stopped. When I turned around, Jack was standing in my doorway. The ruddy complexion had paled to a milky white, and the hair, still the color of sand, seemed somehow wilted, like cut flowers left out in the Florida sun. But he gave me what was left of the old Blackjack smile when he said, "You know, Clark, for a little runt who never could cross-examine worth spit, that wasn't bad. It wasn't bad at all." Then he turned, and went quietly.

A few minutes later I saw him in the parking lot, saw him get in his car and drive away. To the right of the parking lot, out of the line of sight of my one window, is Dade County Jail. It is a large, squat building of grey stone. Its exterior windows are slits, too narrow for a man to escape from. Two front doors open on a lobby area. Its floor is linoleum, or what I take to be linoleum, badly worn but still recognizable as a kind of blue-green color. The lobby walls are painted another shade of blue-green, off just enough from the color of the floor to clash with it. Blue-green seems bizarrely out of place in jail, a cruel reminder of the azure skies and turquoise seas that lie beyond the stone walls. The blue-green wall paint is chipped and covered with scribbling, especially near the pay phone where the phone numbers of bail bondsmen are posted.

At the back of the lobby is a half-wall of bullet-proof glass, separating the public from a booth in which jail guards sit. If he is presented with proper paperwork, the guard on duty will press the buzzer releasing the door to the interior of the jail. The visitor will pass through the door, then through a magnetometer, and halt at the side window of the guard booth. There he must sign in, show identification again, and be issued a jail pass. The guard will press a second buzzer, and a second door will open. The visitor is now in the interior lobby. He is now in jail.

Judges do not go to Dade County Jail. Family members of inmates go during visiting hours. Defense lawyers go at all hours, because the Constitution guarantees a man the right to consult with his attorney. But if a judge has business with a prisoner, he orders the corrections officers to transport the prisoner across the catwalk that separates the jail from the courthouse, and to bring the prisoner to the judge's courtroom. I have not been to Dade County Jail since I became a judge, but I remember going as a lawyer. I remember that the first thing you notice after you leave the jail is how fresh the air smells outside. Jails have a smell you can't describe. All jails have it, to remind the prisoners that they are in jail. Jail-smell.

That night I tried to get drunk. But I'm no good at it, and I ended up with my head in the toilet, puking, and Miriam stroking my back telling me it would be all right, it would be all right.

Epilogue
Another Friday

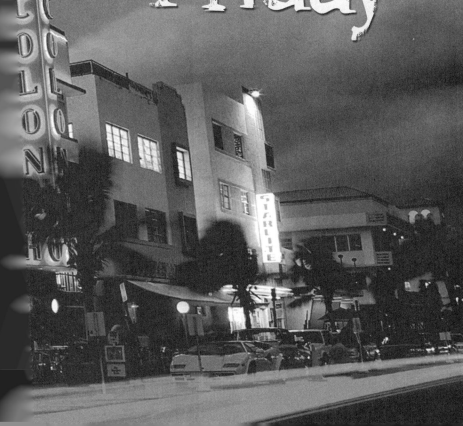

I remember my father as being about average height. That would have made him slightly taller than I am now. I wasn't even a teenager when my father died, I had hardly started to grow, so it may be that he seemed taller to me than he was. I remember that he was thin. Instead of eating his food he picked at it or ignored it, just as I do. I have trouble giving a physical description of him, because he had no particularly distinctive features. I don't mean that he was a bad looking man, just that he was an ordinary looking man. When I try to see him in my mind's eye there is nothing singular, nothing diacritical—hair, eyes, nose, chin—on which I can focus.

The floor of my parents' bathroom was done in alternating green and white tile. The tiles were very small, maybe the size of a matchbook. They weren't ceramic tiles, or polished marble. They were some kind of inexpensive stone, I imagine, with a rough surface even though the house was not new when we moved in and the tiles had been walked on for years. The surface of the floor was not perfectly flat because the tiles were not perfectly flush one with the other. This, as I understood it, was not considered a defect; the tiles were not supposed to line up perfectly, because of their individual textures. The green ones were the color of jade, or perhaps a shade lighter. The white ones were white, not off-white or bone, but because their finish was flat rather than glossy they sometimes looked off-white. In between the tiles the caulking was discolored, particularly near the toilet and the shower stall, where it was almost black. In the center of the bathroom the discoloration was not so noticeable. The rest of the bathroom, other than the tile floor, I remember only in a general way. There were the usual fixtures, of course. I remember that the shower curtain was plastic, not sliding glass.

When they found my father he was wearing dark pajamas; gray, I think, almost black, and with some kind of small pattern. They were long-sleeve and long-pants pajamas that he had bought up north but continued to wear in the Florida heat. Small as the bathroom was, he had managed to fall so that he was not touching any of the fixtures. His head was near, but not touching, the hem of the shower curtain. His right hand, palm up, lay inches from the toilet but not in contact with the porcelain. His left leg was under the sink, his toes pointing at but not reaching the drainpipe. He had swallowed a whole bottle of one of my mother's prescription medications. She told me that he had died in his sleep. I suppose in a sense that was true.

His pajama shirt had a breast pocket, in which was found an envelope. Most suicide notes are terse, a few lines. My father had written seven pages. I wasn't permitted to read it, on the theory that I was too young; and by the time I was old enough I didn't want to. From what I was told there was something in there for everyone: guilt, shame, complaints, explanations, apologies, bequests, requests, you name it. He wanted to leave nothing unsaid. He wanted to make the *why* of it clear, perfectly clear, clear even to himself. Like Jack always says, irony sure is ironic.

Jack's motion to set aside the verdict in the Rodriguez case was on my desk when I got to work that Friday morning. It was neatly typed, with all the legal citations in proper form, and the affidavit from Rasmussen attached. When the motion was called up on the morning calendar I explained that, in light of the new evidence, I would have to set aside the verdict and order a re-trial. Eleanor didn't even bother to object. Teresa Rodriguez was seated in the back row of the courtroom, under the big old Elgin clock. She had sat through her husband's trial without a flicker of emotion; but now a perfect tear formed in one of her dark, perfect eyes, and trickled gracefully down her perfect cheek.

I didn't know it then, of course, but that was the last time I would ever see Jack Sheridan. After a few weeks no one around the courthouse seemed to know where he was, and after a few months no one seemed to care. I drove by the marina where he kept his sailboat, but it was gone. Maybe he sailed away for a while. Maybe he sailed away forever. Maybe Teresa Rodriguez went with him, and maybe she didn't. A week ago I had two best friends. I lost one to death. The other I just ... lost.

It was a slow day Friday, the way Fridays are, and I thought about driving over to the Antibes Mens Wear on Miami Beach and letting Billy Eisenberg sell me a hat. As I was leaving the court-room for lunch one of the corrections officers buttonholed me. He had just gotten back from a few days' vacation, and he had just heard about Ed Barber. It was too bad, he said, a hell of a thing. What did I suppose made a fellow do a thing like that?

What did I suppose made a fellow do a thing like that? In truth I do not know; but I was tired of that answer, so I said, "There must have been something inside him that was building up and building up through the years. I guess every time he saw another stiff, or another cocaine baby, or another twelve-year-old rape vic-tim, it just built up and up. And he never spoke about it, never got it off his chest, never kicked the dog, never figured he could do anything about what he saw except get up tomorrow and put on his pants and see another day's- worth of it. And it built up until it couldn't build up anymore, and then he died."

He nodded carelessly, as if I had just said "How 'bout those Marlins?" "Got anything interesting in trial this afternoon, Judge?"

"No. Nothing special."

"Just another day at the factory, huh?"

In truth I do not know why men kill, and why men steal, and why men cheat, and why men lie. I am a judge of the criminal court of the Eleventh Judicial Circuit in and for Miami-Dade County, Florida, and these things I need to know. Ed Barber had killed, and I did not know why. But I knew what Jack had done, and I knew why he had done it. Knowing about Jack hurt as much as not knowing about Ed, and in that moment it occurred to me that I had been sentenced to spend the rest of my life knowing the one and not knowing the other. *La ley es apenas la sombra de la justi-cia*, the Cubans say; the law is but the shadow of justice. The law produces verdicts. Sometimes it produces justice. It doesn't pro-duce answers.

"Yeah," I said. "Just another day at the factory."

ABOUT THE AUTHOR

Milton Hirsch, a Miami attorney at the firm of Hirsch & Markus, LLP, has handled some of Miami's most notorious and controversial criminal cases. His acquittal of former Los Angeles Dodger/St. Louis Cardinal All-Star Pedro Guerrero on federal narcotics charges prompted the sports editor of *The New York Post* to write: "When the time comes that I finally snap, someone please contact attorney Milton Hirsch to represent me."

After receiving his J.D. from Georgetown University Law Center, Milt joined the Office of the State Attorney in Miami-Dade County, Florida, and rose to assistant chief of narcotics prosecution, then entered private practice. Milt has been a prolific author, publishing principally on the subjects of the Fourth, Fifth, and Sixth Amendments; and his *Hirsch's Florida Criminal Trial Procedure* is the leading treatise of its kind in Florida.

Milt is named in *The Best Lawyers in America*, is listed as one of South Florida's top lawyers in *Miami Metro Magazine*, and is a past president of the Florida Association of Criminal Defense Lawyers, Miami Chapter.

ABOUT THE PUBLISHER

The Shadow of Justice is the first novel in the new series, "Great Stories by Great Lawyers," from the American Bar Association Criminal Justice Section.

The American Bar Association is the world's largest professional membership organization, with over 400,000 members, and represents the more than a million attorneys practicing law in the U.S. today. ABA Publishing, the publishing arm of the ABA, publishes approximately 100 new titles each year, primarily practical legal handbooks useful to practicing attorneys and judges.

The Criminal Justice Section of the ABA (the CJS) has over 9,000 members including prosecutors, private defense counsel, appellate and trial judges, law professors, correctional and law enforcement personnel, law students, public defenders, and other criminal justice professionals. The CJS takes primary responsibility for the ABA's work on solutions to issues involving crime, criminal law, and the administration of criminal and juvenile justice. The CJS plays an active leadership role in bringing the views of the ABA to the attention of federal and state courts, Congress, and other federal and state judicial, legislative, and executive policy-making bodies. The CJS also serves as a resource to its members on issues in the forefront of change in the criminal justice arena.

The CJS primarily produces practical handbooks for practicing criminal attorneys, but, with *The Shadow of Justice,* inaugurates its fiction series, "Great Stories by Great Lawyers." This series is intended to further the mission of educating the public about the inner workings of the country's criminal justice system.